Fair Ways
and Foul Plays

A FICTIONAL INTERNATIONAL THRILLER

J.T. KELLY

1

"Yaaaaah," Jack screamed as he ran down the big hill on the golf course across the road. From the time he was four or five, it was always a thrill for him to tear down the high, gradual slope with his legs churning at breakneck speed – trying not to fall. *I can do this…I can do this.*

"Jack, wake up, you're dreaming," Sara said as she jostled him next to her. "Man, you're scaring me."

"Ugh, what the…" Jack snorted as he began to gain awareness that his loud slumber had awakened her. "Sorry, hon, didn't realize I was making so much noise." Even though Jack hadn't sped down the hill since he was in his early teens, the daredevil thrill often crept into his dreams.

The "big hill" was only 15 yards long but it was always well-manicured like part of the fairway and was made for play by golfers as well as youngsters. It was on the south side of the fifth green but the east and west sides of it were incredibly steep and somewhat treacherous.

Jack McCabe and his girlfriend, Sara Bellamy, had been living at his grandfather's home on the shore of Lake Maxinkuckee for the past few weeks. After Jack's parents had been tragically killed in a skiing accident near Innsbruck, Austria, 12 years before, Jack became the sole heir to Amos McCabe's fortune and his vacation property on the lake.

Growing up, Jack always loved Maxinkuckee and its idyllic setting, where he learned to water ski, play golf and tennis, and appreciate the enchanting beauty of the area. During childhood, he always looked forward to taking rides with Pop in his big Cadillac for ice cream cones at Rossa's Drug Store, or into town where he'd buy him a small toy or a bag of little plastic cowboys and Indians.

Maxinkuckee, which means clear water or diamond lake, was named by its early inhabitants, the Potawatomi Indians, and is the second largest natural lake in Indiana. It is known as a kettle lake that was formed some 15,000 years ago by receding glaciers. Beneath the lake is one of the best-producing bedrock aquifer systems in Indiana. Twenty-one underground springs stemming from the aquifer feed the lake with fresh water.

"I'll make coffee, Sara," Jack sighed as he trundled to the kitchen. "You sleep a little longer if you can."

The two lovers had been in a close relationship for the past year and a half. Sara's his best friend and confidant with whom he can freely share his feelings. *She means the world to me.* They were both in their late 30s but, before they met, hadn't been in a serious, long-term relationship with anyone.

At six foot, 180 pounds, Jack was able to maintain his conditioning with daily runs. Even though his dark brown hair was beginning to turn prematurely grey in the temples, he was told he still had his youthful good looks.

Sara practiced yoga and vigorously rode a stationary bicycle with video training. With an African American father and Caucasian mother, her skin and lithe body were blessed with a perpetually tan glow that added to her sensuous features.

Among her hobbies, Sara loved genealogy and tracing her heritage as well as Jack's.

As partners in an Indianapolis advertising and public relations firm, McCabe and Bellamy, they had been through good times and bad with the business. The agency was hitting on all cylinders now. Jack's role as head of creative was very rewarding. He says they're lucky to have Sara who's a top-notch strategist and a technology geek, of sorts. *She's the best.* While at the lake cottage, they maintained communication with staff in Indianapolis via text, Skype and email.

It was a Tuesday in the middle of June and the morning brought a threat of rain, grey sodden clouds building overhead. With his fingers wrapped around a steaming cup of coffee, Jack sat in the front room and peered out over the blue-green lake, reflecting on the duties he faced to help settle his grandfather's estate. One of his challenges was to dig through Amos' numerous files and try to uncover anything that needed attention. *Hope I don't miss anything important.*

Amos McCabe's finances and trusts had been well managed by his attorneys and CPAs, so much of what they were uncovering related to business, cultural, and philanthropic activities.

"Want some company, buddy?" Sara implored as she joined Jack on the couch.

"Sure, I've been thinking about all the work we still have in front of us," Jack replied. "There's lots of filing cabinets. Hope we've got all the keys and combinations to locks."

"We should have everything, Jack, but I'll be happy to go through your grandfather's notes to be sure," Sara affirmed.

"Thanks, looks like a downpour any time. Think I'll head over to the golf course for a run before we get soaked," Jack exclaimed as he finished the last of his coffee.

Heading across the road to the course in his running attire, Jack didn't see any golfers, but there were few during the week at Maxinkuckee Country Club since many of the cottages and the course only came alive on weekends.

Passing by the seventh tee, Jack viewed the hilly terrain in front of him. *Perfect for a good run.* The big hill came into view almost immediately and he picked up his pace as he neared it.

"What the hell!" Jack screamed out loud as he suddenly approached the steep eastern slope adjacent to the fifth green and the big hill. Strewn awkwardly before him at the bottom of the precipitous hill was the body of a man with an old irrigation hose taut below his chin. His head was contorted in a freakish position with his arms and legs splayed awkwardly.

My God, that's Hugo! Jack echoed to himself trembling, nearing the body of his friend. Jack knew Hugo DeMann very well since their days at The University of Notre Dame. They both spent time together at the lake and maintained their close relationship.

How could this happen? Jack screamed to himself as he shivered at the sight of the lifeless form in front of him. Hugo was always very athletic and even though there was a sharp drop off from the top of the green, it was terrifying to imagine him sliding down the bank and getting tangled in the gnarled hose.

Reaching for the phone in his running pack, Jack shivered as he quickly dialed for help and waited for an answer. When the 911 emergency responder came on the line, Jack sputtered a brief description of his friend's horrifying state and their location on the golf course. *What the hell!*

While waiting for help to arrive, Jack hesitated but slowly bent down to see if Hugo was truly dead. Picking up a limp wrist, he felt for a pulse, but none was present. His worst fears were confirmed. Jack kept repeating to himself, *Can't believe this could happen.*

Both men played sports together and even tried out for rugby at Notre Dame, a very physical club sport with teammates who weren't quite good enough to make the Irish football team. They often water skied at the lake when they were younger. Hugo was even an accomplished barefoot skier at one point in his teens. With an inboard speedboat at full throttle, a skier drops a slalom ski and uses only his bare feet to stay above the water – a feat that takes incredible skill and agility.

The wail of sirens suddenly broke the still air. *Finally*, Jack thought in stunned silence as police and EMTs soon emerged over the knoll of a nearby grass bunker. Hauling in their gear, EMTs bent over Hugo's body to check his vitals. Detective Lewis Tenant, a lanky, middle-aged man with a full beard introduced himself and his stout, elderly deputy, Jerome Atrich.

While Tenant perused the scene, he began scratching notes on a small pad. Atrich pulled a camera from his backpack and began documenting the body and surrounding environment, scrutinizing both Jack and the victim. Matted wet grass wrapped around Hugo's limbs and head.

"How long ago did you find the body?" Tenant queried.

"Less than half an hour ago," sputtered Jack as he tried to control his racing pulse. "I live across the road in the McCabe cottage and was just out for a morning run."

"Can't believe it!" Jack trembled, trying to find words. "I've known this guy for years – even went to school with him. Hugo DeMann has been coming here with his family for a long time. In fact, he's a real estate developer and was just breaking ground for a new resort hotel on the old Potawatomi land on the northeast part of the lake. Right next to Culver Military Academy."

"Very sorry about this awful mess, Mr. McCabe. It looks like a terrible accident," Tenant responded. "I'm new to the area. Just moved here from Plymouth, Indiana, just up the road from Culver. I've heard that the land where he planned to build is sacred ground – Indian burial mounds or something. Hope you didn't touch anything around the body."

"I tried to feel for a pulse, but that was it," Jack mumbled as he gritted his teeth in disbelief, then thinking to himself, *Just don't see how Hugo fell down the hill. Getting tangled up in that water hose. He was just too athletic.*

"We'll be sure to check for fingerprints on the hose to see if we can find anything," Tenant said. "In any case – and sorry to be blunt – but it looks like Mr. DeMann's land developing days have come to an end."

2

W ith their initial examination of DeMann completed, the EMTs left to bring the ambulance to the scene. Deputy Atrich estimated that the probable time of death was the previous evening, near sunset, June 14. With his golf cart and clubs near the green above, Hugo must have been playing some twilight golf alone.

"Please come to the police station in Culver as soon as you're able, Mr. McCabe," ordered Detective Tenant. "I'd like to wrap this up quickly, if we can. We'll have to close off this part of the golf course until our investigation is completed."

When Jack returned to the cottage, Sara was waiting for him. "Just can't understand it, but the most horrifying thing has happened, Sara," he explained frantically, his eyes welling up. "I just found Hugo DeMann's body at the bottom of the hill next to the fifth green."

"Oh no! What on earth?" Sara cried as she threw her arms around him while he shook, trying to hold back her own tears.

"Police and emergency techs came and got the body. They said they're going to try to figure it out," Jack continued as he still couldn't make sense of the painful image. "Hugo had an irrigation hose under his throat. He must have slipped and fallen down the steep bank. Maybe it was too dark for him to see. How could it happen?"

After going over the sordid details with Sara, Jack decided to grab a quick shower and head into Culver to meet with the police. Jack began to relax as the hot, pulsing water soaked his body. *This isn't real,* he repeated to himself.

Since Culver was a small town on the north side of the lake, the police station was easy to find. Jack parked his silver Audi sedan in front and went in. "Thank you for coming to see us so quickly, Mr. McCabe. We know this must be horrible for you," Detective Tenant offered as Deputy Atrich sat nearby polishing off a cream-filled Long John.

"We found some fingerprints on the hose near his neck, but it's too early to know whose they could be – or if they were one of the groundskeepers," stated Tenant. "There was a peculiar clue at the top of the hill, however. We detected two sets of footprints at the edge of the green – one set skidded down the hill and another set of prints was not far behind at the top."

"An autopsy will be performed soon. That should verify his death by strangulation – accidental or otherwise," Atrich chimed in as he wiped a spot of donut cream from his chin.

Before signing his statement, Jack reiterated his shocking discovery of the body and gave Tenant more background on Hugo, his business, and family.

"Would you mind if we got your fingerprints, Mr. McCabe?" Tenant asked respectfully. "Just need to cover our bases.

"Do you know anyone who could have possibly wanted Mr. DeMann dead?" probed Tenant, taking a sip from his steaming coffee mug. "You mentioned his new resort being built on the ancient Potawatomi burial mounds, but we're not sure where to start looking for anyone who may be connected with the Indian tribe."

"It just occurred to me that Hugo had some fierce legal

battles with environmental activists concerning the location of a few of his properties," recalled Jack. "He was actually fearful of physical harm at one point, but I don't recall that it ever amounted to anything."

"Hmmm, we'll see if we can find anything related to those threats in past court filings," Tenant responded, thinking to himself that there may be more to DeMann's demise than a tragic slip and slide from the evening dew next to the green. And with the telltale footprints at the top of the hill, they were all beginning to suspect foul play.

A WEEK LATER, Jack and Sara returned to the lake cottage after attending Hugo's emotional funeral in Indianapolis. Jack did all he could to comfort the family, who was devastated by the loss. His wife, children, and relatives were obviously still in shock from the tragedy. *It's just not fair,* he kept saying to himself during the service.

Jack and Sara tried to set aside their grief by pouring through Amos' filing cabinets as well as boxes of documents and legal notes.

Even as he worked, Jack couldn't get Detective Tenant's comments out of his head, *We detected two sets of footprints – one set skidded down the hill and another was not far behind at the top.* In his mind, Jack could still picture the marks of Hugo's slide, and the horrible image of him at the bottom of the steep bank.

That evening, attempting to divert their thoughts from their recent experiences, Jack and Sara prepared one of their favorite meals on the grill: marinated chicken breasts wrapped in foil along with sliced green peppers, onions, and tiny red potatoes. With a hearty Romaine and tomato salad topped with oil and vinegar, they were ready to enjoy the feast. Popping the cork on a 2016 Chardonnay from the Sonoma Coast, the meal and the evening would be nearly complete. *This is just what the doctor ordered*, he thought.

Before calling it a day, they watched the sun descend through wispy crimson clouds over the western part of the lake. Sitting on the pier and holding hands, the dew was already forming on the white wooden planks. In the distance, fishermen boats were slowly motoring to secret destinations.

The next morning, after a deep, satisfying sleep that followed a passionate lovemaking episode, Jack and Sara were eager to continue sifting through Amos' files.

It was well known even before they began their review of Amos McCabe's papers that he had donated to a variety of missionary charities serving the poor in many parts of the world. His generosity was well documented with folders attributing specific contributions along with numerous letters of appreciation from beneficiaries. Jack and Sara had nothing but deep admiration for Amos' devoted outreach to the poor.

With a cup of fresh coffee steaming in front of him, Jack spread some recently discovered letters over the large, wooden kitchen table. When Sara sat down to join him, he remarked apprehensively, "Check these out. They're letters from organizations I've never heard of – very strange!

"Here's one from The Office of Foreign Relations that dates to the '90s. Another one in 2002 from the United Kingdom is signed by The Royal Guard for International Affairs. Here's one from a European outfit called The Blitzberg Group that came just a few years ago," Jack continued in disbelief. "They're all urging Pop to develop new formulations to replace the asphalt products used by McCabe Industries." Even though the company was one of the largest in its industry, Jack and Sara knew it was extremely odd to draw this type of attention from environmentalists. "What the hell's going on?"

"Very strange indeed – and frightening!" stressed Sara.

"Wow, here's one that's even more disturbing," Jack

exclaimed as he shook the letter in his hand. "It's from another organization called The International Academy of Sciences that also expressed concern over the use of asphalt materials for roads, bridges, and airports.

"It describes how greenhouse gases are accumulating in the earth's atmosphere as a result of human activities, and the use of fossil fuels like asphalt. Petroleum products like this are causing the earth's climate to change and ocean temperatures to rise. Due to this crisis, nations and corporations must take prompt action," Jack snorted. "It closes by saying, consider this a warning."

Astonished at these revelations, Jack and Sara stared at each other, stunned in disbelief. "What in the world is this all about? I don't get it," Jack said.

Just then the phone rang loudly, jarring the two back to reality. "Hello, Mr. McCabe, this is Detective Tenant. Thought I'd give you an update on your friend's death. The autopsy report showed it was indeed strangulation. It appears Mr. DeMann was a victim of homicide."

"Oh my God, Detective!" cried Jack. "What are you going to do now?"

"We'll start investigating people who may have been at the golf course on the day of the murder," responded Tenant. "We're still checking on the extra footprints we found at the top of the hill. If you know anything else we can go on, don't hesitate to call me. Oh, and your fingerprints don't match the ones on the irrigation hose, so you're no longer a suspect."

Jack shared the shocking police information with Sara as they sat transfixed and dumbfounded in front of the jarring letters.

3

Needing some fresh air to clear his head, Jack made his way out the back door for a walk down East Shore Drive. Sweat began beading on his body from his brisk pace and the moisture in the air. Returning home, he stopped by the mailbox. Among several sales circulars and bills, he was stunned to discover a letter from Hugo DeMann! Riveted, Jack tore open the envelope.

Dear Jack,

As one of my closest and dearest friends, I directed my attorney to mail this letter to you if anything happened to me. If you're receiving this, the worst has certainly come to pass.

You may recall that there have been numerous threats on my life from insidious factions who are driven to establish their goals for extreme environmental control. They claim my real estate developments have endangered wildlife and natural resources in multiple states.

As a result of ignoring their demands, I felt that I may have been in grave danger. I urge you to contact my attorney, Mr. Richard Fitzwell, through my real estate development headquarters in Indianapolis to learn more. He may be able to provide you and the police with the name of the organization behind these ultimatums.

Very sorry to bring you into this, old friend, but I know I can trust you.

Sincerely yours,

Hugo

After sharing Hugo's alarming letter with Sara, Jack phoned the local police, but he only got a voice recording alerting callers to leave a message. His next step was to contact Hugo's attorney to learn more. "Hello, Mr. Fitzwell, this is Jack McCabe, Hugo DeMann's friend. I just received his extremely unsettling letter."

"Very, very sad and disturbing situation, Mr. McCabe. We're all devastated," Fitzwell replied. "We've been in a constant battle with those radical environmentalists for the past several years. We've got the police on it and they've brought in the FBI. A variety of activist groups kept sending intimidating letters, but we never thought it would come to this."

"By any chance, have you received a letter from an organization called The International Academy of Sciences?" Jack queried.

"Let's see...yes, I believe they were one of the first ones to criticize Hugo's land development because they said it was encroaching on wetland areas – sites protected by the Environmental Protection Agency," Fitzwell confirmed as he thumbed through case files. "But our property was outside of those lands.

"Unfortunately, the International Academy of Sciences doesn't seem to exist according to FBI research. We're at a dead end for now, I'm afraid."

"The McCabe family business has also been receiving similar demands," Jack echoed nervously. "Our asphalt product has been on their radar. And now it looks like I may be on their hit list!" *How could this be?* Jack wondered to himself.

CULVER POLICEMEN DETECTIVE Tenant and Deputy Atrich pulled into the Maxinkuckee Country Club gravel parking lot for a follow-up visit with a golf course employee. "We're here to question one of your groundskeepers, Mr. Lonnie Moore, about his whereabouts on the night of the DeMann murder," Tenant announced to the preppy golf pro, Jackson Cass. "We're looking into fingerprints found on the hose that strangled DeMann and need a few words with him."

Cass got up from his desk and led the two policemen to a garage area loaded with tools, irrigation equipment, golf carts, and tractors. Moore was wiping his hands with an oily rag as he peeked up from an engine.

"Mr. Moore, we appreciate you coming into the station for fingerprinting last week. We found yours on the hose that was near the victim's body and we need to ask you again what you recall about that night," questioned Tenant.

"We all handle them hoses to water the greens, ya know. As I told ya, I got done mowin' early that day – knocked off about 4:30 for Miller Time," claimed Moore, a stocky, disheveled man in overalls. "Do most of my work on that part of the course in the mornin' before golfers hit the tees.

"I been seein' sompin' kinda odd, lately, though," Moore offered. "Some men been out by the wooded, swampy area near number eight fairway," he said. "Couldn't tell what they was doin' but looked kinda odd to me 'cause people just don't go hikin' 'round in there. Not too safe."

"Just where did you go after you got off work at 4:30?" inquired Atrich.

"Head to the Brewhouse most days," Moore claimed.

"Give us a call if you see anyone out in the swampy area again, okay?" requested Tenant. "We'll check out your Brewhouse alibi."

THAT EVENING AFTER SUPPER, Jack and Sara sat on their pier with stemless goblets of Cabernet. They peered out over the lake, watching billowy, white sailboats cut through the breeze like swans gliding over glass. Then Sara pondered, "I wonder if McCabe Industries has tried to develop an alternative to asphalt for its road paving material? Have you had any contact with them recently?"

"No, I haven't," replied Jack who was not an employee, only its new owner. "Good thinking. I'll contact them to see if they have anything going on in the research and development lab. Since Pop knew about these threats, you'd have to imagine they'd be working on something."

Early the next morning Jack called the head of product development at McCabe Industries, Ellen Mentry. "Hello Ellen, it's Jack McCabe, Amos' grandson. It's been awhile but I wanted to ask you some questions."

"Well, hello, Jack," responded Ellen, a bright, young chemist who had been with the company for seven years. "How can I help you?"

"Did Amos ever discuss developing alternatives to asphalt for the company products?" Jack inquired.

"Actually, we're getting close to something quite extraordinary, but we're still testing it," Ellen advised. "As you may know by now, various environmental activist groups have been putting a lot of pressure on us to stop using the crude oil bitumen.

"We got the idea from scientists in the Netherlands who have used a plant molecule known as lignin to replace bitumen.

Lignin, which keeps water out of plants and binds them together, is chemically much like bitumen. As a result, the two products can be blended to produce a product that replaces some of the bitumen from the usual asphalt mix.

"In fact, we think it's possible to produce a 50-50 mix of bitumen and lignin that works well for paving construction applications, cutting the demand for asphalt in half, and helping the eco system.

"There's certainly lots of lignin in the world, too, because it accounts for almost a third of all the dry material in trees. It's removed as a waste product during the production of paper. There's about 50 million tons of the stuff around the world every year!"

"That's incredible, Ellen!" Jack emphasized. "Have you reported this to the environmentalists?"

"We've sent them letters but haven't received any replies. Have to say that we're not sure of their addresses," responded Ellen. "I'll definitely keep you apprised on the development of our new product – and if we hear anything from the people who have written us."

Just as he hung up, another call came in from Detective Tenant responding to Jack's earlier phone message. "What's the latest, Mr. McCabe?" Tenant asked. "Any news on DeMann?"

"Actually, there are a couple of new developments," Jack replied as he filled in the policeman about the shocking letters his grandfather had received and about the unexpected one from Hugo. "I spoke with Hugo's attorney and the police have the FBI looking into the intimidating letters he received," Jack added. "So far, they haven't been able to get a good lead on The International Academy of Sciences, the outfit that has threatened both Hugo and my grandfather." *This is crazy,* Jack thought.

4

A secret gathering of the group that called itself The Committee met in a remote, stately villa outside Rome, Italy. Their revered director, Adamis Baum, ordered vigorously, "Take your seats. We are very pleased that you could all attend this important session. We have much to discuss."

The Committee was the latest iteration of The New Global Order whose goal was to dominate the political and economic direction of the world.

Fingering a stack of neatly arranged folders, Baum, a wealthy but shady financier whose lawyers had kept him out of prison, set the agenda by restating the group's mission. "We will achieve one global government and a one-unit monetary system. The population will be limited by restrictions on the number of children per family, until there are one billion people who are useful to us. They will be permitted to live in areas which will be strictly and clearly defined. And they will be under our control as part of the new global population."

Those at the ornate round table showed their agreement with nods and grunts. Some lightly pounded their fists to demonstrate support. Coffee cups and glasses clinked from the vibrations.

"There will be no middle class, only those of us in leadership and our servants," Baum expressed heartily. "All laws will be uniform under a legal system of global courts practicing the same unified code of laws, enforced by one global police force and one global unified military.

"Those who are obedient and subservient to the global government will be rewarded with the means to live. Privately owned firearms and weapons of any kind will be prohibited. Those who are rebellious will be starved to death or be declared outlaws. Targets for execution."

It was well known to the group that, in the past, U.S. political leaders who didn't follow The New Global Order agenda may have been killed by the organization's adherents. More recently, a prominent CIA director and a naval commander were possibly assassinated because they weren't doing what they were directed – and tried to expose The New Global Order's plans.

"As you know, one of our recent goals has been to destabilize the U.S. economy," Baum stated almost breathlessly. "In the past, several influential political leaders helped cripple the U.S. by creating wars in the Middle East, Vietnam and Korea. Then, a compliant United Nations Military entered those areas to create an ongoing presence to support us."

Creating fear was a tactic The Committee frequently used to expand its goals and manipulate human emotions. They would establish a rival group to create unrest in a nation they wished to unhinge. That group would initiate a problem – often fueled by misinformation in the media – and then promote a solution.

Baum went on to describe just such an effort involving global warming. "The U.S. proposal for a dramatic climate-change policy, which calls for sweeping changes to American society, has been a masterful strategy. Its objectives include cutting greenhouse-gas emissions to zero over the next decade. And the left-wing political party behind it is promising to provide a free wage for all."

However, The Committee knew this manifesto wasn't totally about the environment. It was also about changing the country's economic model to redistribute wealth and further deteriorate the U.S. economy.

"Secretary Lisbett Kant, what is the latest on the Environmental Disruption Initiative that is beginning to affect the U.S.?" inquired Baum as he peered intently over his reading glasses at a well-dressed, full-figured woman of German heritage.

"Thank you, Herr Director," Kant replied. "We are hoping to see much unrest in the United States – politically and financially – nurtured in large part, as you mentioned, by the radical left wing of the government. We have continued to carry out our campaign to intimidate hundreds of successful businesses and their executives into complying with our demands for environmental purity.

"In several instances, we have had to make examples of those who failed to comply by liquidating them or with other means designed to disrupt their corporations. Without question, it appears that our threats and actions are beginning to have a ripple effect in the U.S."

"Hear! Hear!" shouted Major Oli Klosov, a hefty former Russian military leader with a clean-shaven head and large, black-framed glasses.

"Wonderful to know our work is producing results." Others at the table nodded their approvals with gusto.

THE NEXT AFTERNOON at Maxinkuckee Country Club, Detective Tenant and Deputy Atrich borrowed a golf cart to investigate possible sightings of people roaming in the woods near the eighth fairway. "Can't imagine what someone would be doing out there – it's mostly swampland past this initial wooded area," claimed Atrich.

As they neared the woods along the fairway, Tenant noticed an odd structure 20 or 30 yards away. "Can't tell what that is, Jerry, but I'd like to get a closer look."

Atrich handed him a pair of binoculars but there was too much foliage to get a clear view. "We're going to need a rowboat to get out there. Too much swamp to cross on foot."

When they returned to the grounds-crew garage they found Lonnie Moore moving some golf carts inside as thunderstorm clouds brewed suspiciously overhead. After confirming Moore's alibi the night of the murder, he was cleared. "Say, Mr. Moore," Tenant asked, "would you have a rowboat we can borrow? Need to get out into the swamp near the eighth fairway to check something out."

"Happen to have one inside," Moore offered. "Better take the trailer and one of our ATVs." After getting the boat and trailer hooked up, they returned to the swamp.

Sounds of bullfrogs croaked loudly on the nearby lily pads as the policemen pushed through the swaying cattails that lined the water's edge. They slid the boat onto the algae-laden surface and rowed toward the mysterious object. When they arrived at a small island, they were stunned by what they saw.

With a crack of lightening and dark, thunderous clouds bubbling overhead, they peered at a tree-like effigy fashioned from twigs and limbs covered with strips of cloth of various colors, large bird feathers, several stuffed birds, beaver claws, and cattle horns – all hanging like ornaments on an eerie Christmas tree.

"Holy horse feathers, Lew! What in the Sam Hill is that thing?" Atrich, muttered loudly, as they both peered at the peculiar sight.

"No idea, Jerry. Let's get some photos. Near as I can tell it's some sort of Indian construction. But what Indians are even around here these days?"

After returning the boat and ATV to Moore, they headed back to the police station to collect their thoughts.

"Vishnu Verheer, Notre Dame Professor of Archeology, is the only person I know who's an expert on American Indians," Tenant opined as he recalled attending one of Verheer's Indian culture seminars a few years back.

Fortunately for them, Verheer was on the South Bend, Indiana, campus for summer classes working on student research papers. "Hello, Professor, this is Detective Lewis Tenant of the Culver police. You won't remember me, but I attended one of your seminars a while ago and need some help.

"We're investigating a murder and checking out several leads. The guy who was murdered had broken ground on a new resort hotel on land that was once an Indian burial mound on the shore of Lake Maxinkuckee. I'm telling you this because we've spotted a very peculiar tree-like structure about a hundred yards from the crime scene. And it looks like it was possibly made by Indians. If you have a few minutes, I'd like to email you some photos to see if you can help."

Moments later when the email arrived, Verheer eagerly opened the photos and downloaded them to his computer. He knew right away what the police were facing. "Hello, Detective? Verheer said eagerly when he called back. "Yes, this is unquestionably of American Indian origin. It's made as part of an offering to the Great Indian Spirit. It's very likely for a Ghost Dance.

"Medicine men and others gathered around a tree-like structure, like the one you found, had visions and talked with the spirits of friends who had died. The group chanted and danced around the tree in a circular pattern continuously – which induced a state of religious ecstasy. Believers in the Ghost

Dance spirituality were convinced that performing this ceremonial rite would eventually connect them with their ancestors coming from the spirit world – and ensure that they were at peace.

"With the disturbance to the burial mounds near the lake, it appears that an Indian descendant in your community has resurrected the ancient tradition for the benefit of the spirit world."

When they finished their call with Verheer, Tenant and Atrich sat bewildered, wondering where this strange investigation was headed. "Let's start making some calls to see if we can find any Indians living in the vicinity," Tenant mumbled as he broke their silence and pulled up a search engine on his computer, tapping rhythmically on the keyboard.

5

A fter digging through most of Amos McCabe's documents on the main floor, Jack and Sara descended to the basement to explore further. In an alcove behind the pool table, Sara spotted a small safe they hadn't noticed before. "Do you know the combination to this one?"

"It might be Pop's birthdate...let's see...try 9-26-15," he responded.

Sara rotated the large combination dial, and as the lock tumblers fell into place, the safe door opened. "You got it, buddy!" *Lucky guess,* Jack thought.

Sifting through the contents of investment security stock certificates, bonds, and other financial documents, she came across an envelope that was hand addressed to Jack.

He eagerly reached for the large white envelope and tore open the seal. It was a letter from Amos McCabe that sent instant chills through his body.

Dear Jack,
   I feel obligated to share some information that will no doubt
be quite disturbing. I didn't want to tell you this when it

happened, but your parents died somewhat mysteriously. Their lives ended on a ski slope in the Alps, but records from the Innsbruck police and the U.S. Embassy there indicated they may have perished at the hands of a suspicious criminal force.

You may know by now from letters in my files, I have received threats from a sinister group who I have discovered is interested in global dominance. They claim our business is a scourge upon the earth due to our use of fossil fuels, and they intend to destroy it and the McCabe family. Even though our business is quite large, my connection to it may go back further, possibly to a German Nazi I imprisoned during World War II.

Your father became a target once he took over as chief executive. Now that you're in a capacity of sole ownership, you may be in danger.

I hate delivering such devastating news, but I wanted to give you an opportunity to take matters into your own hands. My advice is to either disappear to save yourself – or expose these villains and help bring them to justice. I wish you nothing but the best and may Godspeed.

Love, Pop

"This keeps getting stranger and stranger," Jack said as he and Sara sat bewildered, barely able to breathe. Moments later, they collected the documents from the safe and returned to the main floor to ponder this new revelation. "Now we have an even better idea who's behind those threatening letters," Jack said, realizing he was probably stating the obvious.

"Sara, you know I love you dearly, but I wouldn't blame you if you wanted to get out now, before it's too late," Jack offered as they sat together on the living room sofa facing the lake.

"You're crazy, Jack! You're my life and I'm here to stay," replied Sara, leaving no doubt about her commitment to him as she wrapped her hands around his.

"Thank God you're with me. I can't help but want to find out all I can about my parents' deaths. It's probably a longshot, but I wonder what we can learn from the police records in Innsbruck. And the U.S. Embassy there," Jack exclaimed. "There's probably six hours difference in time from here, so I'll try calling tomorrow."

After dawn the next morning, with the sun peering through the cottage's eastern windows, Sara searched the web for possible Innsbruck police numbers and came up with several to try. She was also able to identify the number to the U.S. Embassy.

Jack put down his coffee at the kitchen table and dialed the number to the police. "Guten tag, polizei. Wie kann ich ihnen helfen?" came an unfamiliar answer on the phone.

"Uh, hello, my name is Jack McCabe, calling from the U.S. Do you speak English?"

"Oh yes, sir, how may I be of service?"

"My parents were killed during a skiing trip some 12 years ago and I want to see if you still have records going back that far?"

"Yes, sir, we do, but you will need to inquire in person to access them," the young man replied. "For security reasons, we won't be able to provide anything over the telephone. I'm very sorry."

"I understand, thank you," Jack said as he hung up the phone.

Jack quickly made up his mind. "I have to see this thing through, Sara. Do you want to join me on a trip to Austria? I will need to meet the police in person to gain access to my parents' files. Got to figure this out," he said.

Without hesitation, Sara began researching airfare and then booked a direct, one-way flight from Chicago to the Innsbruck airport. They steeled themselves for what they might find.

AFTER MAKING multiple calls to resources and businesses in the Culver area to see if anyone was aware of any American Indian families nearby, Detective Tenant contacted Bigley Orchards to see if they might be employing any. Timothy Burr, head of apple production, came on the line and said gruffly, "Matter of fact we've had the Pokaten family working here – been on staff for several generations, maybe longer. Good people, hard workers. What's the problem?"

"Well, good to know, Mr. Burr. Do you know how I might reach them?" queried Tenant, tapping a pen on his notepad.

"Best way is to call the son, Brandon Pokaten," Burr replied, telling Tenant the number after fumbling through his records. "Actually, he's working in the production line at the processing plant today if you need to speak to him in person."

After Atrich finished his morning coffee and spiced cruller, the two policemen rushed out to the squad car to visit Bigley Orchards. When they arrived, they found Burr at his desk overlooking the processing plant with people busily engaged in sorting and crating the apples, sounds of machinery clattering in the background.

Burr escorted the two men down to the floor and pulled Pokaten aside.

"Brandon, these Culver policemen want a word with you," Burr announced.

"What's the problem, officers?" young Pokaten responded graciously.

"We found an Indian ceremonial structure out near the Maxinkuckee golf course and want to see if you know anything about it?" Tenant asked.

"My grandfather, Joseph, and my father, Edward, have recently performed some ceremonies outside of the course property. They were praying to the Great Spirits to protect our family and those of our ancestors. They weren't hurting anyone."

"We'll need for you, your father and grandfather to come to the police station in Culver for some fingerprints. We need to check out all possible leads, you understand," Tenant ordered as he exchanged quick glances with Brandon and Deputy Atrich. "You or your family may have been spotted on a nearby fairway when a murder took place on the golf course."

As the Lufthansa Airline touched down on the Innsbruck Airport runway, Jack and Sara were awed by the majestic view of the Alps and eagerly anticipated their next steps. They immediately caught a glimpse of gleaming rays of sunlight bouncing off the snow-covered peaks. After claiming their luggage and going through customs, they hailed a taxi and headed to the Hotel Maximilian. Since it was late in the day, they decided to find a nearby restaurant for a meal, then get a good night's sleep.

The next morning, following a breakfast of cappuccinos, chocolate almond croissants, and bowls of fruit at the hotel café, they were eager for their visit to the Innsbruck police station. "This should be interesting," Jack mused.

"Hello, my name is Jack McCabe, and this is Sara Bellamy," he announced to the policeman on duty. "I called recently from the U.S. about my parents who were killed in a skiing accident 12 years ago. I would like to see their file, if I may."

"Of course, Mr. McCabe. I have some forms for you to complete and I will need to see your passports for security purposes," replied Officer Raymond Zenz.

After the formalities were completed, Zenz led them through a well-lit hallway to an elevator, and down to a basement vault where case files were stored. Inside the vault, the policeman keyed in the data on a built-in computer to identify the file's location. He then led them to a storeroom with tall, metal storage shelves.

Moments later, "Here it is, Mr. McCabe," Zenz announced holding a sealed container as he climbed down a ladder. "I will escort you to an office where you may examine the report in detail."

Inside the well-lit room with a small conference table, Jack and Sara broke the seal and opened the box to investigate the contents. In addition to several gruesome photos of the crash site, they were immediately drawn to a profile of the accident that took the McCabes' lives. *Oh my God!* Jack thought.

12 October 2007

Re: Thomas and Julia McCabe, Deceased

The cable car ridden by American citizens Thomas and Julia McCabe at the Nordpark Ski Resort had traveled 300 meters (1,600 ft.) from its starting point. The car suddenly detached from the cables and plunged 90 meters onto the rocky cliffs of the mountainside below. The cable car disintegrated on impact, killing the Americans. Their bodies were airlifted to Innsbruck and later returned to their family's custody in Indiana, USA.

According to the chief engineer of the cable car company, Tyson Knotts, the aerial tramway was built in 1997. Knotts reported that the tramway had been working in "perfect order" prior to the accident. It had recently passed an inspection by the private engineering firm, Displatz, Ltd. During inspection, each component of the cable car had been evaluated, including the cabin, cables, motors and pylons.

Witnesses reported that it appeared that one of the cables holding the car had snapped. Local officials stated that the cable car broke free from one or two cables supporting it, causing a third cable to collapse. Additionally, the ski resort superintendent, Franz Lammer, stated that the car unhooked itself from the cables for some unknown reason.

Initially, the state prosecutor demanded a nine-month prison sentence for the chief maintenance worker, Joseph Kerr, for his contributing negligence in the accident. However, after three months, the court acquitted Kerr of all charges.

Signed: Chief Inspector Raynor Schein

Once again, Jack and Sara stared at each other, horrified by the dreadful documentation and photos of the McCabes. "I don't recall ever hearing that it was such a freak accident," Jack sputtered. "Pop never said a word."

6

At the conclusion of the secret meeting of The Committee, members were engaged in rapt conversation concerning their roles in plots to further the goals of The New Global Order. Sounds of chatter and chairs scooting from the large, round table invaded the air.

"What more can you tell me about the Environmental Disruption Initiative in America, Secretary Kant?" probed Major Oli Klosov in a private conversation, subtly leering at Kant through his thick, black-framed glasses.

"You will be happy to know that the UN Climate Summit in the U.S. went off perfectly," Kant replied, clearing her throat, while delicately adjusting her dress to better cover her voluptuous breasts.

"World leaders of governments – minus those from the U.S. – and the private sector joined to increase and accelerate climate-change action. They focused on heavy industry, fossil-fuel products, and global-warming-initiative finance. Leaders expressed enthusiasm about convening again the following year for the UN climate conference, where commitments will certainly be renewed and hopefully increased."

"I'm afraid another event did not go quite so well," Klosov growled in response. "The high-tech, climate-change conference held in Italy that was attended by wealthy movie stars, entertainers, and politicians, is now being slammed as hypocritical."

"Yes, it was seen as a dismal display of excessive hypocrisy, I'm afraid," Kant agreed, "considering all the lavish yachts that were docked and jets that were flown in by millionaires and billionaires. We won't promote a miscalculation like that again.

"On a grassroots level," Kant continued, "we're making excellent progress against petroleum-based businesses and the enforcement of environmentally protected lands in America. Our threats appear to be received more seriously than ever before. As you know, we've had to use force in some cases – taken the extra step as we say. Director Baum will not rest until we achieve our objectives."

AFTER RECEIVING the shocking news at the police station, Jack and Sara took a taxi to the U.S. Embassy to see if they could uncover anything further about the tragic accident – if it was an accident. When they arrived and confirmed their identities to the guards, they were greeted by an attractive, red-haired foreign service officer, Tessa Steckles. "How may I help you today? I'm Ms. Steckles."

Following introductions and explaining the reason for their visit to Innsbruck, Jack said, "We read in the police report about the accident and the acquittal of the maintenance person involved in the faulty cable that led to my parents' deaths. The record indicated that the cable came unhooked for some unknown reason. There were threats on my parents' lives, and we have to wonder if some person or organization might be behind it?"

Sara quickly added, "Since the entire cable car, its parts, and the cables themselves had just been approved for use by an engineering firm, we have to question how this could happen – unless there was a criminal motive behind it."

"I am extremely sorry for your loss," Steckles replied. "Please come into my office and let's discuss your case in more detail." With a background in U.S. military operations and counter espionage, Steckles' personal radar was immediately piqued by their story. They entered her private office, which was well appointed with a comfortable seating area.

"Have you been aware of any suspicious activities with the Austrian court system?" Sara inquired.

"We don't monitor every court case and certainly haven't kept track of something as far back as your parents' accident," Steckles answered. "However, as part of the Embassy's enhanced surveillance program in conjunction with the U.S. military and Interpol Counter Terrorism Unit, we are aware of some irregularities that have occurred between the court system and outside political groups."

"By any chance are you familiar with an organization that has a desire for global dominance?" Jack asked, thinking of his grandfather's letter.

"I am familiar with an international terrorist group that calls itself The New Global Order, Mr. McCabe," Steckles responded, glancing back and forth between the two of them. "How did you become aware of these people?"

"They may be behind threats to my family and our fairly large business, which manufactures asphalt materials. As you probably know, it's a fossil-fuel-based product they are trying to force us to stop using due to radical environmental concerns," explained Jack.

Sara continued, "Since Jack's father was the CEO of the company when he died – or was killed – he was very likely a target!"

"Hmmm, I would like to put you in touch with the Chief at Interpol, The International Criminal Police Organization. Even though Interpol's headquarters is in Lyon, France, its Counter Terrorism Unit is here in Innsbruck, which is aligned with the U.S. military. In addition to my work at the Embassy, I serve as a U.S. military Combat Liaison to assist in their investigations."

"Wonderful," Jack responded. "Sounds like we're meeting the right people." *Wow, this is encouraging,* he thought.

"His name is Samuel Aritan, and he has a lot of experience in these matters," Steckles advised, handing them her business card. "And here's the Chief's phone number. I will get in touch with him and provide an initial briefing."

"We are very grateful for your help, Ms. Steckles!" Jack said, feeling more relieved than he had since his arrival in Innsbruck.

"If Aritan gets on board, you'll see me again," Steckles replied. "We occasionally work in tandem on cases."

The Interpol office was a short taxi ride from the U.S. Embassy, so after Jack phoned to set up the meeting, they quickly reached Chief Aritan's office. "Tessa filled me in on your situation. Have to say how sorry I am that you've had to deal with this kind of crap," Aritan offered when they were ushered into his office. "Please excuse the cigar smoke. It'll probably be the death of me, but I'm a sucker for good tobacco."

Aritan paused then said, "There's a lot of rotten characters in this world that we have to deal with, but The New Global Order may be one of the sickest. They're very well financed and have many shell organizations operating for them. Hate their asses."

Chief Samuel Aritan was a well-built, bearded African American in his late 40s who had served in the U.S. Army for several tours during the Middle East wars. He was an expert in reconnaissance and intelligence work and dealt with his share of troublemakers around the world. His knowledge of The New Global Order went back several decades. His love for fine cigars, especially those from the Dominican Republic and Nicaragua, and his rough language were two distinguishing characteristics people got wind of quickly.

"Do you think there's any way we can find out more details about my parents' cable car accident?" Jack inquired as Sara blinked her watery eyes in reaction to the fumes in the air.

Aritan explained the process he would initiate on their behalf and told them to sit tight in Innsbruck until he completed some research on the case. "I'll be in touch in a day or two and let you know what I've uncovered. Can you stick around here for a while if you have to?"

"Yes," Jack responded eagerly. "We are most grateful for your help! If I can, I'd like to share some additional information that The New Global Order may be behind. There is an investigation going on in Culver, Indiana, regarding a possible murder of a good friend of mine, Mr. Hugo DeMann, who also received intimidating threats. We spoke to his attorney who confirmed that the group behind the threats may have had all the earmarks and aliases of this organization."

"Hmmm...damned shame about your friend, Mr. McCabe," answered Aritan as he made notes on a legal pad. "We'll start working on your parents' case and see what turns up."

BACK AT THE Culver Police Station, Deputy Jerome Atrich completed fingerprinting the three Pokaten men, Brandon, Joseph, and Edward, handing them a box of tissues to wipe their fingers. "Can you tell us where you were on the evening of June 14?" Detective Lewis Tenant inquired as he squinted at the three men of American Indian heritage. "As you may know, that was the night Hugo DeMann was murdered on the golf course. You might have been seen nearby on that day, which is why we're checking all possible leads in the case."

"We were honoring our ancestors' spirits for over a week in

that location," stated Joseph Pokaten, the eldest of the three. "Since our family's ancient burial site on the banks of Lake Maxinkuckee was desecrated by the construction of the new hotel, we prayed that the spirits of our ancestors were still at peace."

Then Edward Pokaten spoke up. "We are not violent people, Detective. Our ceremonies are peaceful, and we do not seek revenge. However, I did see a man on the golf course on that evening. He was someone I have never seen in the area before. And as far as I could tell, he was not playing golf."

"Hmmm, can you describe this person?" asked Atrich.

"I wasn't totally focused on him, but as I watched the sunset, I caught sight of him and believe his arms were heavily tattooed – in what looked like swastikas. I think he may have worn a shirt with the sleeves cut off, and jeans with work boots. He looked unshaven with dark hair. He didn't seem to belong there."

"What time did you leave your ceremonial location near the eighth fairway that day?" questioned Tenant.

"It was before sunset, and I recall that the man was still prowling along the edge of the fairway," Edward said, distinctly remembering the person's image, as he looked past the late-day sun that was filtered through fluttering foliage, with nearby cattails swaying like sentinels in the wind.

7

During a romantic dinner at the Ottoburg Restaurant near their hotel, Sara had beef in a delicious bouillon broth, served with creamed leaf spinach, roasted potatoes topped with horseradish, plus apple mousse. Jack enjoyed the wiener schnitzel, served with a dish of cranberries, parsley potatoes, and a mixed salad perfectly dressed with oil and vinegar. They both savored a bottle of Austrian red wine.

After the meal, Jack asked if he ever told her about some of the famous people who spent time at Lake Maxinkuckee. "Don't recall you ever bringing it up," Sara responded quizzically.

"You've certainly heard of former New York Yankees owner George Steinbrenner. He owned a place on the lake after attending Culver Military Academy. His four children and five grandchildren also went there."

Sara sipped her wine and nodded as she listened attentively to Jack's fascinating history lesson.

"Are you familiar with the old songs *Night and Day, Anything Goes,* or *It's De-Lovely*? They were from popular musical composer Cole Porter, who was a Maxinkuckee regular.

"How about the author Kurt Vonnegut? He had lots of

popular books like *Cat's Cradle*, *Breakfast of Champions*, and *Slaughterhouse Five*.

"Let's see, another big name was author Lew Wallace who wrote *Ben Hur*, which was made into a movie. And the Hoosier poet, James Whitcomb Riley, was also a frequent visitor. I'm sure there were others whose names escape me."

"Wow, that's amazing," Sara responded and then chuckled. "I had no idea. Now Maxinkuckee has another famous name: Jack McCabe!"

Even though the candlelit dinner was very enjoyable, they were eager to learn more about Jack's parents' deaths.

After several days passed since their meeting at Interpol, the phone buzzed in Jack and Sara's suite. "Hello, Mr. McCabe, I have some news about your parents," Chief Samuel Aritan explained. "If you have a few minutes, come by my office today and I'll fill ya in."

Aching to learn more, they grabbed a taxi and made it to his office in less than five minutes. When they sat down with Chief Aritan, he had an international newspaper opened on his desk. *What's this?* Jack wondered.

"Since your family's business has likely been threatened by factions of The New Global Order, you'll be interested in this story," Aritan offered, putting his cigar in a nearby ashtray. "It's about a scientist by the name of Cyrus Burnett, murdered just two days ago after a meteorological conference in Denmark. He'd just presented his research that countered global warming theories. Someone must have had it in for him – 'cause now he's dead."

Aritan read aloud from the article. "Burnett stated in his speech that a study he published in the American Meteorological Society's *Journal of Climate* showed that climate-change models exaggerated global warming from CO_2 emissions by as much as 45 percent!" Aritan paused then growled, "Guess the damn media only reports the bad news."

"That's incredible," Jack responded as he and Sara exchanged glances.

Aritan continued citing another part of the article. "Burnett also said that the official NASA global temperature data from February 2016 to February 2018 showed that average global temperatures actually dropped by 0.56 degrees Celsius – the biggest two-year drop in the past century.

"If this murder's linked to The New Global Order, it's another in a long line of strikes against them. Problem is, they hire local contract hitmen to do their dirty work. Makes it difficult to pin crimes on 'em.

"This may be what we're facing with your parents, Mr. McCabe. It's possible the maintenance man, Joseph Kerr, who was charged with negligence for the faulty cables, was paid off indirectly by The New Global Order. But we'll have to prove that in a court of law. Won't be easy. If we can find supporting evidence, he could be charged with accessory to a double murder. It's one hell of a cold case."

Sounds like we're getting somewhere! Jack said to himself.

"I've asked our field agents to investigate Kerr's bank statements. Since it was 12 years ago, we're having a little problem getting his old records, but we expect to find what we need. Hang in there for several more days. We'll know if Kerr received a big payoff for his dirty deed."

BACK IN CULVER, the fingerprints of the three Pokaten men did not match those on the irrigation hose – the weapon used to strangle Hugo DeMann. As a result, they were no longer suspects, but they could be valuable witnesses since they saw a man on the golf course the night of the crime.

Wondering out loud, Deputy Atrich asked, "Where are we

going to find a guy with swastika tattoos, Lew? Almost sounds like some sort of Neo Nazi type."

"Well, using the information we got from our meeting with the Pokatens, I did some research and found a group in Warsaw, Indiana, not far from here," Detective Tenant said as he scanned his computer. "Their name is the White Aryan Resistance. Says they share a hatred for Jews and a love for Adolf Hitler and Nazi Germany. They also hate minorities, gays, lesbians, and Christians."

After calling their police contacts in Warsaw, the Culver policemen learned that several Neo Nazi types had been booked for crimes in the past. Some had seen prison time. "Can you fax us some photos of people in those gangs?" Tenant asked his Warsaw contact, Officer Woodrow Forrest. "We're looking for a guy with swastika tattoos on his arms."

"Sounds familiar but I'll have to check our files," replied Forrest.

Later that day, the fax machine hummed and Atrich put down his glazed donut to see what turned up.

"Well now, Lew, this looks hot," Atrich enthused as he pulled out a mug shot of a man named Terrence Boll, who could be a possible match for what the Pokatens described. His arms were heavily tattooed with swastikas.

"Looks like we'll be paying the Pokatens a house call," agreed Tenant who carefully studied the faxed image.

An hour later, when the Culver police squad car pulled up to the Pokaten house on the outskirts of Culver, the grandfather, Joseph, was relaxing in a rocking chair on the front porch, smoking a large wooden pipe carved with Indian icons. An elderly woman with white braided hair rocked next to him. "Hello Mr. Pokaten, we'd like to see your son Edward. Is he home today?" Asked Tenant.

"He should be out back doing some repair work on the house, Detective," the old man answered. "Is there a problem?"

"Just have some questions," Tenant answered with a smile as they started moving to the back of the house.

Edward stopped repairing a rear window when he saw the police coming into view. "Don't want to alarm you, Mr. Pokaten. Just need you to look at a photo of someone who might match the description of the person you saw on the fairway the night of the murder," Tenant said in a friendly manner.

After putting on his reading glasses, Edward scrutinized the faxed photo he now held in his hands. "Can't say I saw his face real clearly, but the arms appear to be the same. Those tattoos look like what I remember," he stated calmly, glancing up at the policemen.

"Would you be willing to testify to that in a court of law, Mr. Pokaten?" Atrich inquired. "It could be critical to convicting this guy if his fingerprints match."

"I'll do what I can to help," Edward responded, even though he realized it could be stirring up a hornet's nest for him and his family by doing so.

On the ride back to the Culver police station, Tenant asked, "Do you see the irony in this situation, Jerry?"

"What's that, Lew?"

"There's a possibility that Edward Pokaten – whose family has been in mourning after DeMann's company desecrated their Indian burial ground – may help convict DeMann's murderer!"

"Well, I'll be, you're right," Atrich agreed with a wry smile. When they returned to the police station, Tenant called Officer Forrest in Warsaw. "It looks like we may have a visual identification of the guy with the tattooed arms – Mr. Terrence Boll. Do you happen to have a set of fingerprints on him? We need to compare them to what we pulled off the murder weapon."

"Sure, I'll email the images we've got on file. I'll tell you, he's a mean S.O.B., so it will be a challenge bringing him in if he's your man. If his gang's around, they'll try to protect him."

About 20 minutes later, the email came through with the fingerprints on Boll. "Jerry, can you get these to the lab A.S.A.P. to see if we have a match?" Tenant asked when the printer chugged out the forensic evidence.

After dropping them off at the lab, Atrich stopped by the Culver Coffee Company for some lemon meringue pie, and to catch up on a local newspaper and eavesdrop on the gossip amid the clattering of coffee cups. An hour later, the lab called his mobile phone telling him the test was completed.

When Atrich returned to the station, he announced excitedly, "The lab determined that Boll's fingerprints were indeed a match to those found on the irrigation hose."

"The next step: charge him and book him," Tenant responded as he glanced at the weapons case in the back of the office. Based on Boll's violent reputation, he knew it wouldn't be easy.

8

Chief Samuel Aritan from Interpol called Jack the next day with some encouraging news. "Hello, Mr. McCabe. We've got some evidence incriminating Joseph Kerr, the damned maintenance man at the ski resort. He was paid a week before your parents' deaths by a company called the Luzar Group. Believe that's only a shell organization, so we're investigating further.

"The one-time deposit from Luzar was 10 times Kerr's monthly salary, which tells the tale. Once we locate Kerr, we'll bring him in for questioning. We'll get answers."

"Do you have any leads on his whereabouts?" Jack asked.

"Gotta believe he's working as a maintenance person at another ski resort. Should track him down soon," Aritan said hopefully, flicking the ash from a Nicaraguan. "I'll get back in touch as soon as we know more."

THREE DAYS LATER, two young, well-built Interpol officers approached Joseph Kerr behind the Kitzbuhel Ski Resort, where he was working on a tractor inside a garage. "Mr. Kerr, I'm Officer Melvin Loewe and this is Officer Phillip Wright," Loewe announced as he showed his Interpol identification badge. "We are here to question you about the cable car accident 12 years ago at Nordpark."

"Hey, already served time for what they called *negligence*," Kerr stammered, beginning to tremble at the presence of the policemen. "Can't do nothin' more 'bout that."

"You're right, Kerr," Loewe responded, "but this isn't about negligence; this is much more serious. We have evidence that you received a large payment the week before the cable car *accident*, and we need you to come with us for questioning."

"Hey, I'm working here. Can't just leave my job."

"We've explained the situation to your boss; you're coming with us," Loewe replied as he cuffed Kerr and then physically escorted him to their unmarked cruiser.

Several hours later, Kerr was brought to a room with a two-way mirror, a single metal table, and a glaring light overhead. "I'm Chief Samuel Aritan, Mr. Kerr. We got an order to search your bank records. Found a big payment from a company called the Luzar Group. That's a lot of money – out of the blue. Tell us what you know about that company?"

"Just did a little side job for 'em, that's all," Kerr said feebly.

"Well, just what sort of blasted job was that?"

"They was doin' research on cable cars and asked me to help document the steps in approving a car and the cable system inspection," Kerr explained sheepishly.

"So, you helped them falsify the documents showing the cable car was in perfect working condition?" Aritan grilled as he tapped his pen on the table.

"It wasn't like that! I explained how the cars were approved and then showed one of their technicians how I go about helping the engineering firm, Displatz."

"So, you allowed a stranger – someone with no friggin'

authorization – get access to the equipment?" Aritan responded, glaring at Kerr. "Who was that person? Need a name. Contact information."

"The guy contacted me. I'd recognize him if I saw him. Name was Lasch...Ivan Lasch, I think."

"So Lasch was your only contact from Luzar?"

"Yessir."

"Need you to look at some photos. See if you recognize him," Aritan ordered as he pushed his chair back from the table. Fifteen minutes later, Aritan returned with several books filled with photos of criminals or suspected criminals. "Take your time and let me know if you see the guy you worked with – Ivan Lasch," Aritan ordered as he sat back and folded his arms impatiently, glaring at the suspect.

Kerr spent the next hour flipping through pages of photos showing one potential criminal after another until he spotted Lasch. "This is him," Kerr said as he fingered the image of the man he met 12 years before. Lasch was described as average height and weight, with a thin face, bushy black hair and eyebrows, and wore wire-rimmed glasses.

"Kerr, we're going to hold you here while we investigate this further," Aritan stated gruffly as he pulled the photo books together. Kerr slumped in his chair, his head shaking. "You're being charged with aiding and abetting a potential murderer. Hell of a bad decision on your part, Kerr."

With that, Officer Phillip Wright got Kerr and led him down a well-lit hallway to a holding cell, clanging the door as it locked.

"We need to find this fellow, Ivan Lasch," Aritan growled to Wright after they had secured Kerr. "He knows something about the McCabe murder. Need to find out what he can tell us about the Luzar Group."

AFTER MAKING plans to meet up with the Warsaw Police Department, Detective Lewis Tenant and Deputy Jerome Atrich packed their weapons and bullet-proof vests in the squad car and headed east out of Culver. When they entered the Warsaw station, Officer Woodrow Forrest was there waiting for them. Forrest had completed Officer Training School only a few years before, but he displayed the confidence of a seasoned veteran.

"We're ready to show you the way to Boll's place whenever you're ready. If you've got your protective gear, better put it on before we head out there."

Forrest brought along his partner, Officer Alvin Dente, and the four of them loaded into the station's police van.

"Have you ever searched Boll's bank account, assuming he has one?" asked Tenant.

"As I recall, his bank records were pretty sketchy," replied Forrest.

"We'd like to find out if he has received a payment recently for the potential hit on DeMann," Tenant stated as they drove along a country road lined with rows of growing corn stalks.

"Here we are, men," Forrest exclaimed as the van crunched on a gravel road. "We better go the rest of the way on foot, so we don't announce ourselves too early." Climbing the front steps of the house, they knocked, but there wasn't an immediate answer. Inside, Boll was suspicious and pulled out a semiautomatic pistol and gripped it in his right hand.

When he opened the door slightly, he greeted with a sneer, "What can I do for you, officers?"

"Are you Terrence Boll?" Tenant inquired.

"Maybe I am, what's the problem?" Boll grunted disrespectfully.

"We'd like to ask you some questions about your whereabouts on the night of June 14. Your fingerprints match those we found on a murder weapon." Tenant charged, with his hand on his sidearm.

All at once, Boll swung his right arm around the door and fired. He hit Deputy Atrich in the chest, forcing him off his feet. Then he aimed at Tenant, but he was too late. Tenant had pulled out his weapon and wounded Boll in the shoulder, knocking him off balance and onto the floor. The police crashed through the door and kicked Boll's weapon away, spotting the swastika tattoos covering his arms.

As Officers Forrest and Dente frisked Boll and handcuffed him, Tenant went back to check on Atrich, who was thrown back by the power of the bullet. "You okay, Jerry? You took a good one in the chest. Thank God for your vest."

"I'll be okay, Lew," Atrich slowly replied, gritting his teeth in pain.

After helping Atrich stand and regain his footing on the front step, Tenant went back into the front room where Boll was sitting on the floor with his hands bound behind his back. Forrest was applying a bandage to Boll's bleeding shoulder as Tenant read him his rights and charged him with the murder of Hugo DeMann.

"Where's the rest of your gang, Boll?" Tenant asked accusingly.

"Nobody else, just me," Boll snarled as he glanced at his wound.

After searching Boll's house, they picked him up and led him to the van that Dente had pulled up to the house.

When they returned to the Warsaw station, they transferred cars and drove back to Culver, with the suspect in the back seat. "Jerry, call the St. Joe Hospital in Plymouth. We're going to have to get him patched up before we lock him up."

After the stop in Plymouth, they made their way back to the Culver Police Station and booked Boll for his potential murder crime and for firing a weapon at the police.

"I need a lawyer. Got my rights," Boll growled angrily as the cell door closed loudly behind him.

"You'll get a lawyer, no problem," Tenant responded. "We need to find out who paid you to take out DeMann."

As Tenant walked back to their office, Atrich appeared to be back to normal, enjoying one of the chocolate-covered donuts he purchased earlier that morning.

9

The phone in Jack McCabe's suite rang early the next day. "Hello, Mr. McCabe, it's Chief Aritan from Interpol. We've ID'd the guy who paid Kerr. Name's Ivan Lasch. We're doing a search to see if we can locate him. Not sure how long this will take but wanted to let you know. In the meantime, we're holding the maintenance man, Kerr, for his role in a possible double murder," Aritan growled with a well-chewed cigar tucked firmly in his teeth.

"Sounds like Interpol is making good progress!" Jack reported to Sara as they finished their room-service breakfast of eggs, toast, fruit, and coffee.

"That's really encouraging!" Sara agreed as she warmly squeezed Jack's hand. "I'm going to call our office in Indianapolis to make sure everything is going okay. We need to weigh in on that important client presentation coming up soon."

ARITAN and his team were actively tracking the whereabouts of Ivan Lasch and thought they may have a lead. "His last known address was in Bruges, Belgium," Officer Phillip Wright reported. "He lived in a little place on the canal at Verversdijk 22. We'll get our people there to check it out."

Wright got in touch with Officer Cameron Payne, the local Interpol agent in Bruges and gave him the lowdown on Lasch. "This guy may be connected to The New Global Order, so be careful. Plan on him being armed and dangerous."

Officer Payne, a seasoned veteran with gray hair and mustache, alerted his partner, Officer Jeanette Poole, a stunning, 30ish brunette who was a former martial arts competitor. They gathered their gear and made their way to Lasch's last known address. Fortunately, they knew the streets in Bruges, which could be tricky for the uninitiated. When they arrived, they approached the entrance with caution. "Hello, Mr. Lasch, are you home?" Payne questioned loudly as he knocked on the door. No answer. Tried again. Still no answer.

"Let's check the neighbors to see if anyone has seen him recently," Poole offered as each approached an adjacent home to Lasch's.

"Hello, sorry to bother you. My name is Officer Poole from Interpol and we're looking for your neighbor, Ivan Lasch. Have you seen him recently?" she asked the bleary-eyed neighbor as she displayed her ID and badge.

"Sorry, he doesn't show up there often, so can't help you," the neighbor asserted.

"When's the last time you remember seeing him?" Poole responded.

"Been a few weeks at least, but I haven't been looking for him either."

On the opposite side of Lasch's place, Payne asked the same of the person who answered the door. "Don't know the guy at all – he's quite a loner. I think I saw him leave in his car a week or so ago," the elderly lady offered kindly. "Guess you could say I keep an eye out for the neighbors."

"Well, that could help. Do you recall the model of the car and color?" Payne asked.

"Let's see, I think it may have been a sporty, black Alfa Romeo. Yes, that's what it was. Is he in some sort of trouble?"

"Thank you very much, ma'am. That could be very useful. I'd rather not say right now, but we may want to get back to you. Don't suppose you recall his license plate number?"

"Don't remember – uh, wait, maybe a number ending in 48-something," she recalled vaguely, rubbing her forehead.

As they headed back to their office, Payne described the car and partial license plate the neighbor identified. "Good thing she was a nosy neighbor. I'll search our database when we return to the office," Poole remarked as she made notes in her mobile phone.

BACK AT THE Culver Police Station, Detective Lewis Tenant had just escorted Terrence Boll into a small room for questioning. He had invited a public defender to join them. "We weren't able to locate the person you identified as your attorney, so Mr. Kellogg Greene, a public defender from South Bend, has agreed to take you on as his client," Tenant advised. Boll mumbled that Greene would be okay, as he wrestled with his hands cuffed to a round anchor on the table, clinking metal on metal.

Tenant tapped on the recorder in front of him. "Mr. Terrence Boll, your fingerprints match what we found on the irrigation hose that was used in the murder of Hugo DeMann. Plus, we have witnesses that identified you on the scene the night of June 14. We need to know what your motive was for the murder. Or, did someone pay you to do this hit?" Tenant inquired calmly as he fingered the notes of the crime in front of him.

"Can't say who would have paid me, or if I was even there. Not saying I did it," Boll deflected.

"Well, we have all the evidence we need, Boll," argued Tenant. "If you cooperate, it might be better for your sentence."

Boll looked cautiously at the attorney sitting next to him and seemed to be seeking advice on how much to say. "Might be better for you to just tell the truth," Attorney Greene advised.

"You're supposed to be helping me, right?" Boll grumbled as he squinted at his new attorney.

"Based on the evidence, this is what I would advise," Greene retorted.

"Well, damn... Okay...I was approached at a bar in Warsaw by a guy who wanted to see if I'd take care of someone in Culver," Boll offered.

"What was the name of the bar? Do you remember the guy's name?" Tenant queried.

"It was The Tethered Goat near Sand Lake Road. His last name was Lester. His first name might have been Michael or Morris, something like that."

"How much did he pay you?"

"When I said I'd help him, he gave me an envelope with $5,000 in cash with a photo and address of DeMann. Then, when I finished the job, I'd get $5,000 more."

"Do you happen to have the phone number of the man?"

"Never got a call from him. He found me at the bar and came back later," Boll said, gritting his teeth and rubbing his handcuffs.

"How did you know DeMann would be on the golf course that night?" Tenant inquired with squinted eyes.

"Tracked the rich S.O.B. for several days, and followed him over there," Boll explained, admiring his tattoos.

After their meeting, Boll was returned to his cell and Tenant thanked Greene for his visit. Then he turned to Deputy Atrich, who was shuffling through some old parking tickets.

"Boll gave us just about everything we need, Jerry," Tenant remarked with a wry grin on his face. "Now we have to pay another visit to Warsaw and see what we can find at the bar where Boll met his contact for the murder. See if you can get a warrant for the surveillance tapes at a bar called The Tethered Goat."

On the drive over to Warsaw the next day, Detective Tenant called Officer Woodrow Forrest to see if he was familiar with the bar Boll described. "Yep, they've got a rough bunch of patrons. Lots of biker guys as I recall," Forrest remarked.

When they arrived at The Tethered Goat in the middle of the day, Tenant and Atrich slowly crunched onto the gravel parking lot. There were already a bunch of Harleys and other motorcycles parked in the front. When they entered through a squeaky door, they could feel at least 20 pairs of rough-looking bikers' eyes focused sharply on them amid sounds of clinking glasses.

"Hello," Tenant said to the bartender who was wiping out a beer glass. "We're investigating a crime and want to see if you have video surveillance tapes we can look at."

"You're going to need a legal paper to see the bar's videos," mumbled Dean Gilberry, an overweight man with long stringy hair pulled back in a ponytail.

Tenant looked over at Atrich who fumbled in his bag for the warrant. "Here you go," Atrich offered, smoothing the wrinkled document.

"I'll have to check with the owner," Gilberry snarled. He left the bar and disappeared down a hallway and presented the warrant to his boss. "Two cops have this warrant to look at videos of the bar," Gilberry grunted. "They say they're looking for someone who was here in the last few weeks. Something about a possible crime."

A few minutes later, a disgusted Gilberry returned and barked for the police to follow him. He led them down a dingy hall to a smoke-filled office where the owner, Manford Akin, was seated at a rickety wooden desk counting receipts.

As Atrich explained the warrant, Akin stopped what he was doing and reviewed the document again. "Okay, let's see what we got," Akin replied with disdain as he got up from his chair.

He limped over to a cabinet loaded with small digital surveillance tapes and thumbed through the stack of recent ones. "Here's some from the past three weeks. You're welcome to the tapes, but want 'em back," Akin offered, grabbing a box to carry them.

As they were leaving the bar with the box of tapes, the evil eyes continued to track them out the door. "Not a friendly place, Jerry. But mission accomplished," Tenant said gratefully as they climbed in their squad car and peeled away, spitting gravel behind them.

10

In their hotel suite in Innsbruck, Jack and Sara linked up a Skype video conference call with their Indianapolis advertising and PR firm, McCabe and Bellamy. They were eager to review the trial presentation to a client that was a major sporting goods retailer with locations in key markets throughout the Midwest. The company was launching stores in four new cities and the team was proposing ad buys for TV and radio, social media, search optimization, web applications, media relations, press releases, new signage, special promotions, and events to all be timed for maximum effect to tantalize the target audiences.

The pitch was led off by Maria Richman, the stunning account supervisor. "We are very excited to be part of the introduction of these strategically placed stores in key markets," she extolled with confident articulation. Richman detailed the plan for the entire ad campaign and creative concepts, including all the research they had conducted on the locations and customer personas to support their decisions.

Next, Martin Graw, the shrewd, well-spoken public relations director, described the extensive plans for the media blitz, along with special events that included appearances by popular sports and entertainment celebrities.

At the conclusion, Jack and Sara applauded and expressed their appreciation for the team's hard work, creativity and attention to detail. They provided their own insights to help shore up a few branding and timing elements and were confident the client would love the overall approach. To date, the agency had helped the company gain a substantial market share in most of its locations, so this was anticipated to be another step in their mutual success, and a win for both.

When they wrapped up their online meeting and clicked off the Skype connection, Jack and Sara sat back and discussed the pros and cons of the agency's account team, and potential needs for new hires if their growth continued.

Later in the day, the phone rang in their suite. It was Interpol Chief Samuel Aritan with an update. "Hello, Mr. McCabe, wanted you to know that we're closing in on tracking down Ivan Lasch. A neighbor gave us an excellent description of his car and part of a license plate number, so it's just a matter of time," he explained as he unwrapped and lit up a new stogie.

NOT LONG AFTER his call to Jack McCabe, Chief Aritan took a call from Officer Cameron Payne in Bruges, who was zeroing in on the location of Lasch's car. "The latest we have on Lasch is that he is now in Innsbruck, so have your people on the lookout," Payne stated emphatically. "Word could be out on the street that the McCabe fellow has been personally investigating his parents' deaths. If there is a hit out on McCabe and his friend, they could be in danger. It's very possible Lasch is still working with The New Global Order."

Aritan sat up straight in his chair and clenched his fist. "Good work, Payne but, damn, not good news for the McCabe couple," he replied as his blood pressure started to rise. "I just got off the phone with McCabe and they're in their hotel. I'll let them know of some possible danger."

He immediately dialed McCabe's suite but got no answer, so he called the front desk concierge and was told they had gone out for lunch. "Do you know where they might have gone?"

"I'm very sorry, sir, they didn't tell me about their plans. May I ask them to return your call if I see them?"

Aritan gave him his number and called the Innsbruck team of Officers Phillip Wright and Melvin Loewe for a quick meeting. "We've got a potential problem. Ivan Lasch has been spotted here in Innsbruck and I haven't been able to reach McCabe and his girlfriend, Bellamy. Get out there and search the restaurants near Hotel Maximilian. After you locate 'em, give me a call."

After putting his men into action, he called Tessa Steckles at the U.S. Embassy to alert her of the possible trouble ahead. "Tess, this is Sam, we may have an issue with the Americans," he said as he tapped his pen on the folder open to McCabe's inquiry.

When Steckles was briefed and received a faxed photo of Lasch, she eagerly offered to join the search. After changing into more casual clothing and shoes – and grabbing her Barretta sidearm – she hopped in a cab and headed to the vicinity of the hotel.

Upon her arrival, she contacted Wright and Loewe so they could coordinate their coverage of the area, which was suddenly threatened with darkening storm clouds rolling in from the mountains.

After 30 minutes checking out several cafés and bistros with claps of thunder overhead, Steckles walked briskly to another good possibility a half block away.

At the same time, Jack and Sara were sharing a piece of torte pie, a specialty of the house at the Café Sacher. Just as they were finishing, Ivan Lasch, dressed as a server, entered the main restaurant from the kitchen, searching the diners. Underneath a towel draped over his forearm, he was carrying a Glock pistol that he was ready to discharge. His contact had paid him handsomely 12 years before for the murder of the two Americans. Now, after being contacted again, he was ready to put an end to this generation of the McCabe family, and the new owner of the large asphalt company, McCabe Industries.

Simultaneously walking through the front door, Tessa Steckles immediately spotted Jack and Sara and scanned the rest of the Café environment and its other patrons. Stunned for a split second, she caught a glimpse of the gun Lasch had under the towel and yelled, "Everybody down, active shooter!"

When Lasch heard Steckles and eyed McCabe and Bellamy, he turned to fire, but he was too late. Steckles fired first and blasted Lasch in his gun hand, with the Glock skittering across the polished wooden floor. People screamed, quickly ducking below their tables. But one bullet from Lasch hit a mark. Sara was bleeding from her left arm and fell to the floor, with Jack yelling and then sliding on top of her for protection. "Oh, Sara, no!"

Steckles rapidly reeled in a nearby chair and rammed it on top of Lasch, pinning him to the floor. Hearing the shots, Wright and Loewe ran into the Café and joined Steckles, who had begun reading Lasch his rights, and charging him with the attempted murders. The two officers bound his hands and pressed the towel he had been carrying to his wound to stop the bleeding. Grabbing the Glock that had fallen to the floor, they pulled Lasch up and escorted him out of the restaurant.

"My God, Mr. McCabe and Ms. Bellamy, how terrible!" Steckles said as calmly as she could.

"Thank God for you, Ms. Steckles! You saved our lives!" Jack responded appreciatively with tears in his eyes.

"Your timing couldn't have been much better, Ms. Steckles,"

moaned Sara as she gritted her teeth from the bleeding wound on her arm that Jack had compressed with a cloth napkin.

"Looks like it could have been a *little* better, but you should be okay. I'll call an ambulance. They'll take care of you quickly," Steckles replied, grateful for getting a lucky break to see the couple – and spot Lasch – with no time to spare.

After the EMTs arrived, they bandaged Sara's arm, helped her out to the ambulance, and sped to the nearby hospital, siren blaring and rain beginning to splatter on the vehicle's windows. Jack knelt next to Sara on the way and comforted her as best he could, while she grimaced and endured the throbbing pain.

Steckles called a relieved Chief Aritan and described the intense action that took place at the Café Sacher. "Great work, Tess!" Aritan exclaimed happily as he rubbed his head. "You saved the day, for sure. And good to know that Lasch will be available for us – to grill him to get the name of his contact. If we can force him to talk, we may have all we need to put him away. Not only for the attempted murder today, but the cold case 12 years earlier."

When the ambulance arrived at the hospital, the EMTs brought Sara in on the gurney and rushed her to surgery to remove the bullet and repair her wound. Jack followed along, holding her hand and praising her for her bravery.

"You're doing great, Sara! I love you and they're going to take good care of you," Jack murmured softly as they wheeled her through the surgery doors. The gowned and masked medical team was ready to go to work.

Following the procedure, Sara gradually woke up in a hospital bed. Jack was by her side along with a surgical nurse checking her vitals. "Hey, you look as beautiful as ever, Sara," Jack said softly, stroking her hand and watching her protectively as she recovered from the anesthetic.

11

While Culver Police Deputy Jerome Atrich was setting up the computer to load the video surveillance tapes from the bar, Detective Lewis Tenant was pressuring Terrence Boll for a description of the man who paid him for the hit on Hugo DeMann. It was a Michael or Morris Lester he had said.

Boll fidgeted on the hard bed in his cell and tried to come up with a valid description. "Damn... I remember he was tall... light gray hair – almost white – dressed in black it seemed. Might have been in his 50s, but hard to tell. Pretty dark in the bar. Plus, he had a foreign accent...might have been German, which I liked."

Jotting down notes on his pad, Tenant grunted, "That could help for a start. We'll see what we can find on the tapes. Did he say why he picked you?"

"Said people told him I could do the job," Boll subtly boasted.

When he gave Atrich the description, they thought they may have a good clue to work with. For the rest of the afternoon, after scanning through several days of tapes in the time span they determined the meeting took place, Atrich finally found a shot of Boll acting cocky and gulping shots of liquor. But nothing close to the description of Lester showed up, so he moved on to the next tape.

He continued to scan the tapes until Boll appeared again. This time, a man matching the description of Lester moved next to Boll. They appeared to be in a conversation for a long time and then, suddenly, Lester pulled an envelope from inside his jacket and slowly slid it along the bar to Boll. After he fingered the contents, probably the cash and what must have been a photo of DeMann, they obviously made a deal. Then Lester moved out of sight. Looking around suspiciously, Boll tucked the thick envelope in his pants and headed for the exit.

"Bingo, Lew!" Atrich almost shouted to Tenant. "Looks like we have him, but who the hell is he?" After showing a replay to Tenant, they high fived and began laying out plans for locating Lester. Atrich made a still-frame photo of Lester and printed it out for Tenant. After Boll confirmed that was the guy who paid him, the two policemen began their work.

Not long after, the office phone rang, and Tenant answered. It was Jack McCabe. "Hello, Detective, I wanted to give you a heads up on our latest situation in Innsbruck," Jack explained as he and Sara had returned to their suite after Sara was released from the hospital. "Sara and I have been looking into my parents' deaths and quite a bit has transpired. Interpol's Anti-Terrorism Group has been helping us and so far we have two people being held for their part in the murders. Sad to say Sara was injured by a bullet from one of the men but, thank God, she is okay and recovering."

"Wow!" Tenant exclaimed as he put down his coffee, stunned by the news. "Very sorry to hear about Sara – but fortunately she's okay!" Tenant paused and continued, "So, you're working with Interpol?"

Jack described the process they went through to review his parents' file at the Innsbruck Police Station. Then, how the

American U.S. Embassy representative they met, Tessa Steckles, connected them with Interpol. And how Steckles saved their lives by shooting the killer.

"That's an amazing story, Mr. McCabe. You've really made progress – and you're really lucky," Tenant responded. "Here in Culver, we've got DeMann's murderer identified. Matched his fingerprints on the hose and have an eyewitness to his presence at the golf course the night DeMann was killed. In fact, the murderer has admitted his guilt."

"Sounds like justice will be served!" Jack agreed.

"Well, we still have a problem," Tenant said as he scratched his beard. "There was a man who paid off DeMann's killer. We have a name and a photo but no idea where to look for him."

"I think I told you about the information my grandfather shared in a letter we found in his files," Jack said calmly. "He described an organization that I've since learned is called The New Global Order. They're apparently behind the threatening letters he received and may be the same group that intimidated Hugo DeMann. The Interpol agents know this group and hope to get information from the guy they're holding – the guy who tried to kill us and may have killed my parents."

"Hugo's killer, Terrence Boll, described the person who paid him and said he had a foreign accent – maybe German," Tenant continued. "Wonder if the Interpol people can help look for him?"

Jack gave Tenant the contact information for Chief Samuel Aritan to hopefully cover both cases. Jack described Aritan as a well-built, bearded African American in his 40s who was said to be an expert in reconnaissance and intelligence. After reviewing the conversation with Deputy Atrich, Tenant placed a call to Innsbruck and explained his background with Jack and requested help in locating Lester. Chief Aritan offered support and asked Tenant to email the photo and any other details on the case against Lester.

When he received the email and reviewed the files, Aritan called back. "You've got a damn good case against Boll, but we'll have to do some research to see if Lester turns up on any of our databases. I'll get back to you when I know more."

As Aritan studied the photo of Lester, he called Officers Phillip Wright and Melvin Loewe into his office. He briefed them on the case and ordered a search on Lester. The guy seemed familiar, but he couldn't place him. Only thing that seemed to make sense was that he was somehow connected to The New Global Order.

LATER THE NEXT DAY, Officer Loewe escorted Ivan Lasch into an interrogation room for more questioning, accompanied by his attorney. So far, he wasn't willing to give up any names of people who had hired him. When they assembled, Chief Aritan clicked on the recording device and initiated the conversation.

"Won't do you any good to keep stalling, Lasch," Aritan pressed as he peered at the criminal. "We've got you for the attempted murder of the McCabe couple, and there's lots of evidence you were behind the cold case 12 years earlier. Make it easy on yourself. Give it up. Who's behind the big payments you received?"

"My client doesn't have to answer any questions," claimed attorney Louis Poule, a handsomely dressed, middle-aged man with slicked-back, gray hair.

Aritan knew they were fishing for a plea agreement, but he wasn't sure how far to go, so he started with a bargaining salvo. "What's it going to take to get what we need, Poule?"

"Let's start with a lightened sentence, of course," Poule offered. "And Lasch will need protection."

"Protection from what?" Aritan growled back. "Only damn place he's going is behind bars."

"As you know, that can be a dangerous place for a marked man," Poule stated emphatically, tapping his pen on his note pad for emphasis.

"We're going to need information on the deaths of the McCabes 12 years ago before I can do anything," Aritan demanded. After glaring at them with no response, Aritan stopped his recorder, got up, and stormed out of the room. He then convened with Officer Loewe who was viewing the meeting through a two-way mirror. Lasch and Attorney Poule seemed to be in muted discussions while they looked on.

"I'm going to call the prosecutor's office to see what he might be willing to offer this scumbag," Aritan grumbled.

After a long discussion with the prosecutor, they agreed on a prison term of 10 years for the recent murder attempt, and 20 for the possible two murders 12 years earlier. Lasch would receive special protection in prison and early parole for good behavior.

A few minutes later, Aritan reentered the interrogation room and turned on the recorder. He explained the possible offer to Lasch and Poule and sat back, arms folded, waiting for them to respond.

"We will need something better than that," Poule stated, glaring smugly back at Aritan. "He'll need 5 years for the recent incident and 10 years for the event that took place 12 years ago."

Aritan once again stopped the recorder and huffed out of the room, knocking his chair backward as it chunked loudly on the floor. After reviewing the demand from Poule with the prosecutor, they agreed to go with seven years and 15 years respectively.

Back in the room once again, Aritan made the counteroffer to Poule. After discussing it in hushed voices with his client, Poule reluctantly agreed.

The next day, with the offer signed by Lasch and his attorney that the prosecutor's office faxed over, it was time for Lasch to provide some answers.

Lasch hesitated but then begrudgingly detailed his involvement in the McCabe parents' deaths. He had received the information for the cabling mechanism from Joseph Kerr, the maintenance man being held as an accomplice. Since Lasch was unable to determine an easy way to rig the cables at the bull wheel of the cable car terminal, he decided on another scheme.

He positioned himself, well-hidden in the mountain above the cable car, with a Savage Model long-range rifle with silencer. He knew that by knocking out one cable, possibly two, that the third would collapse and the car would no longer be supported.

"Okay, we'll buy that," Aritan said disgustedly. "I need names. Who paid you then? And who was your contact to try to take the lives of the younger McCabe and his friend?"

With some reluctance and considerable squirming in his chair, Lasch grunted that the same person contacted him both times. "His name is Michael Raffone, that's all I know. They were hits, plain and simple. Paid well."

12

Chief Samuel Aritan and his Interpol team were now searching for two criminals, both likely connected to the terrorist group, The New Global Order. Michael Raffone paid Ivan Lasch for the Innsbruck murders 12 years before and for the recent attempted murders on Jack and Sara. Michael or Morris Lester paid Terrence Boll for the hit on Hugo DeMann in Culver. "Any trace of either of them?" Aritan barked to Officers Phillip Wright and Melvin Loewe who were busily scanning through computer names and photos to find a match, with images speeding by. They had been at it for several days with no luck.

Then, Officer Loewe, who was searching for Lester, got a hit with a computer match. "This looks good, Chief," Loewe said with enthusiastic relief, pushing the console screen around for Aritan to confirm.

"I owe you lunch," grumbled Officer Wright, who was still coming up blank on his search for Michael Raffone.

"That's got to be him," Aritan agreed. "Says it's *Morris Lester*, last spotted in Dusseldorf, Germany, a year ago. I'll contact our people in Bruges, Belgium, and have them track him down."

That afternoon, Aritan got Officers Jeanette Poole and Cameron Payne on a conference call after emailing a photo and description of Morris Lester. "This guy could be dangerous; no doubt he'll be armed, so watch yourself. We need him alive so we can find out who ordered the hit on Hugo DeMann in Indiana."

With the briefing behind them, Officers Poole and Payne packed their gear and flew to Dusseldorf from their private airbase in Bruges. Their IDs allowed them to check through security with weapons as well as protective vests and other belongings. They rented an Audi RS3 sedan for speed and headed for the Novum Hotel Plaza and got a map to determine their next steps. Lester's address was on Karlstrab, which would take them about 20 minutes by car.

When they arrived at Lester's home, Poole knocked on the door, but there was no answer. She tried the doorbell – and waited. Finally, an attractive, middle-aged woman opened the door. "Yes, what can I do for you?" she asked politely.

"We're from Interpol and we're looking for Morris Lester, ma'am," responded Payne, showing the woman his badge. "Is he home?"

"You must have the wrong address, he doesn't live here," she bluffed coyly.

Just then, tires squealed out of the driveway adjacent to the house. A BMW 328D was in a big hurry to get somewhere fast. "Friend of yours, ma'am?" Poole asked sarcastically.

Payne and Poole ran back to their rental car to give chase. "Let's see what this thing can do," Poole said excitedly as she jumped behind the wheel and peeled out, laying black tire marks on the street. Not only had she been a martial arts pro, she had also spent time on the junior racing circuit of the Belgium Grand Prix.

Lester had nearly a one block lead, but Poole kept pace. He veered left onto Kolner Strabe and tore through traffic. Up ahead on the straightaway, Morris Lester made a call on his mobile phone using the hands-free device. "I've got a tail on me and need help!" he yelled to his government contact, a New Global Order disciple, and gave his location.

"Turn right on Am Wehrhahn, then a quick left on Wieland Strabe," the voice stated calmly. "I'll block the road after you pass. You have the BMW 328D, right?"

"That's it, thanks," Lester responded. Just as his contact promised, he screeched left at Wieland Strabe, fishtailing until he had control.

Officer Poole was nearing Lester as she, too, had to speed by one car after another to keep up. Her vehicle was zipping along at a fast clip and she was gaining on him, but then, "What the hell is *this*?" she screamed as a large garbage truck suddenly pulled out and blocked the road. It was all she could do to avoid hitting it as she slammed on the brakes and slid sideways to a screeching stop within a meter from the large vehicle.

Pounding on the steering wheel, she cursed and looked at Payne. "That doesn't just happen!" she yelled. "Nobody's that damn lucky!"

After returning to their hotel, Payne called Chief Samuel Aritan with an update. "We had Lester, Chief, but he obviously had some help. We raced after him for several kilometers but, out of the blue, our road was blocked by a large sanitation truck," he explained, disgusted at the outcome of their initial pursuit.

"Holy crap! Call the local police. See if they have anything on this guy. Where he hangs out, that sort of thing," Aritan advised as he exhaled a plume of smoke from a Nicaraguan. "Might take a while."

IN THE MEANTIME, Officer Phillip Wright finally got a match on Michael Raffone. "Yes!" Wright yelled as the computer synched the photo he was searching. "Check this out, Chief. He was last spotted in Florence, Italy, where he supposedly owns a villa in the hills overlooking the city." Raffone was a husky, middle-aged man with short, curly hair and dark circles under his eyes. "Nasty-looking S.O.B."

"Great work, Wright," encouraged Chief Aritan. "I'll contact our Interpol people in Rome to see if they can locate him." Within minutes after emailing a photo and background, he had Officers Alberto Fresco and Kara Sterrio on the line. Fresco was a lean, muscular Italian with dark features. Sterrio, also Italian, was statuesque with classical Roman looks and long dark hair pulled back in a bun.

"We just got your email about Michael Raffone, Chief," Fresco responded with keen interest. "We'll head up to Florence in the morning and see if we can catch the bastard taking a siesta."

"As you know, he'll be trouble. Be prepared to use the heavy artillery – if needed. But we want him alive if possible."

The next day, the two Interpol officers were on the road, with AR15s, extra magazines, semiautomatic pistols, vests, tear gas, and more. "You ever hear of this guy, Kara?" asked Fresco.

"His name came up last year related to The New Global Order, but he's been quiet since. Last time I was in Florence, I was looking for someone else."

Once their car reached the city, they took the winding Renaissance Ring Road up the side of the mountain overlooking the city. As they neared the address, they slowed to peruse the landscape around the villa. "Let's park and get a view from the hill above his house – see if there's any activity," Fresco recommended.

Grabbing their AR15s and other gear, they began their ascent. In minutes they found a good location behind a large boulder. "Must be having a party, Alberto," Sterrio whispered as they scoped out several cars parked in front. With binoculars, they got an even better view through the windows.

"Let's move around the mountain so we can see if there are people behind the villa," Fresco ordered. When they were in their new position, they could see four armed men having drinks on a large stone patio, while a few scantily attired women were relaxing in a hot tub.

"Do you recognize Raffone?" Fresco asked his partner.

"He's the husky one on the right, with the short, curly hair," Sterrio determined as she focused her binoculars. "Don't underestimate him, though. I understand he's a tough customer who can handle himself in a fight."

"We need him alive, so let's wait for the party to break up. Maybe he'll be alone," Fresco said as he scanned the terrain around the villa, hoping to identify the best route down to the house. "If it comes to a shootout, don't go for the kill."

As the sun began to set over the Tuscan mountains, the guests started to depart the Raffone residence. When all the vehicles had rolled out of the circle drive, the two Interpol officers slowly descended the mountain. Approaching the house, they could see clearly through windows in multiple locations.

Raffone was in the kitchen – alone – fixing a sandwich on a large, granite island. As Sterrio crept along the exterior, she accidentally stepped on a small twig, *CRACK*, creating enough noise to get Raffone's attention. Suddenly, looking up from his meal, he spotted Fresco and checked for his sidearm. Then ducked behind the island.

"Oh shit!" Sterrio whispered to Fresco.

"I'll go around to the side entrance. Looks like sliding glass doors." Fresco whispered back. "Stay here and be ready to take a shot – in his leg – if he heads this way." Suddenly, a young, sexy Italian woman came walking naked through the house toward the kitchen.

They could hear Raffone yell in Italian to get down – that they were being attacked. The woman screamed and ducked behind a large column. Raffone started moving from the kitchen while staying low and out of visible shooting sight.

The officers waited to see if he would emerge so they could take a shot. No sign of the woman either. Thirty seconds later, they heard an engine revving on the far side of the house. Moonlight reflected sharply from Raffone's red Ferrari as he tore out of his garage and squealed onto the mountain road, spitting gravel as he sped away. Sterrio was closest and got off a shot. But she was only able to shoot out one of the taillights before he was gone.

13

A week after Lasch attacked Jack McCabe and Sara Bellamy at the Café Sacher in Innsbruck, the couple decided it was time to head back to Indiana. Sara needed time to recover from her bullet wound and get therapy, if needed. Rather than go back to their vacation cottage in Culver, they went directly to their comfortable English Tudor-style home in the historic Meridian-Kessler neighborhood of Indianapolis.

Jack was confident that, while they were away from Culver, their home's caretaker, Hans Kriechbaum, would continue to keep a watchful eye on their place, just as his father, Fritz, and grandfather, Driscol, had done before him.

With the murderer, Ivan Lasch, and his accomplice, Joseph Kerr, in police custody – and prison time destined for them both after their court dates – the case against Jack's parents seemed to be resolved, at least temporarily. But Jack knew it probably wasn't over. The terrorist group, The New Global Order, was likely still after him and his family's business. As ruthless as they appeared to be, one failed murder attempt was not going to stop them.

Before heading to the airport to catch their flight, Jack called

Tessa Steckles at the U.S. Embassy to thank her again and to offer to help if she needed it in the future. He also reached out to the Interpol Chief Samuel Aritan and wished him well in his search for Lester and Raffone. Having been apprised of the person behind DeMann's murder, Jack knew they had a rough schedule ahead of them.

IN THE MEANTIME, Bruges-based Interpol Officers Jeanette Poole and Cameron Payne continued to explore background for more information on the possible whereabouts of Morris Lester. Up to that point, he had eluded them in Dusseldorf.

"Finally! Here's some new intel I just received!" Poole stated excitedly as she read an email from the local police. "Lester frequents a nightclub called Chateau Rix on the left bank of the Rhine, which is known to attract affluent characters who love excessive partying. It's a place that supposedly has a rebellious vibe."

"Hmmm, sounds like his type of place – and the people he'd hang out with. Let's visit tonight and see what turns up."

Dressed in casual nightclub apparel, the two officers drove to the bar at 10:00 p.m. to see if Lester would show up. Looking especially alluring in a loose top and tight pants, Poole would surely gain attention. They both carried concealed sidearms in case there was trouble.

As they entered, a pulsating techno beat reverberated throughout Chateau Rix, with a glaring lightshow strobing overhead. Subtly scanning the environment, they didn't see any sign of Lester. They ordered drinks at the bar and moved to a table to keep watch.

It was easy to see that their intel about the bar was on target. There was a diverse mix of clubby, urban people, many of whom were on the huge octagonal dance floor, writhing to the thunderous sounds from the DJ.

As they waited for a sign of Lester, a tipsy German stopped by their table to ask Poole for a dance. When she declined he started to get physical by twisting hard on her forearm. In seconds, Poole spun up from her chair, took the guy's arm and got his wrist in a vice grip – immediately putting him in agonizing pain.

"Get lost," she ordered, releasing the man and pushing him away. Shocked, he slinked back into the dancing crowd, cringing and holding his arm.

"I need another drink," Poole said disgustedly. "Want one?" Payne nodded as she moved back to the bar.

Ordering cocktails from a shirtless male bartender, she scanned the surroundings. Suddenly, she spotted Lester at a table with two seductive Asian women, one with pink hair and one with blue, about 40 feet away. They were obviously enjoying the night and unaware of Poole's presence. Since the two officers were both wearing earpieces and communication devices or coms on their wrists attached to bracelets, she alerted Payne to join her at the bar.

"How do you want to do this?" Poole whispered as they both took stock of the potential ramifications of trying to arrest Lester in his friendly environment.

"He won't recognize either of us," Payne responded. "Why don't you do your thing and gracefully slide over to his table and ask him to dance. I'll move to the side of them and if he gets up, I'll move in for the arrest."

Poole nodded and moved away from the bar toward Lester's table. As she got Lester and his friends' attention, she alluringly asked him to dance as he looked up and stared back with a suspicious slant to his head.

"Well, thank you for the offer," Lester responded after pondering Poole's request for a few seconds, music blaring and lights flashing around them. "As you can see, I have guests, and it would be rude for me to leave them. I'm sure you can understand."

"Oh, c'mon, just one?" Poole requested with a sexy glint in her eye to match a subtle, flirtatious smile.

"Well, I suppose it won't hurt – please excuse me ladies," Lester finally agreed as he slowly got up from the table to join her. Poole noticed immediately that he looked lean and muscular through a tight, silky shirt. And taller than she expected.

As Lester joined Poole, they began moving to the dance floor. Out of the corner of her eye, Poole could see that the two Asian women had also gotten up and were slowly following them. Payne was tailing closely behind all four.

Just before Poole and Lester reached the octagonal dance floor, she turned to show him her badge and let him know he was being arrested. As she did, he pushed away from her and his two Asian girlfriends immediately responded by attacking Poole.

Simultaneously, Officer Payne stuck his pistol into Lester's ribs and told him to get down on the floor, which he did begrudgingly. In seconds, Payne had Lester cuffed as he dug a knee into his back.

Unaware of Lester's predicament, the two female bodyguards began throwing karate kicks at Poole, who deftly defended herself with her own expertise. Poole caught the pink-haired woman's leg and flipped her upside down as she sprawled across the floor. The blue-haired companion caught Poole in the side of the head with a kick and momentarily stunned her as she fell to a knee. With the music blaring intensely and lights flashing, Poole needed a moment to regain her composure. Shaking it off, she got up and fought back with a fist punch to the blue-haired woman's throat, causing her to recoil in pain.

Deciding they were overmatched, the two Asian women

glanced at each other and slowly scampered away from the threat.

Just then, one of the onlookers from the dance floor raised a sidearm and aimed at Poole. Watching the action closely while covering Lester, Payne quickly pulled up his pistol and fired at the dancer, hitting him in the arm and rendering him momentarily harmless.

Knowing they were in hostile territory, they decided to escape the nightclub before more threats came their way. Payne stood Lester up and they moved to the door. Poole had since grabbed her own sidearm as they exited, searching the environment for more attackers.

Most of the onlookers seemed frightened as they sulked back in the pack of dancers, but Poole spotted the shirtless bartender pointing a pistol in their direction. She quickly fired and hit the man in his shoulder, dropping him to the floor.

They continued slowly leading Lester out of the bar and into the street, staying alert to any other protectors who could be lurking in the shadows. Finally making their way to their rental vehicle, Payne forced Lester into the backseat. Poole jumped behind the wheel and they peeled off.

On the way to the local police station to hold Lester, Poole phoned their local contact, policeman Christopher Coe. "We're bringing in Lester and need to keep him in a cell overnight. Got room for him?"

"We'll be here when you arrive," Coe responded. "Got a space reserved just for him. Great work!"

When they arrived at the station, Coe was there to meet them at the door. They quickly fingerprinted and booked Lester for accessory to murder. But there were likely many other crimes.

"Hope you're secure here, Coe," Officer Payne questioned. "Don't know how many friends he's got, but there are people in government ready to help him. No bail for this guy, got it? Stay alert."

With Lester in a cell, the two Interpol officers called Chief Samuel Aritan to report on the evening's events.

"We'll send a plane in the morning to pick you three up at the airport. Take him back to the Bruges headquarters for interrogation," Aritan ordered as he made notes on the case file in front of him. "Need to find out his friggin' connection to The New Global Order. Let's hope nobody tries to spring his ass before morning."

14

After The New Global Order's secret gathering outside of Rome, the hefty former Russian military leader, Major Oli Klosov, had returned to his luxury flat in St. Tropez on Rue des Charrons. It was late in the evening and he was ready to collapse au naturel onto his large, comfortable bed with silk sheets. Having consumed his usual number of martinis, sleep would be a welcomed respite.

Just as he closed his eyes, his mobile phone, laying on a bedside table, began ringing loudly. Grumbling to himself, he answered, "Yes, this is Klosov, who the hell's calling at this hour?"

"Very sorry to disturb you so late, Major, but we have a serious issue in Dusseldorf," reported Kenneth Dahl, who was the attorney for Morris Lester. "Our man, Lester, has been captured by Interpol and is being held at one of the local police stations." Dahl, a well-groomed senior advisor for The New Global Order, had already attempted to meet with his client, but the officer on duty declined his requests.

"Totally outlandish! Unacceptable!" Klosov yelled into the

phone. "Get our team posted near the police station with two of our large, fast SUVs. If they attempt to move him, track their vehicle, kill the guards, and get Lester out of there. He knows too much! We cannot afford to have him interrogated."

———

BACK AT THEIR hotel in Dusseldorf, Officers Payne and Poole were finding it difficult to sleep, so Payne got up and knocked on the adjoining door to Poole's suite. "Hey, you still up?"

"Can't sleep either? Looks like we're both in the same boat," Poole responded as she opened the door, wearing only a t-shirt and panties.

"Been thinking that we might need an armored truck to get Lester to the airport with the enemy possibly ready to pull out all the stops to free him," Payne said as he flopped onto a large, comfortable chair, and logged onto his mobile.

Without hesitating, Payne rang Interpol's Chief Aritan, knowing the late hour would not be received kindly. "Hello, Chief, hate to disturb you but I'm worried about transporting Lester to the airport in the morning. His people may be planning something big and we need to be prepared."

"Damn, Payne, you know how to ruin a good night's sleep... Sorry to say, but you're probably right. We need to get you an armored vehicle and some police assistance to make sure you don't get hijacked. I'll also make sure the pilot of the plane has some help."

Aritan called his contacts in Dusseldorf and arranged to equip his people with an armored German SWAT vehicle and provide four additional armed guards for the transit. He knew the people behind The New Global Order would do everything they could to free Lester – and he had to do what he could to prevent it.

The next morning, Officers Payne and Poole, dressed in combat gear, arrived at the police station and found policeman Coe waiting for them. "Not taking any chances with this one," Coe asserted eagerly. "We have an armored truck parked underground and we can get you ready to go as soon as you say. There are four armed military guards here for the trip to the airport."

They brought the shackled Lester down an elevator to a basement garage and found the vehicle set to go. It would be a twenty-minute drive to the airport and the plane should arrive by 8:00 a.m. One of the guards drove and Payne rode shotgun. Poole was in the back with the three other guards and Lester. As they exited the garage drive, the sun was already heating up the city as rush hour was building.

They scanned the street for possible conflict, then pulled out to Heinrich Strabe in the middle of traffic. After a few kilometers, they took a left on Gewerbegebiet and suddenly found themselves trailed closely by a large, black SUV. Then another one darted directly in front of them, attempting to slow them down. Innocent cars on the road quickly darted to one side or the other to avoid them, horns blaring as they passed.

"Run that son of a bitch off the road if you have to," Payne ordered Officer Barron Kaide, a muscular young man with tattooed arms.

When the SUV in front started slowing, Kaide rammed it several times, forcing the lead vehicle to swerve out of control from left to right. As the SUV veered to one side, Kaide jumped on the accelerator and side-swiped the enemy, causing it to crash loudly into a large light pole on the side of the street, and forcing several vehicles in traffic to run off the road.

In the back of their armored truck, one of the guards suddenly began to raise his MP5/10 submachine gun to fire at Poole, but she was too fast. "What the hell, buddy?" she screamed as she pulled up her firearm and hit him in the forehead before he could get off a round. "Thought you were on our side. How about you two?" she growled breathlessly, aiming at the other guards as Lester recoiled on his metal bench.

"Don't know where that guy came from, but we're on the up and up," responded Officer Darren Deeds convincingly.

"Better be," Poole exclaimed loudly. "Don't need to cover you *and* the prisoner, do I?"

Hearing firing in the back, Payne called Poole to make sure she was okay. "Yeah, looks like one of the enemy guards infiltrated our force. Had to put him down."

Turning right onto Danzinger Strabe, the other black SUV still tailed them closely. They veered onto Flughafenbrucke Strabe to the airport and Payne knew what they were facing, so he called to the back of the vehicle with orders.

"The vehicle behind will surely follow us onto the airport tarmac. Be ready for a fire fight. We may need to wipe them out to get the prisoner on the plane."

Chief Aritan called Payne while they were in route and gave him an update on the plane and its location at the airport. "You make it okay?" Aritan questioned somewhat bleary eyed as he put his coffee mug back on the desk and searched for the stub of a Dominican.

"The enemy's on our tail and we've had some issues, but nothing we couldn't handle," Payne barked back in the mobile. "Hope there's some armed support at the plane because the enemy will give us trouble once we reach the tarmac."

When they arrived at their destination and found the plane, the armored Interpol vehicle pulled to a stop in front of the plane, with the black SUV stopping a half block behind. Officers Payne and Kaide jumped out on the side closest to the plane and positioned themselves for a battle.

"Keep a close eye on him!" Officer Poole yelled to the other two guards as she climbed through the gated divide to the front passenger seat, then hopped out to join Payne and Kaide. From the plane, two armed guards emerged and rushed down next to them.

Four armed men in military attack gear peeled out of the SUV and started to fire, missing their targets behind the armored car, but hitting the plane's fuel tank. Suddenly, flames erupted and started to engulf the rest of the military transport, forcing the pilot to rush out of the cockpit and hurriedly duck behind the armored truck.

"Holy hell! Looks like we'll need another plane – fast!" Payne barked.

Poole and Kaide looked at each other and grabbed M367 hand grenades from their belts. As a former semi-pro baseball player, Kaide had a rifle for an arm. He flung his grenade as far as he could. It landed with an explosion – harmlessly – just short of the SUV.

During continued armed fire, Poole gave him one of her grenades. He pulled the pin and tried again. This time he had the distance and the accuracy as the grenade detonated and the SUV burst into flames with the four armed men blasted violently in several directions.

"Strike, and they're out!" Poole screamed, giving Kaide a hearty pat on the back.

In the meantime, the pilot had been on the phone with the military attaché at the airport, urgently requesting another aircraft. Firefighting units soon reached the flames spewing from the plane and the SUV and got the explosive fire under control.

Opening the back of the armored car, the two officers were keeping Lester closely guarded. They unshackled him and led him out, stepping over the dead enemy officer's bloodied body.

Soon, a new transport plane taxied to their vicinity on the

tarmac and the team, along with its prisoner, boarded for the flight back to Bruges.

"That was too close for comfort, Chief," Payne said anxiously, briefing Aritan on his mobile as the plane lifted off on its western route.

15

J ack McCabe and Sara Bellamy had settled comfortably into their home in Indianapolis when the phone rang. "Hello, Jack, this is Tessa Steckles from the Embassy in Innsbruck. I hope you are well, and that Sara is getting better every day." Steckles had saved them both when Ivan Lasch attempted to kill them at the Café Sache in Innsbruck. Sara was injured during a gun fight but had since recovered.

"Ms. Steckles, what a nice surprise!" Jack responded cordially but apprehensively.

"I wanted to report a couple of things to you," Steckles said as she reviewed the notes in front of her. "First, you'll be happy to know that Ivan Lasch and Joseph Kerr are now awaiting trial for the crimes they committed against you and your parents.

"Secondly, I hate to alarm you, but we have valid intel that you still may be in danger," she alerted him calmly. "Our sources from Rome, Italy, report that someone probably connected with The New Global Order has continued to identify you as a target, so please take all precautions. They may be unaware of your location in Indianapolis, but they certainly know about your residence on Lake Maxinkuckee, which could be threatened, possibly with arson – or explosives, I'm afraid."

Stunned by this frightening but not totally surprising news, Jack replied anxiously, "Oh my God, I appreciate the warning! I need to get word to my caretaker and the local police so they can be on the lookout for any shady characters."

After relaying the potential danger to Sara, Jack called his caretaker Hans Kriechbaum. "Hans, it's a good thing you have a military background, because you may need your sharpshooter skills in the days ahead," he explained as gently as he could, and went on to describe the threat to him and possibly the house.

"That's awful, Mr. McCabe!" Hans responded excitedly after he turned off the riding mower he was operating. "What can I do to help?"

"I'm sorry to ask you to do this but I fear that my cottage may be subject to arson and I'd hate to lose everything. Lots of my grandfather's files and documents are still there as well as priceless family heirlooms, as you know. Would you be willing to sleep at our place for the next few weeks or until we move back there? I'll certainly make it worth your while financially."

As a single man with no family responsibilities, Hans was amenable to help Jack as much as he could. Having known the cottage all his life and after helping his father and grandfather care for it, he felt a cherished attachment that he was ready to protect. And the McCabes had been like family to him.

"You can count on me, Mr. McCabe!" Hans said valiantly. As a former Army marksman, he was prepared to clean his AR15 rifle and move it to the McCabe cottage. At 25, Hans was lean but muscular with wavy blond hair and a wispy beard. His high school buddies affectionately called him "Hans-some" for his all-American good looks.

With Hans providing the kind of assurance he was hoping for, Jack called Detective Lewis Tenant at the Culver Police Station. "Hello, Mr. McCabe," Tenant responded graciously as he stopped working at his office computer. "What can I do for you?"

Jack went into detail about his call from the U.S. Embassy and the potential problem that existed in Culver. "I wonder if you would keep an eye on my place on Lake Maxinkuckee?" he gratefully requested.

"Of course, and we will also stay in touch with your caretaker to make sure he's okay," Tenant responded. He then went on to discuss the latest on the DeMann murder trial, in which Terrence Boll had pled guilty due to irrefutable forensic evidence against him. "Boll is waiting for his court date. Fortunately, we have not seen any sign of revenge against Pokaten by Boll's pals in the Neo-Nazi group from Warsaw. As you recall, Edward Pokaten was an eyewitness to Boll's presence the night of the murder."

"Good to know that S.O.B. will eventually pay for his crime!" Jack responded, appreciating all the hard work the police put into bringing the guy to justice. *He's got it coming*, Jack mused to himself.

After Tenant finished his call, he relayed the information to Deputy Jerome Atrich, who was in the middle of devouring a cinnamon twist donut.

"That family can't catch a break, Lew. How do you want to handle it?"

"Well, we can't afford to pull a continuous stakeout on his house, but we should do a daily drive-by for a while," Tenant recommended as he returned to his computer research on a recent robbery suspect.

AFTER RENTING a car at the South Bend Airport, Richard Rasch was on his way to Culver for some unfinished business. Rasch was wiry but strong with dark, slicked-back hair. The

Committee needed someone they could trust. So, without hesitation, they sent Rasch, confident that the business would be handled professionally. Rasch had been a key player for The New Global Order and they trusted his ability to remain under the radar, even in a small town like Culver, and get the job done. *This shouldn't take too long,* Rasch assuredly thought to himself. *I'll take care of McCabe and torch his house. That should send a signal to other people who have refused to comply. We got rid of the father, and now it's time for the son to pay. Can't imagine there's anybody in that hick town who can stop me.* His contact at The Committee – better known as The New Global Order – had shipped lethal weapons to a small gun shop in Plymouth, just north of Culver. He expected to pick up a Lugar pistol and a Heckler & Koch MP7A1 machine gun for his business trip.

AT THE McCABE COTTAGE, Hans was finishing his supper of beef stew and homemade bread, which he grew accustomed to in the Army. He loved getting fresh bread at the Sugar Magnolia Bakery in Culver when he could. It reminded him of the delicious loaves his mother would bake several times a week. His friends always begged him to come over to sample them.

After cleaning his AR15 earlier in the day, he had time for some target practice out by the cornfield near his home. He could still clip off a corn tassel from more than 1,000 feet, so he felt like his aim was true. That first night, he decided to position himself in the dining room on a recliner where he could see the front and back doors and many of the large windows. With the lights off, he pulled the blinds up, so his visibility was good.

For the first week, he didn't see any sign of an intruder or hear anything unusual other than some pesky raccoons that enjoyed invading the chimney. He started to wonder if Mr. McCabe had the right information.

Each evening near dusk, Detective Tenant and Deputy Atrich took a slow drive down East Shore Drive, scanning the terrain for any suspicious visitors or cars. Problem was, with so many tourists and people visiting friends who had cottages on the lake, it was almost impossible to tell.

A few days later about 12:30 a.m., undetected by the local homeowners or Culver police, Rasch parked his rental car on East Shore Lane – off the main road and several blocks from the McCabe house. He had cruised by the McCabe's multiple times since he arrived in Culver, so he was aware of the environment. He hadn't spotted McCabe or his girlfriend, but someone was living there. He thought he'd go ahead and take out whoever was in the house and torch the place. Then he'd lay low until McCabe showed up. The local hicks would never know he had been there.

Carrying a can of gas and his weapons, he stealthily crept along the grass next to East Shore Drive under a cloudless, moonlit sky. When he got to the McCabe house, he hid behind a large oak tree to scan the rear entrance. He didn't see any activity or lights, so he moved slowly toward the house, put down the gas can, and poked his head up to look through a window.

Inside, Hans' eyes and ears perked after as he saw a moonlight reflection of a shiny weapon and movement from a window on the outside garage behind the house. He quietly slid off the recliner and prepared his rifle. *Am I just seeing things?* he wondered.

Feeling secure that no one was downstairs, Rasch jimmied the backdoor lock and slowly opened it. No alarm...he snuck in...his pulse rising. Once he was inside, he held steady momentarily to see if anything stirred.

All at once, Hans shouted in a stern voice, "Who goes there?"

As soon as he heard him, Rasch pulled his Lugar and fired.

But he was not fast enough. Hans blasted Rasch repeatedly with a full load of ammo, knocking him through the back door. Springing up and sprinting to the bullet-riddled rear entrance, Hans looked outside.

The intruder was lying motionless on the asphalt driveway below, with a gas can nearby. A pool of blood was puddling from his now lifeless body. Switching on the outside lights, Hans immediately saw Rasch sprawled in front of him, his eyes still open, staring up at the summer moon.

16

Moments after the failed attack on the McCabe cottage, Culver Police Detective Lewis Tenant's mobile phone buzzed on his nightstand. "Uh…yes, Tenant here," he coughed and replied wearily, disturbing his wife who was lying next to him.

"So sorry to call, Detective, but you asked me to contact you if anything happened here. Well, sir, it did! You better come over – and bring an ambulance."

"Oh my God, Hans!" Tenant whispered loudly in return. "You okay?"

"Yes, sir, some guy was looking for trouble with weapons and a can of gas, but he won't be bothering us anymore."

After rousing Deputy Jerome Atrich from his deep slumber, Tenant picked him up at his home and they sped to the McCabe house, driving down East Shore Drive. On the way, Atrich sipped on some coffee and called for an ambulance to meet them.

When the squad car turned into the McCabe driveway, they immediately saw the body lying motionless behind the rear entrance to the house, with part of the back door blown away.

Hans gave the policemen all the details he had on the intruder, and how he had ordered the man to halt. But when he drew his weapon and fired, Hans defended himself – and the cottage.

"Thank God for the Second Amendment, Hans," Tenant responded, grateful to see that Hans was able to protect himself. "Looks like this must be the guy McCabe was warned about from the U.S. Embassy."

"Chalk one up for the good guys," Atrich chimed in as he began staking yellow crime-scene tape around the back of the house.

Just then, the ambulance drove up next to the garage and the EMTs came rambling down the driveway to join them. Moments later, one of them confirmed the man was certainly gone – closing his open eyelids.

ITALIAN OFFICERS ALBERTO Fresco and Kara Sterrio had contacted Chief Samuel Aritan at Interpol and described their missed opportunity to capture Raffone. The only thing they knew was that one of his taillights had been knocked out, but he would surely get that repaired quickly.

They had entered the Raffone premises and took a beautiful Italian woman, Piper Roni, in for questioning. While there, they searched his house for any incriminating evidence and ties to The New Global Order. From their initial surveillance, however, there was nothing outstanding they could use.

After gaining a search warrant, they requested the Florence police do a more thorough examination of the house. When they questioned Roni at the police station in Florence, it appeared she was a call girl paid by Raffone and didn't seem aware of his criminal activities.

In the days that followed, Sterrio reported, "My source here tells me Raffone frequently dines at the Trattoria Fratelli Briganti on Piazza Giovanbattista Georgini. Don't suppose he'd be ballsy enough to show up in public – this soon – do you?"

"No telling what he might do, but he likes to eat and probably thinks he's protected, so let's check it out. I've heard they have some of the best pasta in Florence. If he's not there, we can grab a meal."

Before heading to the restaurant, they changed into undercover casual attire, but still covertly packed their weapons and wore protective vests. Driving down Via Sallustio Bandini, they parked a block away and walked to the restaurant. A summer rain was threatening overhead among darkening clouds, which they hoped might end the intense humidity they had been having this July.

They entered the crowded Trattoria and sat at a booth near the front door. There was no immediate sign of Raffone, so they opened the menus to order. Soon, a friendly young waiter brought them some sparkling water and rolls and told them about *la specialita: spaghettino al pomodora*, which they ordered. Before the waiter left, they asked if there was a private dining room, and he confirmed there was one near the back by the restrooms. But it was currently in use.

"You don't suppose our friend is back there with his pals, do you?" Sterrio asked with interest. "I'll head back there and take a peek."

Moving around tables to find her way to the restrooms, Sterrio arrived in a hallway and scanned the rooms that led from it. The door to the private dining room was ajar, but she couldn't see inside. Without hesitating, she made her way into the kitchen and presented her badge to the head chef. He reluctantly agreed to allow her to change into a waitress uniform so she could enter with a cart full of dessert choices as the guests were finishing their meals. She contacted Fresco, who quickly joined her in the hallway.

Knocking on the private room door, she smiled and pushed her cart near the table. Quickly searching the faces of the six men at the table, she spotted Raffone downing a glass of Chianti. *Can't believe he's out in public already*, she thought. Without giving any notification, she pulled her semiautomatic pistol from under her apron and announced her intention to arrest him.

Suddenly all the men reached for their weapons and Raffone lifted the dining table up and flipped it on its side with plates, glasses, and bread rolls flying everywhere. One of the men fired and hit Sterrio in her left shoulder, but her right hand held the pistol and returned fire, striking two of the men.

As soon as Fresco heard her voice, he stormed in with his weapon ready, shooting the other three men and putting holes into the dining table. During the melee, Raffone was able to escape through a back door.

"You okay, Kara?" Fresco yelled as the other men lay wounded and bleeding on the floor next to the overturned table and chairs.

"I'm fine, get Raffone!" she screamed back, wincing from the bullet she took, but holding her gun on the men writhing in pain near her.

Fresco tore out of the private dining room backdoor, scrambling after the criminal. He was able to spot Raffone hopping on a Powersports Max Moped at a rental shop a half block away. Fresco ran and jumped on another one and ripped after him down Via Sallustio Bandini, weaving in and out of traffic. Raffone was headed to Piazza Pietro Leopoldo, took a sudden right, skidding onto Via Ubaldo Montelaciti, with Fresco making up ground behind, as rain began to fall.

Raffone zipped to Via Giandomenico Romagnosi, and took a quick left in front of several cars on Via Giovanni Maria Lampredi toward a series of industrial buildings. The criminal then darted into a parking lot. Fresco thought he had lost him but continued his pursuit.

When he entered the facility, Fresco could hear the squeal of the scooter's tires heading up the circular ramp above, so he followed. Reaching the end of the ramp, he spotted Raffone's abandoned scooter. He was nowhere in sight. Jumping off his own scooter and roughly tossing it on the side of the ramp, Fresco opened a door to the roof to check the sight lines. Raffone had eluded him. Fresco scanned the roof but there was no sign.

Suddenly, a small Fiat revved up and was heading toward the exit not far from Fresco, who aimed his sidearm and fired. The bullet pierced through the driver-side window and buried in Raffone's temple. Immediately, the Fiat lost control and sped toward the side of the roof and careened over – seconds later crashing on the empty street below. Fresco ran to the edge of the building and watched as the Fiat burst into flames.

Using his mobile, he got Sterrio on the line and asked how she was doing. "I've been better, but I'll survive. Any luck with Raffone?"

"He led me on a wild chase but ended up taking a dive in a Fiat over the side of a building," Fresco said as he calmly described the frantic events that had just transpired.

"Three of the men at the restaurant didn't make it. We have two in custody, headed to the hospital under armed guard. They'll have some tough interrogation coming their way. Surely these guys know something about the organization we're after."

As a gentle rain began falling harder, Fresco called the police and their sirens were soon heard above the noise from the city. Firemen quickly followed to douse the burning Fiat. But there wasn't much left of Raffone, who obviously had his *last supper*.

17

Back in Rome, Italy, Major Oli Klosov arranged to visit The Committee's stern leader, Adamis Baum, for an urgent meeting at his luxury estate. "Director, as I said briefly on the phone, there are several operations we need to discuss that did not go well," Klosov explained sheepishly. "Our people failed to capture Lester in Dusseldorf. Our man Richard Rasch was killed in Culver, Indiana, trying to take out a guy on our hit list, Jack McCabe. And Michael Raffone was knocked off in Florence with two of his men captured."

"This is totally unacceptable, Klosov! How are they making such fools of us?" Baum growled back, pounding his fist on his polished mahogany desk. "If you can't get the job done, we will need to find someone who can."

"We have a team ready to make a move in Bruges, but the Interpol base there is almost impenetrable," Klosov explained as he wiped his bald head with a handkerchief. "Morris Lester, who paid off a local to kill Hugo DeMann, was captured. His attorney, Kenneth Dahl, is headed to Bruges to sit in on the upcoming interrogation, so we will have someone getting inside. We'll position the rest of our men to pull a surprise attack when the opportunity arises. We're also ready to move in Florence and Rome when the time comes."

"Have you ever heard of the *Trojan Horse* story, Klosov?" Baum asked rhetorically as he began doodling a drawing on his open folio pad. "Well, as you recall, the Greeks hid inside a large wooden horse statue to attack Troy once it was pulled inside its walls. In a similar fashion, tell attorney Dahl that if things aren't going well once he's inside, he needs to give Lester a poison cyanide tablet to do the honorable thing and take his own life. If Lester refuses, take the next step and tell Dahl to use a poison syringe."

After the meeting with Klosov, Baum buzzed his assistant, Bendrick Dover, for some tea. Baum took a moment to admire his prize possessions: the fine art masterpieces he had accumulated over the years. He was passionate about his Rembrandt, Titian, Caravaggio, Picassos, and a recently acquired Van Gogh. But he wanted more.

But enough of that for now, he thought. *Back to business.* Accidentally picking up his *personal* mobile phone, Baum called a close ally in the U.S. Senate, Russell Fossett, to discuss the lingering problem in Indiana. "Senator, I hope you are hale and hearty."

Baum and Fossett had grown close while they orchestrated the proposal for the government's dramatic new climate-change initiative. "Greetings, Baum," Fossett responded warmly but felt a sudden sense of alarm. "To what do I owe this unexpected call?"

"We have a little problem in a small town in Indiana, Culver to be exact," Baum explained. "There is a man named Jack McCabe who is now the owner of a very large asphalt manufacturing business he inherited. We have sent his family repeated demands to cease operations, change its fossil-fuel ingredients, or face the consequences. We ended the lives of his parents and now need to finish off the son. Do you have any contacts in that area?"

"As a matter of fact, I have a connection in Indianapolis who is willing to take on this type of job...for a fee," Fossett replied confidently.

"Money is not an issue, Senator. Just let me know what it will take," Baum confirmed.

MEANWHILE, near Bruges, Belgium, the military plane carrying the Interpol team and its prisoner, Morris Lester, was nearing a touchdown at its private airfield. Interpol frequently used this airstrip to get in and out of the city, especially in matters of urgency. After capturing Lester in Dusseldorf and flying him back for questioning, getting him in a prison cell was a high priority.

Lester had been identified paying off Terrence Boll in the murder of Hugo DeMann. But who was Lester's contact from The New Global Order? And how many layers were there to get to the top players?

After they landed in Bruges, Officers Barron Kaide and Darren Deeds joined Officers Cameron Payne and Jeanette Poole in transferring the prisoner to their headquarters.

During the flight, Chief Aritan, based in Innsbruck, phoned Payne with some critical intelligence. "The enemy may try to attack the Interpol base in Bruges to rescue Lester. If they can't free him, they may try to kill his ass. Lester's attorney, Kenneth Dahl, could be a problem. No doubt he'll demand to be present for the interrogation. Have to think Dahl is linked to the enemy."

While driving to the headquarters, "Great work on the tarmac in Dusseldorf, Kaide," Poole said with sincere praise for

Officer Kaide, who destroyed the enemy SUV with a long grenade throw. "Must be fun having a rifle for an arm."

"Happy to be of service, ma'am," Kaide responded respectfully. "And good thing they parked close enough to be in range, huh?" he continued, giving the team a brief chuckle. Kaide had attended Furman University in Greenville, SC, on a partial baseball scholarship, and was in the pitching rotation for the Paladins. After college, he played semi-pro ball for a few years before joining the military, which led to a position with Interpol.

"When did you get all those tattoos on your arms?" Poole wondered.

"Mostly after college while I was playing ball. One thing led to another you know. Got a few in the military."

After they reached their base, the team escorted Lester to a holding cell and prepared for his interrogation. "I need my attorney," Lester complained loudly as they locked the door to his cell.

"We'll see about that," Officer Payne responded, knowing he would likely need to allow Kenneth Dahl to be present during questioning. But he hated to delay their interrogation any longer than necessary.

It didn't take Dahl long to make his way to Bruges and request to attend Lester's probe. "Hello, this is the attorney for Morris Lester. I demand to be involved in the questioning of my client," he announced to Officer Poole, who took the call.

"We plan to begin in the morning, so be here by 9:00 a.m.," Poole responded coldly.

Later that evening, Officers Poole and Kaide had some time off and decided to grab dinner together. They were of similar age and wanted to find out how much they might have in common. They enjoyed their time alone and, after having a few drinks, Poole invited Kaide back to her apartment for a nightcap.

On the way to her vehicle and preoccupied with each other,

they passed a large black van next to the sidewalk. Just as they walked by, three men darted from their vehicle. Even though Poole and Kaide were armed, they had no time to react. The men quickly stuck syringes with strong sedatives into their necks. With Kaide collapsing in a heap on the sidewalk, they pulled Poole into their van and sped off.

As they drove to a warehouse location outside of Bruges, the men in the back disarmed Poole, tied her up, and put a black hood over her head.

Two hours later, Kaide slowly regained consciousness, rubbing his head and feeling the injection point in his neck. Even though he was still groggy, he eventually got his bearings. He checked to see if he still had his weapon and then pulled out his mobile. "Sir, something terrible just happened," he reported to Officer Payne. "Poole and I were jumped outside the bar. I was injected with something that knocked me out, and they've obviously taken Poole!"

"Damn, Kaide! We didn't need this kind of crap. Any idea who it was or where they went?"

"No, Sir, I didn't see them. It happened too fast. They were on us before we could react," Kaide explained, disgusted with himself.

At a secret warehouse facility, Poole was bound with her hands and feet lashed to a chair, the hood still over her head. As she regained consciousness from the drug, she realized she had been captured but had no idea of her location. She could barely see through the gauzy black hood. A bright light glared from above.

The next morning at 8:00 a.m., Officer Payne received a call at the Interpol headquarters. The voice sounded like it was artificially deepened so it could not be detected. "We have your officer and need to discuss an exchange for Lester. We will call back in one hour and want an answer."

Payne was not in the habit of dealing with terrorists nor did

Interpol exchange prisoners. But Poole was his partner – he wanted to protect her at all costs. He needed to do whatever it took to get her back.

At 9:00 a.m., Lester's attorney, Kenneth Dahl, arrived on site for the interrogation. Major Klosov had alerted Dahl to Poole's kidnapping but was not going to tip his hand. "Good morning, I am here to meet with my client."

"What do you know about Officer Poole, Dahl?" barked Payne.

"Why, what happened? I'm afraid you have me there, Officer," Dahl responded coyly.

As another officer led Dahl to Lester's cell, a hidden video camera recorded their actions.

Finally, Payne's phone rang, and the deep voice was on the line. "We hope you've come to your senses and are ready for the exchange."

"What do you want?" Payne replied bitterly, making notes on a pad in front of him, while Officers Barron Kaide and Darren Deeds listened in on the conversation.

"There is a dead end on Mosselstraat on the east side of Bruges. Be there at midnight tonight. We'll have our prisoner and will exchange for Lester at that time. Don't try anything foolish...or Poole dies," the deep voice demanded and abruptly clicked off.

18

After discussing the exchange of prisoners with Interpol Chief Samuel Aritan in Innsbruck, it was decided that they would surround the area of the exchange with men fully disguised and hidden under foliage in the nearby terrain. They would also wear night vision goggles on this cloud-covered night. Once the exchange was made – and Officer Jeanette Poole was in the clear – they would destroy the kidnappers. Additional military officers were called in to assist Officer Cameron Payne and his team in this touch-and-go operation.

It was nearing the exchange time. The enemy grabbed the kidnapped Officer Poole, dragged her out of the warehouse, and tossed her into the back of the van. Her arms were still tied in back, but her legs were free as she composed herself after the rough treatment. The three men sat in front and left her alone in the back, which gave her a chance.

Quietly pressing on the floor of the van with her bound hands, she was able to lift herself up and slide her rear end past her hands. Then she slowly pulled her legs behind them. Finally, she got her feet past her wrists, so her hands were now in front of her. *Yes!* She thought. Pulling the hood from her head, she waited for the opportunity to strike.

The enemy van slowly drove down Mosselstraat to meet for the exchange. When they neared the meeting place, its headlights brought the Interpol vehicle and Lester into view. Two officers were positioned closely behind him.

Stopping a block away, the enemy waited a few minutes, then exited the van. One of them opened the side door. Poole had positioned herself out of obvious view. When the guard leaned in to locate her, she kicked his weapon away from him to the inside of the van. She then leapt forward with her legs getting a scissor lock around his neck. With her hands still bound, she leaned over, grabbed the weapon, and shot the guard in the head. Another guard came around to check on his partner. Poole fired at his temple, killing him instantly.

Seeing the entire situation blowing up in his face, the van's driver quickly jumped on the gas and drove in reverse, speeding to escape. Instinctively, Poole tumbled out of the van, and kept rolling when she hit the ground to avoid further injury.

As the van continued to speed backward down the street, the officers hidden in the terrain had seen Poole escape from the van and began firing. They immediately riddled the enemy vehicle and its tires with bullets. The van spun out of control and flipped off the road, kicking up a huge cloud of dust and debris.

Sprinting rapidly to his partner, Payne reached the bruised and disheveled Poole, who otherwise seemed okay. "What took you so long, Payne?" Poole joked, as he quickly untied her hands and hugged her.

The other military men soon reached the enemy van, which had come to a rest on its side. They pulled the remaining man out of the driver's seat to check on him. He still had a pulse but was wounded severely from the rapid blast of ammo. One of the men called for an ambulance in hopes of saving him for questioning. In the meantime, Officers Barron Kaide and Darren

Deeds, who had been guarding Lester, shoved him back in their vehicle to return to the base.

THE NEXT DAY after his breakfast at the Senate dining hall, Russell Fossett, who had agreed with Adamis Baum to hire another hit on Jack McCabe, moved into a hidden alcove to make a phone call on his burner mobile. "Yeah, this is Downe… speak," Patrick Downe answered in his usual gruff manner. Downe was a wiry but tough African American who had a criminal record for armed robbery and escaped being caught for several murders he was suspected of committing.

"Why yes, Downe, this is Fossett calling. I may have a job for you in Indiana."

"Must be important for you to contact me, Fossett," Downe replied. "Give me the skinny and I might be able to help."

Fossett proceeded to brief Downe on the location and details and made an offer that they both agreed on: the usual $25,000 for the hit.

ABOUT THAT TIME, Jack had driven to Culver to check on Hans and begin arranging for his grandfather's documents and other valuables to be put into storage. Sara was going to stay with family in Indianapolis while he was away. Jack also wanted to make sure the repairs to the back door and any other damages from the earlier gunfire were completed to his satisfaction.

When he pulled into the driveway in late afternoon, Hans was painting the railing along the steps to the back door, which appeared to have been repaired. The sun was glistening off the lake, warming his heart to be back. "Hello, Hans, great to see you!"

"Hello, Mr. McCabe, happy to see you again at the lake."

After praising Hans for his bravery while protecting the house, Jack asked if he would join him for dinner. They cooked some steaks on the grill, made baked potatoes, and prepared a salad. Jack even popped one of his favorite bottles of Merlot for the feast.

After their meal, Jack described his plans to move all of Amos McCabe's files and private belongings to a safe storage facility in Culver. Hans was happy to help. They also discussed that the potential threat to Jack and the house was probably not over.

"How are you with a weapon, Mr. McCabe?"

"Haven't done much with guns, I'm afraid. I was never in the military and we didn't hunt with rifles. I did learn how to use a bow and arrow quite handily during several hunting expeditions, but I'm not sure how well I'd do in battle."

"I'll be happy to train you, if you'd like. I've got a firing range not far from here and I can get you up to speed in no time." Without hesitation, Jack took him up on his offer and they planned to begin the next day after moving Amos McCabe's things into storage. Hans had an extra rifle that belonged to his father that Jack could use for as long as he wished.

Jack was not used to packing a gun, but with the danger they faced, he purchased an M17 sidearm for himself and one for Hans, who had used that model in the military. After several days of practice, Jack felt comfortable enough with the rifle and pistol to take care of himself, if danger warranted.

SENATOR RUSSELL FOSSETT and Patrick Downe were unaware that the Indianapolis police had wiretapped Downe's mobile phone after he avoided prosecution for two murders. Homicide Detective William Wynn overheard their conversation and called the Culver Police to warn them of the potential trouble. "Hello, this is Detective William Wynn from the Indianapolis P.D. We just got some information you need to know."

"Yes, Officer, what's going on?" Detective Lewis Tenant replied as he paused from filling out the day's agenda.

"There's a bad apple here in Indy that we tried to prosecute for murder on two occasions but couldn't make 'em stick," Wynn explained as he reviewed case folders on his desk in the busy police station.

Wynn detailed the crimes against Downe and how he had alibis for both crimes. "Now he appears to have taken a job for a hit on a guy who lives on Lake Maxinkuckee. Do you know a fellow named Jack McCabe?"

"Sure do, and he's had more than his share of threats from terrorists," Tenant responded, breathing heavily and wondering if McCabe's problems would ever end. After his call with Wynn, Tenant contacted Jack to alert him of yet another possible attack. "We'll provide extra protection for your home, Mr. McCabe. Hope you take precautions."

A few days later, after arriving in Culver, Patrick Downe had driven by the McCabe house at different times and noticed a local police car stationed across the street on each pass. He needed another way to get to his target. To disguise his visit, he brought his trailer and fishing boat with a high-speed motor to survey the McCabe house from the lake. After launching his boat from the public access, he powered up and made his way toward the east side, reviewing a map of the homes. It was nearly sunset, so he flipped on his boat light to avoid any problems with the lake police. Slowly he cruised to McCabe's cottage.

19

W*hat luck!* hitman Patrick Downe thought to himself as he slowly circled past the McCabe house and saw two men sitting on the long, white pier. Pulling up his binoculars, the older guy looked like the photo D.C. Senator Russell Fossett had emailed him. He knew he had the right person.

As Jack and Hans were relaxing, sipping beer, Jack peered out across the lake. It occurred to him how many new houses seemed to be popping up on the distant shore. They almost appeared like mushrooms springing up from mossy ground.

After making a loop about 50 yards from the cottage, Downe put his motor on idle and drifted closer to his firing range, but he still had to stay outside the buoy, which marked the safe distance for boats. The waves made his balance less than ideal, but he reached for his weapon with a silencer and prepared to fire.

Just then, Jack spotted the boat and its driver and whispered loudly to Hans, "Hey, what the hell's that guy up to?" They both jumped up, pulled their sidearms, and got down behind a large, wooden bench on the pier.

A bullet whizzed toward them, hitting the bench as they

watched the attacker aiming their way. Jack and Hans fired back, one hitting the boat and the other apparently hitting the man. Quickly, the boat sped away toward the center of the lake.

Hearing the shots, Culver policemen Detective Lewis Tenant and Deputy Jerome Atrich jumped from their squad car that was parked across the street from McCabe's and ran toward the lake. When they reached the front of the house, Jack and Hans were slowly standing up from their positions behind the bench, focusing toward the lake. In the distance, the two policemen could see a fishing boat speeding away.

At that time of dusk, boats weren't allowed to go over a minimal speed for safety so, after hearing the shots, a nearby lake shore patrol boat spotted the offender and quickly gave chase. Patrolman Oliver Sutton of shore patrol grabbed his loudspeaker and loudly ordered the speeding boat to slow down and kill his motor. But Downe's boat kept tearing through the water to the western shore.

Patrolman Sutton phoned his staff on shore to be ready for the boat heading toward the public-access beach. As Downe sped to the western shore, he could see a patrol car driving up with lights flashing, so he made his way toward the south side of the lake. The shore patrol boat kept gaining on the offender and Patrolman Sutton yelled again into the speaker, but Downe wouldn't stop.

Downe looked back to see how much the shore patrol boat had gained, keeping his throttle at high speed. When he looked back in front, a moored fishing boat came into view, but it was too late. Downe hit the anchored boat straight on. His boat careened over the top, flipping in the air before slamming violently back onto the water. Downe was thrown from his boat. He sank momentarily after crashing to the water, but came back up, splashing frantically. The shore patrol slowed, circled around the sinking man, and threw him a life preserver.

Several minutes later from the east side of the lake on the

McCabe pier, Detective Tenant phoned Patrolman Sutton. "Hello, Detective Tenant here from the Culver Police. Looks like you may have apprehended the guy who fired a weapon at the McCabe house on the east side. They fired back. We had a tip that Patrick Downe was hired to make a hit on McCabe."

"We heard the shots but couldn't tell where they were coming from. Yes, we've got this guy under arrest now. He has a bullet wound in his thigh, which we've bandaged."

Tenant went on to explain the recent history of attacks on McCabe and his caretaker. He also told Sutton that when information surfaced about another threat, McCabe and Hans had been armed and were prepared to defend themselves.

"We'll need to get him to the Plymouth hospital to take care of his wound, then get him back to our police station in Culver for questioning," Tenant explained as Jack, Hans, and Deputy Atrich looked on.

"Looks like you warded off another potential disaster, Mr. McCabe," Tenant said gratefully after finishing his call.

"Thanks to Hans, we were prepared. I think a bullet from the guy lodged in this bench," he said as he looked around for the evidence.

Moments later, Atrich offered, "Here you go, Mr. McCabe," as he pointed to a fresh slug in the white-painted bench with his pocketknife. "I'll dig this out for future comparison to the man's weapon, if we can ever locate it from the bottom of the lake."

The next day, after Patrick Downe's bullet was removed from his leg and the wound was patched up in Plymouth, he was brought back to the Culver Police Station. Detective Lewis Tenant called Detective William Wynn at the Indianapolis P.D. to give him an update on the recent events. "Hello, Detective, Tenant here from Culver. Downe did attempt a hit but he wasn't successful, thank God!" Tenant said as he looked back toward the jail cell that was holding the new prisoner.

"Well, good to know you were able to stop him!" Wynn

replied jubilantly. Tenant went on to describe the shooting and subsequent boat chase that led to Downe's arrest.

"Did you happen to catch the name of the person who ordered the hit?" Tenant inquired as he made notes in his case file.

"The guy's name was Fossett, but that's all we got," Wynn advised. "We weren't able to get his number. Must have been some sort of burner phone. If you happen to get Downe's phone, maybe it will be listed."

"We've got Downe's car with his belongings but didn't find a phone. The guy went into the lake, and his weapon and phone may be under water. Our dive team is searching that part of the lake to see if they come up with anything."

Later that day, the station phone rang and Atrich put down his old-fashioned donut and answered, "Hello, Culver Police."

"This is Patrolman Oliver Sutton from the shore patrol. Our dive team located a pistol with a silencer on the lake bottom near the spot where we captured Downe. They also brought up a phone, but not sure it's any good now after being in the water. I'll drop them by the station."

"Great, thanks, Sutton!" Atrich said gratefully and updated Tenant on the underwater discoveries.

After Sutton dropped off the weapon and phone, Tenant asked Atrich to take them both to the forensic lab. They needed to compare the bullet found at McCabe's pier for a potential match to the gun and see if they could get anything from the phone.

Later the next day, the forensic lab called with an update. "Hello, forensics here about your requests. Got some good news. The bullet is certainly a match with the gun, so your prisoner appears to be liable for the shooting. As for the phone, we were able to get a call list but not much else. A recent call came in from Washington, D.C., but no way to connect it with anyone. Sorry."

"Great work!" Tenant responded as he looked over at Atrich who was making a new pot of coffee. "The info on the phone should give us something to go on. Thanks!"

After the call, Tenant went back to the jail cell and stared at the prisoner. "We've got you for attempted murder, Downe. Why don't you make it easy on yourself and tell us who ordered the hit?"

"Not a chance. Need my lawyer here before I say anything." Downe then gave him the name of his attorney, Phillip Rupp, who had represented him well in the past. Tenant located Rupp's contact information and called to request his presence for the interrogation.

Two days later when Rupp arrived at the Culver Police Station, the attorney requested to post bail for his client, but it was denied. Downe was too connected to the ongoing threats and the police needed answers. They also figured Downe would certainly be a flight risk.

Phillip Rupp was a short, pudgy African American attorney who wore large, black-framed glasses, and seemed to be all business. When the questioning began, his impatient demeanor wasn't winning any favors with Tenant.

With the recorder running, Tenant asked again, "What's it going to take to get information on the guy who ordered the hit? We've already got you for attempted murder. No alibis this time. It's a *fait accompli* as they say."

20

The Italian criminal Michael Raffone had been killed by Interpol Officer Alberto Fresco on top of the parking garage. During the preceding gunfight in the Florence restaurant, two of Raffone's buddies had been injured but survived. Toma Bacco and Torino Nado, who had underworld pasts and were closely tied to Raffone, had been injured but were mending well. They had been returned to the Interpol office in Rome for questioning.

Fresco's partner, the resilient Officer Kara Sterrio, was recovering nicely after suffering a bullet injury to her left arm during the restaurant gunfight.

Raffone had been identified as the person who hired Ivan Lasch to kill Jack McCabe's parents 12 years before, and then ordered the hit on Jack in Innsbruck. They knew Raffone had connections with The New Global Order, but who paid him? That's what they needed to find out from Bacco and Nado.

Prior to questioning Raffone's two associates, Officer Fresco called Interpol Chief Samuel Aritan in Innsbruck. "We're about ready to grill Raffone's two buddies and want to see if you have any input," Fresco inquired as he sat at his desk savoring an espresso. He had researched their criminal cases and knew they were already the subjects of several crime investigations.

"Need to get something on 'em that'll stick, or we won't be able to hold 'em," Aritan responded authoritatively.

"They've both served time for armed robbery," Fresco replied, leafing through case file folders. "And it appears they were wanted for fencing of stolen auto parts as well as illegal drug distribution, so we should be good. We have the evidence, now we have the perpetrators."

The attorney for both was Tomaso Moro, a thin, well-dressed, middle-aged Italian who walked with a cane. They started their questioning with Torino Nado, a heavyset man in his late 50s. "We've charged Mr. Nado for several unsolved crimes," Fresco acknowledged to set the record straight, and then proceeded to list the details of the charges.

"We know that your friend, Michael Raffone, was involved in paying others to commit murder under the direction of an organization that calls itself The New Global Order," Fresco began. "Are you familiar with anyone else connected to that organization?"

"Nah, don't know 'em," Nado replied as he adjusted the handcuffs in front of him, feeling the pain in his wrists.

"Well, we think you do. In fact, we believe you know just about everything that Raffone did, since you were his partner."

"Didn't know Raffone that well actually. Just got together with him for drinks and dinner sometimes. Got a lot of friends in Florence."

"Won't do you any good to play hardball, Nado," Fresco alleged.

"You're badgering my client, officer," attorney Moro claimed.

"Not only do we have you for fencing stolen auto parts and drug dealing," Fresco reminded him, "we've also got you for firing at a police officer! You're going to spend time in prison, so make it easier on yourself and give us the information we need."

"Let me have a word with my client," Moro requested, turning and whispering to Nado. With that, Fresco turned off the recording device, got up, and walked out of the room.

He joined Sterrio who was viewing the questioning behind the two-way mirror. "What type of prison term do you think he's looking at, Alberto?"

"Probably at least 30 years, if you ask me, but I'll have to talk to the prosecutor's office to know for sure."

After rejoining the prisoner and his attorney, a plea deal was discussed, so Fresco called his friend, Prosecutor Morto Talliti, to see what he could do. "You're probably on the money with about 30 years," Talliti suggested. "See if you can get anywhere with a deal of 25."

After bargaining back and forth for several hours among Nado, his attorney, and the prosecutor, they all agreed on 20 years for all crimes, if he would provide the information.

With more questions and runaround answers, Nado finally gave it up. "For all I know, Raffone got his orders from a middleman named Salvatore Amie. Think he lives here in Rome somewhere, but I was never in on the meetings."

Fresco went through the same process with Toma Bacco, a tall, thin Italian with slicked-back grey hair and goatee. Attorney Moro represented him as well and they arrived at the same deal. "Only name I heard of is Salvatore Amie," claimed Bacco. "A middleman, Raffone called him." Fresco realized that the attorney likely advised Bacco on the name for consistency, so they had to go with Amie to see where that led.

The next day, Fresco and Sterrio spent hours in front of their computers trying to get a match on Amie. Finally, Sterrio got a hit. "There's a Salvatore Amie who has a penthouse in Rome but apparently travels a lot," she read from the profile. "He has had legal troubles from loan sharking and ponzi schemes. His place is on Via della Vite, not too far from the Spanish Steps. He's in his 50s, good looking and dresses well."

"Want to pay him a visit, Sterrio?" Fresco inquired rhetorically. They packed their gear, put on their vests, and hit the street. Sterrio wasn't 100% cured from her bullet wound, but she was still capable of doing her job. On the way, Sterrio called Interpol Chief Aritan in Innsbruck to give a report.

"Watch yourselves with this guy," Aritan warned. "No doubt he won't hesitate to try to take ya out."

Fresco and Sterrio parked a half block down the street and walked to the address. They knocked on the front door and presented their IDs to a small, elderly Italian woman who answered the door. She said she was Amie's housekeeper, but hadn't seen him for a while because he was away on business.

"Do you know how to reach him?" Sterrio asked in her most genteel Italian.

"Sorry, he just comes. He just goes," the housekeeper responded, gesturing wildly with her hands.

When they left they decided to put a couple of officers on a stakeout to keep an eye on his place. They didn't know how long it would be before Amie returned, but they wanted to be aware of it when he did. After returning to their office, Fresco and Sterrio briefed Officers Bella Gamba and Enzo Ferno. Gamba was a striking Italian beauty and Ferno was a muscular former boxer. They were both experienced professionals and ready for the stakeout. The team also got a warrant to tap Amie's home phone in case he called his housekeeper.

Later that evening The New Global Orders' Salvatore Amie was dining with the voluptuous Lisbett Kant at her villa in Venice on the Grand Canal. She was left millions after her wealthy husband passed away mysteriously, so finances were of no concern. Amie and Kant had been lovers for several years and he had been living with her for the past month. Tonight, they were celebrating their relationship with a bottle of one of her finest champagnes, a 2008 Dom Perignon Brut.

"Tigre," Kant called him, "let's toast to our beautiful friendship."

"Si, Amore, we do make classical music together," Amie replied affectionately as they toasted and drank from crystal goblets.

"It's been so lovely these past few weeks, but I'm afraid tomorrow I've been called to meet with Director Adamis Baum in Rome. It appears we have had trouble on multiple fronts, so we are planning our next steps."

"Would you like to stay with me while you're in Rome, Amore?" Amie asked flirtatiously.

"Of course, if I could, Tigre. Unfortunately, the director often insists that we stay at his villa for additional security. You understand, don't you?"

"Si, Amore. When will I have an opportunity to be part of the famous round table group of The Committee?"

"If there is a good time, I will try to inquire. I'm afraid this meeting will not be pleasant. It appears that heads are going to roll. Let's just enjoy the evening together." They continued watching colorful boats drifting below with gondoliers singing on the canal. After finishing their bottle, they moved to her luxurious boudoir for a more intimate expression of their amorous affair.

21

The next day, Salvatore Amie was driving back to his flat in Rome after a long absence. He called his housekeeper to tell her to make preparations for his meals and other domestic requirements. "Si, senor Amie, I will take care of everything as I always do. You need to know that there were two policemen here recently inquiring about you. I told them I didn't know how to reach you. They said they had some questions."

"Good to know, thanks for the heads up," Amie responded curiously. With this information, he decided to rent a hotel room for the night and check his place for any sign of surveillance.

Interpol Officers Bella Gamba and Enzo Ferno had rented a place across the street from Amie's, so they wouldn't be easily spotted. After several days, they had not seen any sign of him.

Back at the station, Officer Kara Sterrio got word from the team that the wiretap on Amie's house phone came through with a call from Amie. He was planning on returning but his housekeeper alerted him that police had visited, which could possibly delay his homecoming. The Interpol analysts were able to get Amie's phone number and would attempt to track its location. They also alerted Officers Gamba and Ferno to be on high alert.

After checking into the hotel for the night, Amie drove by his place and watched for any suspicious activities or people. Nothing looked amiss. He sped around the block and parked several houses down the street to see if anything was unusual. Nothing caused him alarm. *I'll give it another day and investigate again,* Amie thought, checking his sidearm to make sure he was prepared for any confrontation.

The next day, Amie called his housekeeper to say he was delayed but would arrive in a day or two. In the meantime, Officer Sterrio got the phone wiretap order she was waiting for and saw where Amie was biding his time. He had a room at the Inn of the Spanish Steps on Via del Condotti, just a few blocks from his home.

Officers Sterrio and Fresco decided to go undercover and sit at a table outside the Cafe Greco across the street from Amie's hotel. To avoid being too conspicuous, they had cappuccinos, then leisurely strolled down the block under the warm Roman sun. Later they returned for lunch. Just as they were being served pizza al taglio at the Cafe, they spotted Amie leaving the hotel, apparently waiting for a valet to bring him his car. The two Interpol officers paid their bill, got up and slowly moved across the street toward Amie. He suddenly caught sight of them, pulled his pistol and fired, but missed. Fresco and Sterrio had ducked and Amie quickly slipped back inside the hotel and ran through the kitchen.

When the officers arrived in the hotel, they loudly asked the concierge if he had seen a man rush by. The concierge pointed to the kitchen and the two officers gave chase. After entering the busy restaurant kitchen with pots and pans clanging, one of the staff pointed to the back door, but there was no sight of Amie in the alley behind. Knowing the area well, Amie fled down one narrow alley after another until he had escaped. On the way, he smashed his mobile phone with his foot, realizing it had been wiretapped.

"Damn, Sterrio! We lost him."

THE MEETING of The Committee was about to begin and its leader, Adamis Baum, was in a particularly foul mood, barely acknowledging the members as they entered the hall and began seating themselves at the large round table. The attendees had arrived at the Baum estate outside of Rome the night before and knew this may not be pleasant. Trouble was brewing.

Before he called the gathering to order, Baum sneered as he looked around at his various associates. Finally, after a few moments of unnerving silence, he almost screamed, "What is becoming of us? We have not been successful in multiple attempts to defeat our enemies, except for the few executions that included the climatologist Cyrus Burnett and the real estate developer Hugo DeMann! Our men in the field have been killed, captured, imprisoned, and overall outmaneuvered! We must fight back!

"The time has come for our destiny to begin its final evolution!" Baum bellowed as the members sunk back in their overstuffed chairs. "Permit me to reiterate our primary goals: we will become one global government with one monetary system. The population will be limited by restrictions on the number of children per family, until there are one billion people who are useful to us, in areas strictly and clearly defined.

"The current global population is 7.7 billion. Thus, we need to eradicate 6.7 billion. But how will we carry out such an unprecedented scheme?" Baum continued, looking more maniacal than ever. "I have accessed an ample quantity of the Ebola Zaire virus – one of the deadliest in the world, which is currently being stored in an offshore shipping vessel, ready for secure access and dissemination at my command." Gasps were heard among the attendees at the round table, as they exchanged startled glances with each other.

"We will unleash this most deadly germ via water sources around the globe! But how will we be saved you ask?" as Baum paused and searched those at the round table. "Well...I have also secured a new drug that will not only be an effective antidote for this virus, it will enable us to live healthy lives, beyond 100 years of age!" he stressed enthusiastically as audible exhales were heard by the members.

"It's called RGB101, which is nearing approval by the U.S. Food and Drug Administration. It is the first of its kind, an anti-aging drug that will also counteract the Ebola strain.

"Those who are with us will be provided an ample supply of RGB101. Those who are against us...will perish. We will control who lives...and who dies!" Baum stated euphorically. Immediately, those at the table looked around at one another, then stood apprehensively and applauded their leader.

"Please be seated!" he responded loudly. "Initial work is being laid in all corners of the globe with newly recruited militia and technicians who will be coordinated to begin distribution of the virus upon my order. We expect to begin mass production of RGB101 in several weeks. Everything is falling into place beautifully.

"Sir Douglas Greaves is heading up our mass distribution operation. Greaves, please stand and provide an update on our plans," Baum ordered. Greaves was a tall, thin man of English heritage who had curly brown hair, a long nose and a bushy mustache below it. In his belted tweed suit and round, wire-rim glasses, he made a distinctly British impression.

"Thank you, Director!" Greaves intoned. "Yes, our forces are being assembled as we speak, including a network of high-tech staff along with newly recruited militia who are preparing for what we are calling *E-Day* to commemorate the Ebola dissemination launch.

"At the same time, we are coordinating the timing of E-Day with the production and distribution of the RGB101 antidote." With that, Greaves passed out a binder that outlined details of the plan and the associated global network grids to each of the assembled members, who were stunned by this unexpected master plan.

"May I ask a question, Director?" Secretary Lisbett Kant asked sheepishly.

"Yes, of course," Baum responded as he stopped tapping his pen on the pad in front of him and reached for his cup of tea.

"This is such a comprehensive endeavor, Director," Kant began. "You are to be heartily congratulated for your vision and ingenuity. I am curious how you were able to gain control of the Ebola Zaire virus and the RBG101."

"We had a person on the inside at the Centers for Disease Control in Atlanta, Georgia," Baum explained.

"He was able to covertly smuggle the virus strain out of a containment area and it is now on the offshore vessel that I described.

"I am proud to say that I recently purchased NuPharma Corp., a U.S. biotech company that's manufacturing RGB101. This revolutionary drug will counteract problems with the immune system, colds and flu, pneumonia, respiratory diseases, heart disease, urinary tract infections, and even dementia and Parkinson's disease, to name of few of its prolific anti-aging powers.

"While we continue to make preparations for E-Day, there's some unfinished business with several of the failed attempts by people in the field," Baum admonished. "Some of them who know too much are being held for trial. Plans are underway to have them terminated – as soon as possible."

22

Later in the week toward the end of July, Chief Samuel Aritan, Interpol's anti-terrorist leader based in Innsbruck, conducted a conference call with his team for an update on the various criminals who were killed or were being held in connection with The New Global Order menace. He had faxed a summary listing the various perpetrators in murders, attempted murders, and other crimes.

Terrence Boll was captured in Indiana and is awaiting trial for the murder of Hugo DeMann. He was paid by Morris Lester.

Morris Lester was captured in Dusseldorf and is being held in jail in Bruges. His attorney is **Kenneth Dahl** who may have links to the organization.

Jackson Goff is a militant who was captured in Bruges and is being held for the attack and kidnapping of Officer Jeanette Poole.

Ivan Lasch was captured in Innsbruck and is awaiting trial for the murder of Thomas and Julia McCabe 12 years ago. He paid ski-lift maintenance man Joseph Kerr for engineering information on the cable car.

Joseph Kerr was captured at a ski resort in Austria and charged with accessory to murder. He is also waiting on a court date.

Ivan Lasch also attempted the murder of Jack McCabe and Sara Bellamy. Lasch's attorney is **Louis Poule**, another possible connection to the enemy. Lasch was paid by Michael Raffone for both crimes.

Michael Raffone was killed in Florence but two of his associates, Toma Bacco and Torino Nado, were captured.

Toma Bacco and **Torino Nado** are being held for various charges and gave the name of the man who paid Raffone: Salvatore Amie. They are both represented by attorney **Tomaso Moro**.

Salvatore Amie was spotted in Rome but evaded capture.

Richard Rasch attacked Jack McCabe's cottage on Lake Maxinkuckee but was killed by caretaker Hans Kriechbaum.

Patrick Downe also attacked Jack McCabe at his cottage. He was captured by lake shore patrol and is being held in jail. Downe was hired by a man named **Fossett** from Washington, D.C. Downe's attorney is **Phillip Rupp**.

IN BRUGES, Belgium, Interpol Officers Cameron Payne and Jeanette Poole along with Officers Darren Deeds and Barron Kaide were preparing for the interrogation of Morris Lester who had been captured at the bar in Dusseldorf. They also planned to question Jackson Goff for his role in the recent abduction of Officer Poole. Attorney Kenneth Dahl agreed to represent Goff as well as Lester.

Attorney Dahl had secretly informed Lester to consume a cyanide pill to take his own life rather than agree to a plea deal and give information about The New Global Order, which was ultimately behind the termination orders. Lester was given the pill but wasn't immediately willing to die for the cause. He was unaware that Dahl was carrying a small syringe of poison to inject him if he refused to take the pill. But with video surveillance in all the cells and interrogation rooms, it would be difficult for Dahl to conduct his execution without being seen.

Officers Payne and Poole began their questioning of Lester as he sat handcuffed next to Dahl. Payne pressed the recording device. "Okay, Lester, we have you for accessory to murder among other crimes. We need to know who gave you orders to pay Terrence Boll for the murder of Hugo DeMann in Indiana this summer."

"I am not going to divulge who my contact was, regardless of the pressure or threats you put on me," Lester responded indignantly, banging his handcuff chains on the metal table.

"You will serve life in prison without a chance of parole and possibly receive the death penalty," Poole stated. "Is that what you want? You know we have you on video paying off Terrence Boll in Indiana, the criminal who identified you. There is no question of your guilt. Is that how you want to play this?"

"I've said all I'm going to say," Lester persisted as attorney

Dahl sat next to him with a subtle smirk, making notes on a legal pad.

With that, Payne and Poole rose and left the interrogation room. Moments later as they looked on through the two-way mirror, they discussed their options. "What's the next step with this jerk, Cameron?" Poole asked.

"If he continues to stonewall, we'll have no other choice than to take him to court and see what sentence he gets," Payne responded, pulling on his mustache. "Makes me wonder what leverage the organization has on him."

"What can we do to get something on Dahl, because we know he has to be connected?" Poole inquired.

"We don't have anything on him now, so there isn't much we can do," Payne responded. "However, let's try to get a warrant to wiretap Dahl's phone to see if that gets us anywhere."

After returning Lester to his cell, Payne and Poole prepared to question prisoner Jackson Goff who also had attorney Dahl by his side. Dahl had warned Goff not to let Interpol know who hired him to kidnap Poole. If he did, he would pay for it with his life.

"Okay, Goff, you've been clearly identified as one of those who kidnapped Officer Poole and held her hostage," Payne began. "Give us the name of the person who hired you."

"Can't say who it was," Goff replied with his eyes staring off in the distance. "My buddy brought me in on the job, but he's dead."

"Well that's a bunch of crap and you know it," Payne said disgustedly. After several more unsuccessful attempts to get some information, the two officers left the interrogation room and convened across from the two-way mirror.

"Not getting anywhere with this guy either," Poole said, stating the obvious. "Looks like it's a court date for him, too."

Later that day, Officer Barron Kaide, the former baseball player, was able to get a wiretap warrant for Dahl's phone and proceeded to track his calls and survey his call list. "Great work, Kaide!" Poole said excitedly. "You may help us take this guy out like you did with the grenade you threw at the enemy in Dusseldorf!"

AT THE CULVER POLICE STATION, Patrick Downe was being prepared for interrogation by Detective Lewis Tenant. Downe's attorney, Phillip Rupp, sat next to his client studying the case notes. As Tenant pulled on his full beard, he pressed the recorder. "Okay, we have you for attempted murder and a phone wiretap by the Indianapolis Police indicates you spoke to a guy named Fossett from Washington, D.C. He's got to be the person who hired you for the hit. What can you tell us about Fossett?"

"Don't know the guy that well, so don't have anything to say about him," Downe grunted disrespectfully.

"Sorry, that doesn't wash, Downe," Tenant responded. "You obviously had previous conversations with him. Otherwise, why would he contact you? Make it easier on your jail time and come clean."

"We need to see what you can offer us before we help you with anything," attorney Rupp grunted.

With that, Tenant put the interrogation on hold, went to his office, and put a call into the prosecutor's office in South Bend. The prosecutor recommended 20 years but would drop it to 10 years if Tenant got the information he needed. He advised Tenant to start with 15 years and see how it went.

"Well, you're looking at 20 years for your crime, but we will consider dropping it to 15 if you work with us," Tenant told Downe.

"Let me talk to my client," Rupp responded as he made more notes on his legal pad.

Fifteen minutes later, Tenant returned to the interrogation room, with Deputy Jerome Atrich watching through the two-way mirror, eating a glazed donut and sipping a cup of fresh coffee.

"Okay, we'll bite for 15 if that's the best you can do," Rupp insisted, mistakenly thinking his client wasn't going to get a much better deal. "Plus, we want early release for good behavior."

"Agreed. Tell us what you know about Fossett," Tenant demanded.

Despite trying to delay the information, Downe reluctantly spoke, "Well...he's a senator and his name is Russell Fossett. He's called me a few times for jobs. That's all I know." Tenant continued to probe for more details, but Downe stonewalled.

Disgusted, Tenant concluded the interrogation and led the prisoner back to his cell. A few minutes later, Tenant asked Deputy Jerome Atrich to begin looking into the whereabouts of Senator Russell Fossett. "Surely he is high up on the food chain with the bad guys," Atrich responded as he tapped on the keyboard to a search engine on his computer. "I'll contact the D.C. police. See what they can tell us."

23

Culver Police Deputy Jerome Atrich made several calls to Washington, D.C., police stations and finally hit on one that was receptive to helping him locate Senator Russell Fossett. "Officer Jackson Tupp, here. How can I help?"

Atrich described the situation indicating that Senator Fossett had been identified through a phone wiretap as ordering a hit on a civilian, Jack McCabe, in Culver, Indiana. Tupp was a lanky, seasoned officer who was not a fan of Fossett's politics and was eager to assist in his arrest.

"Send us the warrant for his arrest, Atrich, and we'll track him down," Tupp offered.

Within minutes, Atrich emailed the details of the charges along with the warrant, and Tupp had what he needed. The D.C. policeman briefed his partner, Officer Jameson Shorts, an athletic-looking African American, about the arrest. They hopped in their squad car and headed to Capitol Hill and the U.S. Senate Chambers.

At the security checkpoint, they presented their IDs, badges, and warrant to Senate Chamber armed guards who accompanied the two police officers to Fossett's office. When they arrived, they were told that Fossett was in a committee meeting and would not be available for several hours. Tupp and Shorts decided to wait outside the committee meeting chamber for their suspected man.

As the meeting doors opened and senators and aides began filing out, they spotted Fossett talking with one of his aides and rushed to block his way. "Senator Russell Fossett, you are being charged as an accomplice to attempted murder of a civilian in Indiana," Tupp alleged as Shorts handcuffed Fossett and escorted him out of the Senate building.

During their exit, media began closely following them, badgering the two officers and Fossett with questions. Other senators and staff were aghast and backed away murmuring to each other at the sight of one of their own being led away in such disgrace. Fossett repeated loudly, "I am innocent...This is all a huge mistake."

When Officers Tupp and Shorts returned to their police station, they booked Fossett and called Deputy Atrich to determine the next steps. "We'll fly out to bring him back to Indiana," responded an enthusiastic Atrich.

After making flight arrangements with the South Bend Airport, Detective Lewis Tenant and Atrich jetted their way to D.C. to eagerly pick up Fossett.

Sitting in his jail cell in the D.C. police station, Senator Russell Fossett knew what he had to do. Stashed inside one of his hearing aids he kept a tiny cyanide pill that would do the job. If he allowed himself to be questioned, he would surely die at the hands of The New Global Order and his personal contact, Director Adamis Baum.

Taking the earpiece out, he unscrewed the small device, dropped the pill in his hand, and tossed it into his mouth. In a few minutes, foam began forming around Fossett's mouth and his heart stopped beating.

The officer who was monitoring the jail cells did not react

fast enough. When he witnessed Fossett retrieving the small pill, he initially didn't catch on to what was happening. As soon as he realized the situation, he jumped up from his console of video screens and ran to the cell. But he was too late.

Arriving in D.C., Tenant and Atrich rented a car, put the police station's address on their GPS, and headed there to pick up the arrested Senator. Along the way, Atrich received a call from Officer Tupp telling him of the shocking demise of prisoner Fossett. He hung up and told Tenant the gruesome news. "Holy horse feathers, Lew! That was Tupp telling me that Fossett committed suicide in his cell!" Stunned, the two Culver policemen continued their way to the police station in silence to meet with Tupp.

"It happened too fast, Atrich," Tupp said apologetically as he recounted the officer's story who had been monitoring Fossett. "The medical staff has confirmed his death, so we'll be taking him to the morgue, unless you have other plans," Tupp explained regretfully. He then led them to the cell where Fossett's body was being tagged and bagged.

"He must have had some poison concealed in his earpiece," Tupp offered, stating the obvious, as they zipped the bag and hoisted Fossett onto a gurney.

"Say, would you happen to have Fossett's mobile phone?" Tenant asked curiously. "I'd like to take it back with us to check out his call list. Might find out who got to Fossett to order the hit on McCabe." Tupp agreed and provided Tenant with the only phone he had on him.

BACK IN ROME, Salvatore Amie bought a cheap burner phone and called his lover, Lisbett Kant, who was still in Adamis Baum's estate following the shocking plans he presented to them. "Hello, Amore, this is Tigre. The police had my phone tapped and I was almost captured at my hotel. Fortunately, I was able to get away and am now laying low in another hotel."

"Oh, Tigre, that is frightening!" Kant responded as she grasped the ramifications of his information. If he was being tracked, how long would it be before she was identified as his close contact? "Please stay out of sight for as long as you can, possibly leave Rome until everything cools down. I have some important things to tell you but now is not a good time."

After his call, Amie took her advice, rented a car, and drove south to Naples, Italy, where he had more associates who would be happy to take him in and provide protection.

IN BRUGES, Officer Barron Kaide was assisting Officers Cameron Payne and Jeanette Pool in the investigation of Morris Lester and Jackson Goff in their connection with The New Global Order. He was able to get a wiretap order on attorney Kenneth Dahl's phone and had been assembling information about his contacts.

"Looks like we may have something we can use," Kaide reported to Poole. "There is a phone number belonging to a man named Oli Klosov who had several communications with Dahl in the past month. He looks suspicious as hell." Kaide had run a background check on Klosov and saw that he had a history of criminal activities, some for suspected murder. "He has a residence in St. Tropez on Rue des Charrons."

After contacting Interpol Chief Samuel Aritan in Innsbruck and advising him on the possible lead of Klosov, Aritan ordered Officers Kara Sterrio and Alberto Fresco to head to St. Tropez from Rome to stakeout his home. Sterrio spoke French as well as Italian and the two officers could easily pose as a couple.

When they arrived in St. Tropez, they rented an apartment across the street from Klosov's to begin the stakeout. In the meantime, they studied his criminal background to see if there were other insights they could uncover. They quickly became aware of his physical appearance and crimes but weren't certain of his level of connection to The New Global Order.

Klosov had achieved the rank of Major in the Russian Military until he retired at the age of 40. From that time on he was linked to several nefarious groups of people who were known to be involved in dangerous criminal enterprises, including illegal sales of firearms to Middle East terrorist groups. He had also been connected to the bombings of pro-Democracy headquarters in several European capitals.

At some point in his career, he was apparently contacted by The New Global Order and was perceived as a valuable resource for securing weapons and explosive devices. Following multiple deals, he was invited to be part of The Committee's round table group.

Several days had passed since Director Adamis Baum presented his strategy for the long-awaited global takeover. He had informed the group of his far-reaching plan to have the deadly Ebola virus disseminated into the world's waterways. His acquisition of the biotech company that was manufacturing the virus's antidote and anti-aging wonder drug, RGB101, would protect the true believers.

Arriving back at his flat in St. Tropez, Klosov unpacked and made himself a martini to unwind. Soon, he would contact his favorite call-girl service and arrange for an enjoyable evening.

Officers Alberto Fresco and Kara Sterrio had seen him arrive and called Chief Samuel Aritan to get the orders for raiding his home. "Let the evening progress so he feels safe, then about 10:30, make your way to his flat and surprise the hell out of him," Aritan growled as he puffed on a recently lit cigar. "One of you attack from a window and the other go to the front door. Contact local police for assistance."

At the appointed time, Sterrio made her way to the entrance

and Fresco climbed to a second story window to investigate the premises. Fresco could see Klosov and a nearly naked young woman beginning to enjoy each other's company in a nearby bedroom.

Fresco alerted Sterrio via his com that he could break in through the window and to see if she could jimmy the front door lock. After several minutes, they both made their way into the flat and cautiously crept toward the bedroom with their sidearms ready to fire.

Suddenly, as Klosov was nuzzling the call girl's breasts... "Oli Klosov, you are being charged with murder and illegal arms sales!" Fresco shouted as the young woman screamed and pulled the silk sheets up to her face. Klosov was taken by surprise. But he had a revolver nearby. He reached for the weapon and raised it to fire at Fresco. Too late. Sterrio had him in her sights. She fired and blasted the gun from his hand.

Quickly, they both rushed to Klosov and rolled the large man out of his bed onto the floor. They cuffed him while he grumbled Russian obscenities. With the naked call girl wailing, they bandaged Klosov's hand, got him dressed, and escorted him outside to a waiting police van.

"I'm going with the prisoner to the station. Contact Aritan. Find out what he wants us to do next," Fresco advised Sterrio. "Then search the flat and see what else you can find in addition to the phone on his bedside table."

24

Adamis Baum's history with The New Global Order went back decades when he learned of the organization from his father, Horatio Baum. The elder Baum had served in Hitler's army, and when his military career ended, he started a business buying and selling luxury yachts to Europe's well-to-do industrialists.

Growing up, Adamis Baum was blessed with attractive Germanic features and wore his dark hair long and slicked back. He was educated in his father's enterprise and became acquainted with a variety of wealthy clientele. As his expertise in business grew, he became an accomplished financier and dramatically increased his personal net worth.

Adamis Baum eventually transitioned from buying yachts to the acquisition of fine art masterpieces as investments and to simply possess them. Included in his collection were famous paintings including a Rembrandt, Titian, Caravaggio, and several Picassos. His most recent purchase was a Vincent van Gogh Self-Portrait with Bandaged Ear for almost $100 million. But he had his sights on another masterpiece – a Caravaggio – that could be coming up for auction. When the time came for it to be sold, he planned to send his assistant, Bendrick Dover, to Paris to make a substantial bid and have it returned to his estate in Rome.

One of the mindsets Adamis inherited from his father was an intense hatred for the U.S. military. During Horatio's imprisonment during World War II, he became acquainted with a U.S. military guard by the name of Amos McCabe, who Horatio claimed was cruel and held back food rations to force him to provide German military secrets.

The McCabe name stuck with Adamis, so he embraced a strong desire to exact revenge for his father's treatment during the war. Since McCabe now owned one of the largest asphalt manufacturing operations in the U.S., he was an immediate target of the organization's Environmental Disruption Initiative.

As he matured in business, Adamis' relationships with those connected to The New Global Order became more established and he was pulled in to be more of an active participant. His forceful personality and knack for strategic planning eventually propelled him to the forefront of the global terrorist organization.

In time, Adamis Baum became proficient at manipulating politicians around the globe, and he was able to influence their decisions to serve his purposes. It was this type of skill and his staggering wealth that enabled him to orchestrate connections and payoff leaders within the Centers for Disease Control to gain access to the deadly Ebola Zaire virus.

Amassing a net worth in the billions of U.S. dollars, Adamis was able to force a hostile takeover of the East Coast biotech company that developed the RGB101 anti-aging medication that was also the proven antidote for the deadly Ebola virus.

Buttressed by his leadership position in The New Global Order, Baum planned to work closely with organizations around the world for the launch of E-Day, the dissemination of the Ebola virus into the world's water systems. Among those aligned branches were:

Britain's Royal Institute of International Affairs
The U.S. Council on Foreign Affairs
The Canadian Institute of International Affairs
The New Zealand Institute of International Affairs
The Australian Institute of International Affairs
The South African Institute of International Affairs
The Indian Institute of International Affairs
The Netherlands Institute of International Affairs
The Japanese Institute of Pacific Relations
The Chinese Institute of Pacific Relations
The Russian Institute of Pacific Relations

Inside each of these groups was a collection of people who were committed to his plan to dramatically reduce the population of the globe and establish the long-held goals of The New Global Order.

It was through Britain's Royal Institute of International Affairs that Baum identified Sir Douglas Greaves as a skilled tactician who would serve him well in the launch of E-Day.

———

INTERPOL'S OFFICER Kara Sterrio called Agent Samuel Aritan to give him the news about their capture of Oli Klosov. "Chief, it's Sterrio calling from St. Tropez. We were able to arrest Klosov, and Officer Fresco is accompanying him to the local police station. What would you like us to do? Keep him here or return him to one of our bases?"

"Great work, Sterrio! Watch out. He could be a very

dangerous prisoner. Be sure he's well frisked and make sure he doesn't commit suicide. That seems to be the fail-safe escape from questioning among those in The New Global Order. Especially the friggin' higher ups.

"I'd like to bring him here to Innsbruck, but you'll need some help. Sit tight for a day. I'll send Officers Melvin Loewe and Phillip Wright to join you for the trip."

When Fresco reached the St. Tropez police station with prisoner Oli Klosov, the local police seemed a bit suspicious to him. He was hoping it was just his imagination or lack of sleep. During his ride there, Sterrio had called to tell him of her conversation with Chief Aritan. Two officers from Innsbruck would fly down and help escort Klosov back to Innsbruck.

Fresco hoped the police station would be secure. "I need to frisk this guy from head to toe and inside out," he ordered the station guards. "Can't be too careful. He may have a weapon or something to kill himself, understand?"

Taking the heavyset man into a cell, he removed all his clothing and did an intense body search. Even though he almost gagged, Fresco carefully examined Klosov's mouth and anal cavity, and probed his flesh to make sure he didn't have something sewn under his skin.

In less than five minutes, he contented himself that the prisoner was clean. Soon after, Fresco called Sterrio to say he planned to spend the night in the local police station to personally guard Klosov. He asked her to monitor potential activity outside the police station in their rental vehicle in case there was some sort of unexpected night flight attempt with the prisoner.

That evening, as he sat outside Klosov's cell during the prisoner's meal, Fresco felt secure that he had examined the meal closely to make sure there wasn't anything that Klosov could use as a weapon or for suicide.

After a guard came to get the food tray from Klosov's cell, he stopped next to Fresco and initiated some idle chatter. Without Fresco's awareness, the guard held the tray in one hand, slipped his other hand into his pocket and pulled out a small syringe. In a split second, he plunged the needle into Fresco's neck, instantaneously immobilizing him.

The guard then returned to Klosov's cell, got the man ready and said he would escort him out. In the process, he cuffed Klosov and walked to the front of the station. With Officer Sterrio sitting in her rental car and alert for just such an attempt, she was immediately aware of foul play. She sprang from her car, ran toward the guard and shouted in French, "Halt, that man is our prisoner. Where're you taking him? Where's Officer Fresco?"

Alert to this sudden counterstrike, the guard pulled his weapon and prepared to fire but Sterrio was ready. She shot first and hit the man in his leg, then in his gun hand, while Klosov cowered on the sidewalk next to the street.

Sterrio grabbed the guard's weapon and knocked him cold with a blow to the head. She then pulled Klosov up from the ground and entered the police station, pushing the prisoner in front of her. "Help!" she screamed as another guard on duty ran to assist her. "This prisoner was obviously taken from his cell without orders! Where's Officer Fresco?"

The guard on duty ran back to the jail cell area and saw Fresco regaining his consciousness and rubbing his neck. Sterrio followed, pushing the heavyset man in front of her. "Fresco, you okay?" Sterrio yelled. "Looks like the enemy has infiltrated this place so it's not safe to stay here." More guards approached who appeared to be legitimate.

Fresco said sluggishly, "I can't believe that guy got the jump on me! Guess we can't trust anybody, can we. Let's take him to our rental car, get another place, and wait for the Innsbruck team to meet us in the morning."

After clearing out of their temporary rental apartment across from Klosov's flat, they drove closer to the airport, got a hotel room for the night, and took the prisoner inside. Cuffing his hands and placing a bag over his head, they tied his legs, and hoped for a quiet night.

25

---

ollowing the attack by Patrick Downe at his inherited Lake
Maxinkuckee cottage, Jack McCabe decided to drive back
to Indianapolis and be with his girlfriend, Sara Bellamy. During
Jack's absence, his caretaker, Hans Kriechbaum, would continue
to provide a watchful eye on the property.

Sara had nearly recovered from the bullet wound she
received from the shooting by Ivan Lasch at the Café Sacher in
Innsbruck. With her physical therapy completed, she was able to
return to her workout routine and hobbies, including her
passion for genealogy. She also spent time at their advertising
and PR firm, McCabe and Bellamy.

On the way to Indianapolis, Jack called to say hello. "Hi, hon,
hope you are doing well. Heading to see you and try to get
things back to normal."

"Can't wait to see you again, Jack!" Sara responded
gratefully. Jack had informed her of the latest harrowing gun
fight at the lake and they both wondered if their world would
ever be the same again. After meeting Sara at her family's home,
they both drove to their place in the Meridian-Kessler
neighborhood and immediately felt the warmth of home.

Shortly after they settled in, Jack received a call on his mobile. "Hello, Mr. McCabe. It's Tessa Steckles from the U.S. Embassy. Hope you and Sara are doing well."

Jack felt a close connection to Steckles, but a momentary sense of apprehension coursed through him to receive her call. "Well, hello, Ms. Steckles! To what do I owe this unexpected call?" Jack responded with anticipation. Steckles had saved their lives at the Café Sacher but he wondered what else could be in store for him.

"Interpol Chief Samuel Aritan asked me to give you a call. The court date for Ivan Lasch is coming up in a few weeks and we're hoping you can return to Innsbruck to testify against him." Lasch was not only being charged with the attempted murders of Jack and Sara, but he had also been identified and even admitted to killing Jack's parents in the cable car murder 12 years before.

"I will be happy to do what I can," Jack stated apprehensively. "We'll make reservations and let you know when Sara and I arrive."

WITH OLI KLOSOV being held as a high-ranking member of The New Global Order, Officers Alberto Fresco and Kara Sterrio were ready to join Officers Melvin Loewe and Phillip Wright for the military flight back to Innsbruck. They packed their gear and drove to the airport and found Loewe and Wright waiting for them. They quickly boarded the plane and secured Klosov's handcuffs to a bar behind his seat. All the prisoner could do was continue to mumble Russian obscenities as he struggled with his uncomfortable cuffs.

Following the team's arrival in Innsbruck, Chief Samuel Aritan was relieved when they got the suspected criminal locked up. "Frisk the prisoner again, Wright." Aritan ordered as he clipped the end of a Dominican. "Can't be too careful with this badass."

"I want to see my attorney!" Klosov grunted disgustedly. "Contact Winston Kash in Berlin. I won't talk until he arrives."

As the Interpol officers suspected, Kash was probably another potential link to the organization, and they would need to be particularly careful with him when he arrived. Kash could attempt to execute Klosov or provide him with the means to take his own life.

Officer Loewe was assigned the task of contacting Kash and requesting his presence at the interrogation of his client. It was not easy to get in touch with Kash but when they did, he was willing to fly to Innsbruck to participate. Before leaving Berlin, Kash got word to Director Adamis Baum through an intermediary that Klosov had been apprehended.

Baum was understandably furious and ordered his intermediary to tell Kash what he had to do. "In no uncertain terms, Klosov is expendable. We can't afford for him to talk," Baum nearly screamed into his burner mobile to the intermediary. Kash got the message.

Kash would not be the only attorney connected to The New Global Order who was in Innsbruck on legal business. Since murderer Ivan Lasch had a trial date coming up, his attorney, Louis Poule, was also on hand and Kash gave him a call. "Poule, this is Kash. What's the status of your client's court date?"

"Coming up soon, which is why I'm here in Innsbruck." Poule advised. "As I understand it, Jack McCabe will be at the trial to testify against Lasch."

"Good information," attorney Kash responded. "I'm sure the Director would be most interested in hearing this important news."

After their call, Kash contacted Baum's intermediary and told him that McCabe would be in Innsbruck for the trial. When Baum was updated, he responded eagerly, "McCabe needs to pay! I have a long-standing score to settle with him and this may be perfect timing."

The next day, Jack and Sara's plane touched down in Innsbruck. They hoped to put an end to the gruesome events that occurred earlier in the summer. Approaching the tarmac, the presence of the majestic Alps surrounding Innsbruck took their breaths away.

"I've got the same suite at the Hotel Maximilian, Jack. Our memory of the last visit wasn't great, but the hotel was awesome, don't you agree?"

"Sure, Sara, almost like coming home again, right?" When they got their bags, they hopped into a waiting taxi and sped to the hotel for some relaxation before the trial began.

The next morning after breakfast, Jack rang for room service to pick up their food tray. While Sara was showering, a knock at the suite door indicated the bellhop had arrived. He pushed in a larger than normal cart and prepared to remove the morning's room-service food.

With his back to the bellhop, Jack busied himself getting a tip. The bellhop pulled a towel soaked in chloroform from his cart and stuffed it in Jack's face. There was a momentary struggle, but the chloroform did its job almost instantly, and Jack dropped to the floor. The bellhop turned the cart over, dumped out some dirty sheets, and rolled Jack into it. He then lifted the cart back up and placed the sheets on top of Jack. Quickly, the bellhop moved out of the suite and headed to the service elevator and down to the first floor. A waiting van was parked in the alley behind the hotel. The driver met the bellhop and helped lift the cart inside. Within seconds they peeled away with an unconscious Jack McCabe.

When Sara came from the bathroom with a towel wrapped around her, she quickly scanned the suite. There was no sign of Jack. She initially thought he may have gone out for something but was surprised he hadn't given her a heads up.

She called his mobile. There was no answer, but she heard a muted vibration tone. As she continued to look around the suite, she spotted his mobile partially hidden on the bed under the comforter. Immediately alarmed, she called the concierge to see if he had seen Jack go out, but the concierge had not spotted him.

Becoming frantic, Sara decided to contact Tessa Steckles at the U.S. Embassy. "Hello, Ms. Steckles," Sara shivered, "I hope I'm just exaggerating the situation, but I left Jack a half hour ago to take a shower and when I finished, he was nowhere to be found. And his mobile phone is still here. I called the concierge, but he didn't see him leave."

"Let's hope he slipped past the front desk and went out for something. In the meantime, I'll contact Interpol Chief Samuel Aritan and let him know that there is a possible issue. I'll also ask him to send one of his officers to provide you with security, just in case it's needed.

"I hate to upset you further, but one of the top people at The New Global Order was recently captured and is in custody here in Innsbruck. No telling what type of retaliation they may have in mind."

"Sam, this is Tessa. I just got a call from Sara Bellamy who arrived here with Jack McCabe for the upcoming trial of Ivan Lasch. Sounds like Jack has disappeared or at least is missing. Could one of your officers visit her at the Hotel Maximilian and provide security?"

"Damn, Steckles. Those S.O.B.s could be up to almost anything. I'll send Officer Wright over to check on Ms. Bellamy and see if he can uncover anything she hasn't considered.

"Oli Klosov's attorney is expected in town for the interrogation and I have to think he got word to his damn bosses at the organization. They know we're getting closer to them and they'll stop at nothing to undercut our advantage."

26

The capture of Oli Klosov in St. Tropez by Interpol Officers Alberto Fresco and Kara Sterrio came as a result of the wiretap of Attorney Kenneth Dahl's phone. With two recent calls to Klosov, Dahl was facing serious legal problems of his own.

Dahl had been representing criminal Morris Lester, who had paid Terrence Boll to kill Hugo DeMann. Dahl was also expected to provide legal counsel for militant Jackson Goff, who was involved in the kidnapping of Officer Jeanette Poole. But the tables had turned, and Kenneth Dahl was now being sought in Bruges for his connection to The New Global Order.

Interpol Officer Cameron Payne called Dahl and requested his presence for the questioning of Morris Lester. "Dahl, this is Officer Payne, and we need you to be here at 9:00 a.m. tomorrow to begin the interrogation."

The next morning, attorney Dahl arrived as requested, unaware of the circumstances surrounding his wiretapped phone. "Dahl, you are being arrested for your connection to The New Global Order and the crimes it has committed, including aiding and abetting murder and mayhem," Payne stated forcefully as Officer Jeanette Poole handcuffed him.

"This is absurd!" cried Dahl who struggled against Poole's forceful binding of his hands. "You have no proof that I'm connected with that organization!"

"We were able to get a warrant to wiretap your phone, which led us to your pal, Oli Klosov, who has since been captured," Payne alleged. "It's over, Dahl."

As they led Dahl back to another cell, Payne ordered, "Check him from head to toe and do a full cavity search. The guy probably has the means to kill himself and others."

After disrobing Dahl in his cell, Officers Poole and Kaide conducted a full body search. "I'll check his clothing and briefcase for suspicious items, Kaide. You do the body search," Poole requested.

"Can't blame you for wanting to avoid the body search, Poole," Kaide quipped.

Sorting through Dahl's clothing, Poole discovered several small capsules that she suspected could be poison. As she continued, she spotted a small syringe that could also be deadly. "Let's get these to the lab to find out what the hell they are," she shouted as Kaide continued to search the naked Dahl.

"Can't find anything on Dahl that looks fishy," Kaide stated. "I've done the cavity checks and scanned his skin to make sure there aren't any surgically buried items. Only thing left would be to check his teeth, but we'll need a dentist to get that detailed."

After the search on Dahl, Payne visited Morris Lester and advised him that his attorney would no longer be able to represent him. "Dahl is out of the legal business, at least for now, because we have proof that he is connected to The New Global Order. You'll need a new legal representative, or we can supply you with a public defender. What's it going to be?"

"Give me some time to figure this out," Lester responded,

jolted by the news of his long-time attorney being arrested. "I stand by my earlier claim that I'm not giving any information."

The next day, Poole received confirmation from the forensics lab in Bruges that the small pills and the syringe were indeed poisonous. Their intended targets – the prisoners – would no longer be in immediate peril.

WHEN JACK McCABE REGAINED CONSCIOUSNESS, his arms and feet were bound to a chair and he was blindfolded. The only thing he could tell was that he was cold, hungry, and his body ached severely. His captor, Macon Waite, who had been hired by The New Global Order, had disguised himself as a bellhop and orchestrated the undetected kidnapping in the Innsbruck hotel suite. Waite was told by an intermediary to let McCabe suffer until further notice.

Not long after Sara Bellamy called the U.S. Embassy's Tessa Steckles, Interpol Chief Samuel Aritan ordered Officer Phillip Wright to visit Sara to try to learn more. When he arrived, she answered the suite door. "Ms. Bellamy, we can't express how terrible we feel about Mr. McCabe's disappearance. Sorry to ask you to do this but please review the sequence of events that you described to Tessa Steckles. I just want to make sure we're not missing something." Wright, who was in his late 30s and well-built from a regular weight-lifting regimen, was an experienced military guard, as good as Interpol had to provide protection for Sara.

"As I told Ms. Steckles," Sara began with tears streaming down her face, "when I came out of the bathroom after taking a shower this morning, Jack was gone, but his mobile was still on the bed. No one in the hotel had seen him leave and he hadn't given me a heads up. Something strange has happened to him."

"We'll figure this out, Ms. Bellamy," Wright offered. "In the meantime, I would advise you stay in the suite, and I'll position myself outside in the hallway if you need anything." After their meeting, Wright contacted the hotel manager and admonished him for allowing someone to break security and get to McCabe. In the future, he ordered the hotel to double-check staffing, food orders, and room services to the McCabe/Bellamy suite.

Back at the Interpol base, Chief Aritan met with Officers Loewe, Fresco, and Sterrio who had helped transport Oli Klosov to jail in Innsbruck after being captured in St. Tropez. "Fresco and Sterrio, stick around for a few days while we sort things out. We've got Klosov and figure his attorney, Winston Kash, is probably crooked as all hell. Plus, Lasch's attorney, Louis Poule, likely has the same connection to the organization. Loewe, get wiretaps on the phones of these two legal beagles. Or should I just call them dogs," Aritan barked as he took a drink from a steaming mug.

After the meeting, Officer Jeanette Poole called from Bruges advising Aritan that attorney Kenneth Dahl was now charged and booked, and they had discovered poison pills and a loaded syringe in his belongings. "Good work, Poole!" Aritan responded. "We'll have to check anyone who enters Klosov's cell for the same reason. Can't trust any of those damn people."

JACK MCCABE HAD BEEN KIDNAPPED for more than a day and still hadn't been given any water or food. Then, without warning, the door to his confined space opened and in walked a smirking Macon Waite. "Supposed to make sure you don't die yet, McCabe. I'm giving you some water, but you'll have to wait for food. Get used to it."

The unknown intermediary working with Adamis Baum, who was coordinating with Waite, gave him a call. "The boss wants McCabe to suffer a little bit, just like McCabe's grandfather did to Baum's grandfather during World War II. I'll let you know when he can have some food. Only water for the next 24 hours, got it?"

The water was nourishing, Jack thought, but the excruciating pain from his harshly bound arms and legs continued to gnaw at him and his muscles began to spasm. His body shivered from the cold of the space he inhabited. *They tried to kill me twice, now they want to starve me. This is insane!* he thought, but he was even more frightened for Sara, and praying to God she wasn't experiencing the same fate.

The intermediary received another call from Baum. During the exchange, he ordered him to contact the Interpol office and offer an exchange of McCabe for Klosov. The time and place of the exchange would come later.

When the phone rang at Interpol, an officer answered, and the disguised voice asked for Chief Aritan who picked up the call. "I want to discuss an exchange of prisoners. We'll send McCabe to a meeting place in exchange for Klosov. More to come." The call disconnected.

"Holy moley!" Aritan bellowed as he pounded a fist on his desk. He called Officers Loewe, Sterrio, and Fresco into his office for a briefing. "Just got one of those processed, deep voices calling to say they want to exchange Jack McCabe for Oli Klosov. No details yet but we'll learn more when the next call comes in."

Aritan then called Officer Phillip Wright who was keeping guard on Sara Bellamy at her hotel. "Let Ms. Bellamy know that we have word on Jack McCabe. Be gentle but the enemy apparently has him and is offering a trade of McCabe for Klosov."

After he got off the phone, Wright knocked on the suite door and communicated the information Aritan had provided. With the news, Sara burst into tears. "Oh, thank God! At least I know he's alive!"

27

D ouglas Greaves had been assigned the critical task of supervising *E-Day* – the Ebola dissemination through the world's drinking-water resources. He wanted to make sure his field commanders were prepared for this massive endeavor that would take place in a matter of weeks.

With 30 people on a conference call from around the globe, he provided a status report. "The deadly Ebola Zaire virus has been proven to withstand biofiltering performed by most drinking water systems and, as you now are aware, our goal is to eliminate more than six billion people!" he began and paused for effect. "Not even chemical processes such as flocculation and sedimentation, carbon activation, electromagnetic radiation and ultraviolet light can inhibit the virus' devastating effect through the globe's drinking water systems. Moreover, there are currently in excess of one billion people who don't have access to improved drinking water, so they will be quickly exterminated.

"We are now waiting on the completion of the RGB101 antidote and anti-aging drug before we initiate our revolutionary plot," Greaves intoned. The biotech company had been shipped a small specimen of the Ebola Zaire virus to check the validity of the antidote on human subjects.

"Regan Zultz, the manager of our newly acquired biotech company, is supervising the manufacturing of the medication. Mr. Zultz, do you have an update on the availability of the drug?" Zultz was a bespectacled man in his 50s with a bald head and large stomach.

"Yes, thank you, Mr. Greaves," Zultz responded eagerly. "We are in the final clinical stages of testing and RGB101 has proven to effectively serve as an antidote for the Ebola virus and deliver its unique anti-aging benefits.

"We've moved from lab-animal testing to human testing and all outcomes are positive," Zultz reported.

"To date, we have had no deaths among the human trial group. Therefore, we expect to begin manufacturing in days, with distribution to authorities committed to The New Global Order as soon as we have completed our final trials.

"Once we have supplies securely packaged, boxed and crated, they will be airlifted throughout the world to authorized teams for distribution. Detailed instructions will follow. Individuals will be required to consume daily doses to withstand the ravages of the Ebola virus."

"Very good, Mr. Zultz!" Greaves responded enthusiastically as he made notes on the grid in front of him. "We will continue to keep everyone updated on the delivery of the Ebola virus and its containment and transportation to various check points. But be assured that we will not initiate the E-Day until the antidote is available for everyone.

"Each of you is in the process of screening and hiring technicians to handle the Ebola strains for distribution," Greaves reported. "Don't hesitate to alert me if there are any problems in achieving the staffing we demand."

AFTER MORE THAN 48 hours in captivity, Jack McCabe, who was still tied to a chair and blindfolded, was feeling weaker than he could ever remember. *Hard to even focus...can't see...everything aches...will I survive?*

Suddenly, the door to his captive space opened and Macon Waite walked in with a small amount of bread and water. "McCabe, you just got a break," Waite snarled. "I've been told to give you a little something today."

With that, Waite untied Jack's hands and gave him some bread – nourishment his body desperately craved. "Keep the blindfold on," Waite ordered. "I'll stick around 'til you finish. You may be in luck because there's a possibility of a trade between you and someone being held by the police that my boss wants in return."

Back at Interpol headquarters in Innsbruck, Chief Samuel Aritan, the bearded African American leader, decided he would agree to a swap of Oli Klosov for McCabe. He didn't like dealing with terrorists, but McCabe had been through enough and he needed to be saved at all costs.

That afternoon, the phone rang, and the call was patched into Aritan's office. Once again, the deep voice on the line gave the orders for the exchange. "Meet at midnight tonight at the end of Framsweg Road. Have Klosov ready and we will make an exchange for McCabe. Don't try anything or McCabe will be killed on the spot. Understand?"

"Okay, same goes for Klosov. We'll need proof of life before Klosov is set free." Aritan was aware that Framsweg was near the beginning of the foothills where he could position his people with sight lines to the kidnappers. He called his team in for a briefing.

"We've been given instructions to meet at the end of Framsweg at midnight for the prisoner exchange.

"Hide extra gunmen in the surrounding foothills and be ready to fire if the trade goes haywire. Don't hesitate to take out their people once McCabe is safe. Get our team there early to scan the area during daylight to make sure the damn enemy doesn't try to outflank us."

Before sunset, the Interpol team spread out in the foothills overlooking Framsweg Road, keeping an eye out for enemy militia. But midnight approached and none had appeared. They were all positioned strategically when Officers Loewe, Fresco, and Sterrio brought Klosov to the meeting place in an armored truck. They waited until 12:30 a.m. but there was no sign of the vehicle transporting Jack McCabe.

At 1:30 a.m. a call came to the office and Chief Aritan got on the line. "I thought we agreed to no foul play with your people!" the deep voice charged vehemently. "We are able to survey the location with drones equipped with video surveillance. You attempted to get an advantage on us. Deal's off until further notice."

"Well crap!" Aritan groaned after they hung up. He called his team and told them the deal was scrapped for the night and to come in. *Win one for the bad guys,* he thought to himself. *Next time we need to be a hell of lot more cunning and covert.* He then called Officer Wright who was guarding Sara Bellamy to say she would have to be patient a little longer.

"No deal for now, McCabe," kidnapper Waite informed Jack as he remained tied up and blindfolded in his cell. "You'll have to suffer a bit longer because your guys tried to pull a fast one on us." All Jack could do was tremble as he fought off the gnawing hunger and throbbing pain racking his body from his bound hands and feet. He had never experienced torture like this and didn't know how long he could last. *Hope to hell Sara is safe.*

Two days later – or four days since Jack was kidnapped in his hotel suite – another call came into the Interpol office and Chief Aritan got on the line. He had the call monitored in hopes of tracking its origin.

"We're going to give you another chance," the deep voice stated gruffly. "This time, we'll meet at the end of Burgstadt near an abandoned warehouse. Midnight again and don't try anything. Remember, McCabe is expendable and so is Klosov for that matter." The call ended too quickly to get a track on the phone or its origin.

Not taking any chances, Aritan got a remotely piloted unmanned aircraft involved. The Predator plane flew 30,000 feet above ground, equipped with infrared cameras and hellfire missiles. It would be able to survey the area and detect people who were on the ground or in buildings. If necessary, it could take out any enemy personnel. Aritan was linked to a computer feed of the Predator video and could follow the action and initiate strikes when desired.

"Take Klosov to the meeting spot and we'll have a bird in the air waiting to take out the enemy if needed," Aritan barked. "Once McCabe is free, our airstrike capability will take care of them."

Almost like déjà vu again, Officers Loewe, Fresco and Sterrio escorted Klosov to the exchange destination and waited in the armored truck. Nearing midnight, the enemy's large, black SUV slowly pulled around the corner approaching the abandoned warehouse and parked a block away. The officers had been on the lookout for signs of drones, but they hadn't spotted any.

As the Interpol officers and their prisoner waited in their armored vehicle, the Predator scanned the area and detected thermal signals in the abandoned warehouse building. This could only mean one thing: the enemy had positioned gunmen there – ready to attack.

"Careful! The Predator indicates there are snipers in the warehouse next to your armored truck," Aritan said forcefully to the three officers who were on a communication link. "See what they do before getting out."

After 10 minutes of no contact with the other vehicle, a

megaphone from the black SUV announced, "Okay, we're bringing McCabe out. Start moving Klosov out of your truck toward us." *I'm too weak to even walk*, Jack thought.

The three officers looked at each other and communicated the message they received to Aritan. He immediately gave the order to begin the exchange. Slowly Loewe and Fresco exited the armored truck, pushing Klosov in front of them.

Aware of possible snipers in the warehouse, they were alert to any gunfire. But they knew if the snipers wanted to, they could take them out. Sterrio stayed back with the truck, ready to fire at the snipers. Loewe and Fresco slowly moved the hefty Klosov toward the enemy vehicle.

They could see that McCabe, looking very unsteady, was being led to them with one well-concealed guard pushing him forward. When they were within a half block of each other, the megaphone announced, "That's as far as we go. Send your prisoner to us."

Klosov was then released and he continued walking forward. Jack also slowly stumbled ahead. The two prisoners passed by each other until they reached their own team. Finally the escorts led the released captives back to their respective vehicles and got in. Trade completed.

28

The SUV with Klosov slowly backed out of the road, turned around, then drove from the exchange point. The unmanned Predator had them in its sights but didn't have orders to fire. Instead, another of Aritan's Interpol team tailed the SUV to track its location.

When the SUV drove away, the enemy snipers started shooting at the armored truck, which withstood their ammo and began moving out. At the same time, the Predator refocused on the warehouse and fired its missiles. Instantaneously, body parts of the three snipers were blown out of the exploding building.

As they drove back to Interpol headquarters, Officer Kara Sterrio sat with Jack McCabe and helped him drink water. He was so thankful to begin to satisfy his thirst. He was also extremely grateful for their valiant rescue. "Can...we...get...a... call...to...Sara?" Jack said between sips of water, hoping she didn't have to experience anything like he did.

"We've been guarding her since you were kidnapped. She's safe at the hotel," Sterrio told him as she phoned the suite.

"Hello, Sara, it's Jack! I'm...okay! So happy you didn't get mixed up in the kidnapping," Jack expressed as tears ran down his cheeks.

"Jack!...You're safe!...Thank God!...I love you!" Sara cried as she wiped away her own tears of joy.

THE VEHICLE FOLLOWING the black SUV with Klosov continued driving to a destination in Innsbruck. Not far behind were two Interpol Officers, Gunther Ruener and Harden Knutt. "We've got the SUV in front of us and we're staying about a half block back, Chief," Knutt reported to Aritan at the base.

"Keep me posted on their location," Aritan ordered as he tried to fight off his sleep-deprived night with a steaming mug of black coffee.

The SUV finally stopped at a building on Hottinger Bild in an unpopulated industrial area. They got out and escorted Klosov inside.

"Chief, they've stopped at a building on Hottinger Bild," Knutt advised. "Should we sit tight?"

"Hang in there. Report any other movements."

Inside the building, Klosov was getting eager to return to his routine. To begin with, he wanted to contact Adamis Baum. "Director, this is Klosov," he said, using one of the kidnapper's burner phones to call Baum on his private phone. "As you know, I was captured but now I'm free. Need to know what you want me to do next."

"How dare you call me at this number! You fool!" Baum yelled in the phone. "Are you trying to lead them right to me? I'll let you know what I want you to do. Never...call me again... on this phone. Understand?" After the call, the kidnapper destroyed his burner phone that had Baum's number.

Soon after, Baum's intermediary reached the other kidnapper

to tell him to get Klosov set up with clothes and money, then take him to the airport to fly to Rome. When he arrived there, he would be instructed on the next step. Early the next morning, Klosov and the two guards left the building and headed for the airport, stopping along the way to get Klosov set up for the trip to Italy.

"They've left the building and are heading out, Chief," Knutt said. "Should we continue our tail?"

"Yes, stay on top of them," Aritan ordered, clipping the end of a new cigar.

When Klosov and his escorts arrived at the airport, Knutt and Ruener parked and followed. Since they were still in military gear, they were concerned about being noticed by Klosov.

Klosov made his way to the ticket counter where he purchased a ticket to Rome. When Officers Knutt and Ruener got to the ticket counter, they identified themselves as Interpol officers and asked about Klosov's destination. After buying airfare for themselves, they moved toward the gate and sat a distance from Klosov.

The flight to Rome went off without incident and the two officers tailed Klosov as he left Leonardo da Vinci Airport. They followed him to his hotel, The Empire Palace on Via Aureliana.

"Chief, Klosov has checked into a hotel here in Rome and we need to know how you want us to handle this," Knutt asked after tailing him.

"Good work. I'll contact local Interpol Officers Bella Gamba and Enzo Ferno to take over. Get some sleep and head back to Innsbruck.

"Hello, Gamba, this is Aritan. You and Ferno drop what you're doing and meet Innsbruck Officers Knutt and Ruener at the Empire Palace Hotel. They're tracking Oli Klosov who just arrived and need you to take over." With those orders, Gamba and Ferno packed their gear, dressed in undercover apparel, and headed to the hotel for further updates.

Later, Aritan called Gamba and Ferno again as he thumbed through his open files. "Show your identities to hotel management and tell them you're monitoring Oli Klosov. See if you can arrange to dress as a maid and bellhop so you'll have the run of the place. Get into Klosov's hotel room, set up some audio bugs and video surveillance. Keep me posted."

BACK IN INNSBRUCK, Officers Alberto Fresco and Kara Sterrio stayed on the kidnappers' tail after they dropped off Klosov at the airport. Arriving at another abandoned warehouse, the kidnappers went in and apparently changed to civilian clothes. Then they got back in their SUV.

Making note of the address, Fresco and Sterrio continued to track the SUV until it reached a small residence. One of the kidnappers got out and went in. Fresco left Sterrio to stay and keep watch on the first kidnapper. Sterrio remained in pursuit of the SUV driver. Eventually, the SUV pulled into the driveway of an apartment house. The man went inside.

"Chief, we've got what looks like the residences for the two kidnappers we've been following," Sterrio announced on a 3-way call with Fresco, who had remained near the first kidnapper's residence.

"Good. Give me the addresses. I'll send Officers Wright and Loewe to relieve you. Wright was taken off protection duty for Sara Bellamy, so he's ready to go." Sterrio and Fresco were happy to hear this since they'd been up all night and were desperate for sleep.

Wright and Loewe drove separately to the respective locations and waited to see what happened next. Sterrio picked up Fresco and they returned to their hotel.

Calling the two officers now covering the kidnappers, "Aritan here. These guys will likely get some shut eye, so relax. We could just arrest them, but I'd like to see what goes down." Throughout the night, Wright and Loewe stayed in their unmarked vehicles and kept watch on the two locations. In the early morning, a delivery person stopped at the first kidnapper's place, knocked on the door, and waited. When the door opened, the kidnapper answered and received a small package from the delivery man.

"My guy just got a package of something," Wright said on a 3-way call to Loewe and Aritan, who had managed some sleep time on the couch in his office. "Could it be a payment?"

"Give me the identification of the delivery person or his vehicle," Aritan ordered.

"Looks like an Alpine Delivery guy and I got his vehicle license number, so you can check him out," Wright acknowledged. "With his hat over his head it was hard to tell what he looked like, but he seemed average in size, with dark hair."

Aritan used the Alpine Delivery guy's license when he called the business office. After providing his Interpol identification and the address of the delivery, he asked, "We need to know who the delivery was to, who it was from, and who the vehicle was assigned to."

"The deliveryman was one of our usual drivers and he was making a delivery to a Mr. Macon Waite," the Alpine Delivery operator reported. "Don't know what the package might have been, but I can tell you who it was from: Ms. Suzanne Flay from here in Innsbruck."

"Do you have an address for Flay?" Aritan asked, ready to take notes.

Moments later, "Yes, she lives on 1290 Frau-Hitt Strabe," the operator answered. Aritan thanked her and hung up. Then he ran a search to see if Ms. Suzanne Flay on Frau-Hitt Strabe was legitimate. *Gotcha,* Aritan muttered to himself as he located Flay and then matched her to a criminal profile. *Looks like she's been connected to the bad guys for a while. We'll check her out in the next day or two and eventually bring her in.*

29

Later that day, Officer Melvin Loewe witnessed the kidnapper he was staking out also get a package from Alpine Delivery. He had to assume it was the same as what the first kidnapper received: payment for work completed. After he called Chief Samuel Aritan, he and Officer Wright were ordered to arrest them both and confiscate the day's deliveries. However, they were to wait until they had assistance from Officers Alberto Fresco and Kara Sterrio.

When Fresco met up with Wright, they approached the residence of Macon Waite. "You watch the front. I'll check the back, in case the guy tries to run," Wright advised as he crept toward the rear of the house, checking in windows as he moved ahead.

Fresco knocked on the front door with his sidearm ready. No answer. Knocking a second time he yelled, "Interpol officers! We're here for Macon Waite."

Moments later at the rear of the house, Macon Waite stormed out the back door, heading toward a fence that he was apparently planning to jump. Wright shouted, "Halt, you are being arrested for kidnapping!" Suddenly, Waite stopped, handgun ready. He spun quickly, but Wright was faster and fired, hitting Waite in the shoulder, causing his weapon to shoot wildly before it fell to the turf.

"Down on the ground," Wright ordered as he darted to overtake Waite and handcuff him. Just then, Fresco sprinted around the back of the house and assisted in nabbing him. Wright got Waite up and they walked him back in the house and applied a tourniquet to the wound. "Anyone else here today?" Wright asked.

"Just me," Waite grumbled as they entered the back door, then through the kitchen, and finally to the living room.

"Well, what's this?" Fresco asked as they saw a pile of cash that looked like it was in the process of being counted. "I think we can guess what your payday was for, can't we." They continued to look around the residence and gathered up anything that looked like evidence. Eventually, they came across an array of weapons and a phone that they also confiscated. "We'll come back for more later," Fresco promised as they left, loaded Waite into one of their vehicles, and drove back to the station.

At the other kidnapper's place, Officer Sterrio had joined Officer Loewe as he was checking for any unusual activity. "Ready to get this guy, Sterrio?" Loewe asked rhetorically. Chief Aritan had provided them with the name of the delivery to Owen Moore in apartment 1A. "Let's split up. I'll watch the front. You check to see if there's a rear exit." With that, Sterrio headed behind the apartment building to block any escape route.

Knocking on the front door, Loewe announced himself and stated that he was looking for Owen Moore. Loewe wasn't aware that Moore was inside the apartment, barricaded behind a wooden table. In the back, Sterrio found the door unlocked and slipped in carefully, trying to avoid making any noise.

Without warning, Loewe kicked the front door open and

waited to see if it would draw fire. Moore riddled the open door with bullets without hitting Loewe. Just then, Sterrio yelled for him to drop his weapon. He turned and fired, missing her as she stayed out of his line of sight. As Moore turned to shoot, Loewe darted quickly through the front and fired at Moore, with a bullet grazing him in the back of the head, blood spraying out.

Even though Moore fell hard to the floor, he was still alive, with blood seeping from his head wound. Sterrio grabbed a towel from the kitchen and applied it to the injured area.

"You're lucky to be alive," Sterrio remarked to the new prisoner.

"I'll call for an ambulance and Interpol backup to clean up this mess," Loewe advised. As they waited for help, Loewe scanned the apartment and found the cash, some weapons, a phone, and other incriminating items.

AT THE EMPIRE Palace Hotel in Rome, Interpol Officers Bella Gamba and Enzo Ferno had provided their identities to the hotel management and made arrangements to go undercover as a cleaning maid and bellhop to monitor Oli Klosov who had just checked in.

Gamba was able to enter Klosov's room on the first morning after his arrival and provide a superficial cleaning while he was watching TV in the suite's living room. While there, she placed surveillance audio bugs inside the bedroom phone and a lamp along with a wide-angle micro lens for a camera view. In the bathroom, she added a bug behind the vanity lamp. Now she just had to find time to bug the living room area so she could monitor him for any signs of communication.

Officer Ferno had spent time in the lobby dressed as a bellhop to make sure there were no deliveries to Klosov's room or any visitors requesting to see him. That afternoon, a delivery person came to the hotel with a relatively small but heavy box for Klosov, and Ferno was there to intercept it before it was taken to Klosov. It was from a local service and Ferno took note of the person's company and signed for the delivery.

Ferno called Gamba to meet and they used a private office to carefully unwrap the package and examine its contents. Inside there was a small handgun with ammunition, cash, and what looked like cyanide capsules in a zip bag, but no note or instructions. They repackaged the box, minus the ammunition for the weapon and the poison capsules. Ferno then asked another bellhop to carry the package to Klosov.

Rapido Parcel was the local delivery company and Ferno needed to find out who was behind the package. After calling Rapido and providing his Interpol identification, he learned that the delivery person was a regular who was simply making his rounds. The package was sent from Armoria Guns, a shop on Via Fosso del Poggio.

Ferno questioned whether the actual person who ordered the delivery would be easy to trace. He called Armoria and identified himself. The receptionist took a minute to locate a copy of the receipt. She said it was from a person named Casi Strato. He purchased the weapon and gave them cash to include in the package, along with some small capsules in a zip bag. Then left.

"Do you have surveillance cameras in your store?" Ferno asked the gun shop receptionist.

"Yes, we probably have an image of Mr. Strato that I will be happy to email to you," the receptionist stated.

After the call, Ferno got on his laptop at the hotel and did an Interpol search for Casi Strato, but none came up. Later in the day, however, he received an email from the gun shop with a still image of Casi Strato, which he downloaded and printed off. The image showed a heavyset man in his late 50s with an old Fedora pulled over gray, curly hair, mustache, and dark circles under his eyes.

Back on the Interpol search tool, he copied the image to the device to get a visual match and waited as hundreds of photos zoomed by. At last, one came up that was very likely a match. The man's appearance was slightly different, but it was surely the same person. His name was shown as Marco Fioso, a long-time thug from the area, who was not currently wanted for any crimes. Ferno took down the details of his address and planned to pay him a visit later.

In the hotel suite adjacent to Klosov's, Officer Gamba was monitoring his activities, but nothing unusual had taken place. She noticed when he received his package he was disgusted that the weapon arrived with no ammunition. *Sorry, Big Fella*, she thought to herself.

That afternoon, while Klosov was in the bathroom preparing for a shower, Gamba had an opportunity to quickly sneak into his suite and add an audio bug and micro video camera in the living room space.

Klosov was becoming *stir crazy* after two days in his hotel suite. He dressed and planned to take a walk to a local restaurant for drinks and dinner. He called the Osteria Quarantaquattro restaurant a block from the hotel for reservations and soon left his room. Gamba had listened to his conversation and alerted Ferno to change clothes and be ready to follow him. No telling what Klosov might do once he left the hotel.

Ferno put on his civilian clothing and watched as Klosov strolled through the hotel lobby and out the door. After reaching the restaurant, Klosov was greeted warmly and shown to a private table. He ordered a martini and scanned the menu. Ferno followed him in and went to the bar to keep watch.

Following several cocktails, and with his multi-course meal finally complete, Klosov slowly rose and made his way out the restaurant entrance. Ferno tailed not far behind. Klosov walked leisurely back to the hotel.

When he arrived, Klosov stopped at guest services to ask a question. After a brief conversation, Klosov seemed satisfied, left and took the elevator. Ferno quickly questioned the concierge and was told that Klosov requested information about call girl availability and was given a phone number he could try. Returning to his room, Klosov changed into a bathrobe and made a cocktail. He then called the number the concierge had provided, and eagerly awaited his nighttime visitor.

30

Interpol Chief Samuel Aritan was reviewing the case against the two kidnappers and was interested in learning more about the person who paid them: Suzanne Flay, who lived at 1290 Frau-Hitt Strabe in Innsbruck. He had given Officers Kara Sterrio and Alberto Fresco an opportunity to return to their base in Rome. He then ordered Innsbruck Officers Phillip Wright and Melvin Loewe to check out Flay at the address he was given by Alpine Delivery.

Wright and Loewe drove to her place and stayed in their vehicle to see if there was any activity. While waiting, Loewe pulled up her background on the Interpol search tool. She was a single, divorced woman in her 50s who had served as an intermediary to pay off various criminals. However, there didn't appear to be a direct link to The New Global Order. The next step was to search for a phone number they could wiretap, but none was coming up.

"Hey, check it out," Wright said as they both looked to see Flay leave her home and get into an older Mercedes sedan. She appeared to be rather thin with long dark hair pulled back in a ponytail. Reversing from her carport, she headed into a commercial area. The officers followed a half block back and after several minutes tracked her to a local SPAR supermarket. She parked and went inside. Twenty minutes later she returned with a few bags of groceries. They followed her back to her home.

"Well, that was innocent enough," Loewe stated and decided to contact Aritan for any updates. "Chief, Loewe here. Flay went shopping for groceries. Now she's back home again. Anything you'd like us to do?"

"Let's wait until she goes to bed tonight and see if you can get inside and plant a few bugs," Aritan ordered, puffing on the stub of his cigar. "If you can get near her phone, see what you can get from it."

About 1:30 a.m., well after her house lights went off, Loewe and Wright crept to the house and scouted around to see if Flay had retired for the night. The drapes were partially opened on one window, and they could see that she had indeed gone to bed. But her bedroom TV looked to still be on, with light flickering around the room.

All the windows were locked, so Wright jimmied the front door lock, positioned his night-vision goggles and entered slowly. He quickly placed several audio bugs in her living room and kitchen. Searching around, he caught a glimpse of a mobile phone being charged on the counter. He carefully pulled a device from his pocket that allowed him to download her SIM card, wanting to copy her incoming and outgoing calls, address book and other communication services like email and text. Once completed, he placed the phone back on the charger, returned to the front door, and exited quietly.

"Hopefully, we've got some good intel here," Wright said to Loewe. "Let's head back to the base and check this out tomorrow."

The next morning, "Hell of a good job!" Chief Aritan bellowed when Wright and Loewe reported their previous evening's activity. "Need to find out what her phone tells us. Start analyzing. Let me know when you've come up with somethin' we can use."

Her phone was likely an inexpensive burner device, so she didn't have a lot of older information on it. She'd received several calls within the past few weeks, however, so they were able to identify a few incoming phone numbers that could be of value. They got her phone number as well and put in for an order to wiretap it.

Tracking the incoming phone numbers took some time but they hit on one from Rome, Italy, that looked suspicious. It belonged to a person named Reid Enright that appeared multiple times. Rome seemed to be coming up as a hotbed for the enemy, so Aritan gave Officer Alberto Fresco a call.

"Fresco, Aritan here. Check out someone named Reid Enright who may be connected to the enemy. His personal number was on the phone of the person who paid off the McCabe kidnappers." Aritan gave him Enright's phone number and asked him to wiretap it to try to get more information.

"Will do, Chief," Fresco responded, happy to have finally caught up on his sleep after being in Innsbruck for several all-nighters. With Aritan's call, he figured he and Sterrio would be heading into another interesting investigation.

When Fresco got the wiretap order, he and Sterrio began tracking the calls to Enright's phone. They also determined his address and decided to check him out. They packed their gear and drove to his home on the east side of Rome on the dead end of Via Norma. "Nice little villa, don't you think, Sterrio?" Fresco noticed, looking at the renovated, stone-façade, two-story home. "Let's hang out here for a while and see if anything comes up."

BACK AT THE ROME HOTEL, where Oli Klosov was being monitored closely by Officers Bella Gamba and Enzo Ferno, a sexy call girl showed up to visit her customer. Ferno stopped her before she got on the elevator and advised that she was visiting a very important guest. He said he had orders from the hotel to make sure she wasn't bringing in any weapons. The Italian woman then allowed him to frisk her before continuing to her date. She seemed to be clean so Ferno let her proceed. "And, ma'am, please don't mention my contact with you as it might upset our guest," he requested. She nodded and took the elevator to his floor.

Officer Gamba was in the adjacent suite monitoring the video and audio of the activity in Klosov's suite. When the woman entered, he ushered her to the living room area, made drinks, and paid her fee. It wasn't long before she disrobed. After minutes of idle chatter, she mounted Klosov, who was only wearing a silky hotel bathrobe.

As Klosov moaned loudly and appeared to be nearing a climax, the Italian woman reached up to her hair and pulled out a long pin that was attached to an elegant hair clip. With his eyes shut, the woman jabbed the pin into his neck. Letting out a scream, Klosov suddenly slumped back onto the couch.

Gamba jumped up from her TV monitors and hurried to the door of Klosov's suite. Just as she arrived, the Italian woman – who had quickly dressed – was opening the door. Gamba pointed her sidearm and ordered her to get down on the ground. The woman quickly kicked the gun out of Gamba's hand and swung at her with a closed fist. But Gamba was ready and dodged the blow, punching the call girl in the stomach, knocking her to the ground. Just then, Ferno appeared in the doorway behind Gamba and aimed his weapon at the woman, who realized she wasn't going anywhere.

Gamba pounced on her, pulling her arms back and binding

her hands together with a plastic strap, reading her rights, and charging her with attempted murder.

Ferno raced in to check on Klosov, who was slightly bleeding and unconscious but still had a pulse. He figured she must have punctured him with something poisonous. He called the concierge desk and ordered an ambulance to respond immediately.

Gamba told Ferno that she saw the woman stab Klosov with the pin. She apparently put it back in her barrette because it was no longer in Klosov's neck. While they waited for the ambulance, Ferno unhooked the woman's barrette and placed it in a plastic bag.

"Who ordered you to do this?" Gamba demanded as she kept the woman pinned to the ground.

"Got a call, that's all I know," the woman grumbled weakly.

"What's your name?" Gamba asked as she nudged the woman's back.

"I'm Barba Sevilla," she groused under her breath as she pushed back slightly under the weight of Gamba.

The ambulance arrived and two EMTs hurried into the room with a gurney to check on Klosov. "He's not in good shape but he might make it. Some sort of poisoning but won't be able to tell until we get a blood sample," one of the EMT's responded. They had been told that the person they were coming for was being watched by Interpol, so they knew it was a police matter. They put an oxygen mask on Klosov's face, started IV fluids, hoisted him with a great deal of effort onto the gurney and prepared to leave.

"This guy needs to be put in a secure, guarded location in the hospital until we get there, understand?" Ferno demanded sternly. "Let's get Ms. Sevilla to the station. We'll follow up at the hospital as soon as we can."

31

Back at their headquarters in Rome, Interpol officers Bella Gamba and Enzo Ferno brought the call girl, Barba Sevilla, in and charged her with the attempted murder of Oli Klosov. The officers got word from the hospital that Klosov was still alive from the poison pin Sevilla used to stab him. They had their crime lab checking on the weapon and any residual poison, plus the hospital was running a blood test to determine how to treat him.

Gamba and Ferno moved Sevilla into an interrogation room and arranged for her attorney, Nicolo Thyme, to attend. "Okay, Ms. Sevilla, we had the room monitored and saw you stab Oli Klosov," Gamba began after she clicked on the recording device. "Who paid you to do this extra trick on the victim?"

"I work for a woman who tells me what to do and pays me well," Sevilla said.

"Okay, let's get down to it," Ferno continued. "What's her name?

"What's in it for me?" Sevilla queried as she and her attorney exchanged glances.

"Could mean a lighter prison sentence for one thing," Ferno replied.

"We'll need to know what we're talking about here," interjected attorney Nicolo Thyme. With that, Gamba stopped the recorder. She and Ferno got up and left the room to discuss the next step.

Back in her office, Gamba called the prosecutor to discuss the jail time options for Sevilla's cooperation and learned the possible sentence would be at least 15 years. This could be reduced to 10 if Klosov lived. Early time off for good behavior.

The two officers returned to the interrogation room and offered the option to Sevilla and her attorney.

"If I give the person's name, I'll be murdered, one way or another," Sevilla complained, clinking her handcuffs. "I'd rather take my chances at a trial."

With that, the interrogation ended, and Sevilla was returned to her cell. "We need to check out that phone number Klosov got from the hotel," Ferno stated. "I'll contact the concierge."

"Hello, this is Officer Ferno from Interpol," he began. "I need to speak to the concierge." Moments later the concierge got on the line and Ferno requested the phone number he gave to Oli Klosov to locate the call girl.

"Yes, Officer," the concierge replied. "I offered the numbers to escort services we provide our guests on certain occasions." With that he shared the contacts that were available, courtesy of the hotel.

After the call, Ferno decided to get a warrant to wiretap the escort services' phones to see what he could learn.

While he was taking care of the warrants, Gamba drove to the hospital to check on Oli Klosov. She saw that he was not doing well but was stable. The guards at the hospital seemed to be staying alert and appeared to be legitimate.

"Make sure no one goes in to see him and check all medical staff to verify their security badges," she ordered. "Let's move him to a more isolated area away from potential access by unauthorized personnel."

She then spoke to the nurse in charge of his care and asked about the poison, "Did you get the results of the blood test?"

"Yes, ma'am. It was a weakened form of potassium chloride that could have caused him to go into cardiac arrest. If the EMTs hadn't started IV fluids as quickly as they did, he would surely have died."

Gamba then called her headquarters to have two of their own policemen replace the hospital guards to ensure that security for Klosov would not be jeopardized.

OFFICERS KARA STERRIO and Alberto Fresco continued to stake out the home of Reid Enright who was possibly linked to payments made to the kidnappers of Jack McCabe and for other crimes. They got his number from wiretapping the phone of Suzanne Flay in Innsbruck, who paid the criminals directly.

"I'll be surprised if Enright uses the phone we are tracing for all of his calls. If he's smart he'll have multiple phones for different purposes," Fresco suspected as he searched the computer in their vehicle.

"Let's bug his house if we can get in there later or if he leaves," Sterrio replied. "That way we'll be able to check him out regardless of which phone he uses."

Later, as luck would have it, Enright decided to leave his house for some sort of errand. "I'll follow him if you want to do your magic and bug his house," Sterrio offered.

"Sounds like a plan," Fresco agreed. He grabbed his tools and got out of the car while Sterrio prepared to track Enright. When Enright's Alfa Romeo sped out from his garage, Sterrio stayed behind him at a safe distance. Fresco crept near Enright's house and checked the windows and doors near the front. All seemed to be locked. In the back, however, the sliding door was not bolted, so he stepped in cautiously. No alarm.

Enright was heading to meet a contract hitman who had proven effective in the past. He was confident he'd come through again. Baum wanted Klosov taken care of quickly. He was no longer trusted and knew too much. Enright soon arrived at a bar and went inside.

After Fresco finished bugging Enright's villa, he slipped out the back. Tailing Enright, Sterrio updated her partner. "He drove to a bar, Mole's Pub, several kilometers from his house. I'll check it out. See if he's meeting someone." After parking, she went inside and sat near the front where she had a good view of the patrons. It didn't take long for her to spot Enright at the bar talking to another man. Using her small camera, she took several photos but didn't get a clear view of either of them.

Out of earshot from Sterrio, Enright gave his contact the details for the hit. "Our boss wants this guy taken out. He was moved to the hospital after the call girl botched it. Need you to get in there and eliminate him. See any problem?"

"Should be a piece of cake. I'll let you know when I've finished the job."

Eventually, one of the men got up and presumably went to the restroom. She was then able to get a clear view to snap better pictures. After an hour, the meeting broke up and both men left.

Sterrio paid her bill and got up to leave. Before opening the entrance door, she watched as the two men chatted next to the other man's vehicle in the parking lot. She didn't have a great angle but took a few shots of his license plate. After they both drove off, she hustled to her car to follow Enright again.

"Probably heading back," she alerted Fresco who was waiting down the street from Enright's house. When Enright drove back into his garage, she pulled up next to Fresco and he got in.

"No problem with the house," Fresco offered. "I didn't see anything incriminating while I was there."

"I took some photos of Enright and a guy he met at the bar," Sterrio explained as she downloaded the camera images to her computer. "Let's see if any of these turn up any matches. I also got the other guy's license plate."

A half-hour later, she got a photo match. His name was Thaddeus Pohl who had a criminal background, but there were no current warrants out for his arrest. He was average height and weight with a dark goatee and graying hair. Sterrio made note of his license and matched it to his address in Rome. "I'll call it in to the station and have him checked out," she confirmed.

Remaining a half block from the home of Reid Enright, Sterrio and Fresco were eager to hear if he would have any communication with someone from The New Global Order. Later that night, Enright was on a call on one of his phones, and they were able to capture the conversation, although slightly muffled.

"I met with Pohl and gave him the assignment to take care of Klosov as soon as possible," Enright said matter-of-factly. "Klosov has become a liability, I know…We can't take any chances…The call girl blew it, so we need to do something fast…Klosov's in the hospital…I'm confident Pohl will finish it." The call ended.

"Great job, Fresco!" Sterrio said of her partner's work at bugging Enright's house. "I'll contact Gamba and Ferno to make sure Klosov is safe and to double up the guards if necessary."

"Gamba, Sterrio here. We bugged Enright's home and learned that a guy named Thaddeus Pohl has been ordered to murder Klosov. Find out if it would be safe for us to move Klosov to our station for heightened protection."

"Yeah, we saw your order to double the guards, and we'll find out how they're treating Klosov and move him here, if it's safe," Gamba replied. "We'll alert the guards at the hospital about the new threat and check out Pohl at his house."

After speaking with the nurse in charge at the hospital, it was determined that Klosov could be moved to their headquarters, assuming there was a jail cell with a sterile environment, and if a nurse could be on hand to maintain the medical protocol he was receiving.

With those plans underway, Gamba and Ferno headed to Thaddeus Pohl's residence to learn more about his attempt on Klosov's life.

32

Officers Bella Gamba and Enzo Ferno made their way to Thaddeus Pohl's apartment on Via Suppino in Rome. Reid Enright ordered Pohl to kill Oli Klosov. But Pohl was not aware that Klosov had been moved from the hospital to a secure medical cell at the Interpol headquarters in Rome.

"Looks like Pohl is on the move," Ferno commented as someone from Pohl's apartment left, got into a Fiat 500, and headed out. "Let's see what we learn from his trip." They followed Pohl for 20 minutes until they reached the hospital where Klosov had been a patient.

Pohl parked and entered, with Gamba and Ferno not far behind. "He's not wasting any time in his pursuit of Klosov, is he?" Gamba noted. They tracked him into a hallway that led to a door with a sign reading *Private, Staff Only*. In minutes, Pohl came from the office dressed as a physician with a security badge clipped to his scrubs. The two policemen decided they would see how this would play out and watched as Pohl stopped at an information desk.

In a few moments, he was on the move again and took the stairs. After Pohl left, Gamba asked the person at the information desk who the man wanted to see, and she was told it was a patient named Klosov who had been on the third floor in a restricted area.

They quickly pursued Pohl to the stairway and climbed to the third floor. When Pohl got to the nurses' station, he asked some questions and was visibly upset, pounding his fist on the counter when he learned that Klosov was no longer there.

As Pohl turned to leave, the two Interpol officers spotted him from down the hall. "Dr. Pohl, I presume?" Ferno quipped as Pohl turned, saw them, and began to run. They shouted for him to halt as they pulled their weapons. Pohl drew his pistol and fired back wildly at the two policemen, then darted to the stairs. When the officers reached the stairway entrance, they carefully checked to make sure Pohl wasn't waiting to attack them. He had apparently climbed to the next level. They gave pursuit.

When they reached the fourth floor, they glimpsed him running down the hospital hallway, pushing medical staff out of the way. Ferno yelled again and Pohl stopped, pulling a young nurse against him for protection. She screamed as he yanked on her neck.

"I'll shoot her if you come any closer," Pohl shouted as he moved back down the hall with the gun pointed at her midsection.

"Give it up, Pohl," Ferno yelled. "You're already in over your head." In blinding speed, Gamba pulled up her pistol and fired at Pohl's leg. He immediately recoiled and dropped his weapon, freeing the nurse who quickly bolted away in terror. The policemen then hurried to push Pohl down to the floor as blood puddled under his wounded leg.

"We have evidence that you were hired by Reid Enright to kill Oli Klosov," Ferno shouted. "You are being charged with his attempted murder."

"I didn't do anything but dress up like a medical person," Pohl stated as he grimaced at the two police officers.

"How about firing at police officers and threatening the life of a nurse?" Gamba said as she pressed a towel against his bleeding leg. "We know you were ordered to take out Klosov. You were obviously planning on more than playing dress up today," Gamba responded. "We're taking you in."

———

MONITORING the home of Reid Enright, Officers Kara Sterrio and Alberto Fresco remained patient to hear any further conversations. On their way back to the station, Officer Gamba called Sterrio to let her know that Thaddeus Pohl had stolen a physician's security badge and changed into scrubs, but they apprehended him after a brief chase and gunfire.

"Good idea to move Klosov to our medical cell," Gamba stated. "Pohl is out of the picture for now."

"Great, there are a couple of things we need to follow up on in this case, if you have time," Sterrio requested. "Marco Fioso was the guy who paid for the package that was delivered to Klosov at the hotel. Need to see if we can find out any more about him. And check on the wiretaps at the escort services. One of them was behind the order for Barba Sevilla to kill Klosov."

While waiting on more activity at Enright's villa, Fresco decided to check in with Interpol Chief Samuel Aritan in Innsbruck. "Hello Chief," he began and then filled him in on the details surrounding Klosov and the recent attempts on his life. "We're monitoring Enright and have his home bugged. Anything you'd like us to do?"

"Good to hear, Fresco!" Aritan barked in appreciation for the update. "We've been monitoring his contact here in Innsbruck, Suzanne Flay, but she's been pretty quiet the past few days."

"Hang on, Chief," Fresco broke in. "Looks like a conversation between Enright and someone. Call you back."

"...sent Pohl to do the job but haven't heard from him," Enright said. "...I'm sure he'll call when the job's done, sir...I'm aware that there are *significant events* coming and we want to make sure Klosov doesn't talk...yes, sir, I'll keep you posted."

"What the hell do you suppose that's all about, Sterrio?" Fresco asked very suspiciously. "*Significant events?* What could they be planning? And who the hell is *sir?*"

"Too bad we don't have his phone so we can wiretap it," Sterrio said, stating the obvious.

"Yeah, but who knows how many phones he's got," Fresco responded. "When I was in there I didn't find any, but maybe I wasn't looking in all the right places."

"Klosov should be conscious by now," Fresco mused. "I've been thinking...we haven't used the drug sodium pentothal, the truth serum, on any prisoners lately. I'll check with the Chief for his take on our using it on Klosov."

"Hello, Chief, Fresco again. The conversation was a bit disturbing. Enright discussed significant events that were being planned. What the hell could that be all about? Any ideas?"

"Nothing comes to mind, but I wouldn't put anything past those damned lunatics," Aritan replied disgustedly.

"Chief, we would like to give Klosov sodium pentothal to see if he would provide some secrets about The New Global Order," Fresco submitted.

"Hmmm, not something in our normal protocol but let's give it a shot since things are ramping up," Aritan agreed, scratching his beard. "Keep it confidential. Gamba can substitute a dose in his IV drip while the nurse is out. She will then need to be there to question him. Don't know if he will give us anything. Sometimes it doesn't work the way you want. Worth a try."

Sterrio got Gamba on the line and relayed the conversation

they overheard from Enright, and the follow-up call with Chief Aritan. Sterrio described the dosage and recommended simple questioning once Klosov was conscious.

Not long after she got the medication, Gamba borrowed a nurse's outfit and went into the medical cell where Klosov was being monitored. Klosov had been alert sporadically after being poisoned but slept quite a bit since he was moved from the hospital. She injected the sodium pentothal into his IV and sat next to his bed. In a few minutes he seemed to be more aware but confused about his location.

"You're in a protective area to make sure no one hurts you, Mr. Klosov," Gamba said gently as Klosov nodded groggily in return. "I know you have some significant events coming up with The New Global Order. We hope everything goes well," she probed, with a recording device in her hand.

Slurring his words, Klosov mumbled, "...Globa...Ord... yeh...plans... Ebol...virus...antido...mus...help..."and with that he seemed to drift off into unconsciousness.

Gamba sat by his bed for several minutes to see if he would come to, but he was out.

After she left Klosov's cell, she shared the recording with Ferno and they both sat stunned at what they heard. She then called Sterrio and played the recording for her and Fresco. "My God, Gamba! That sounds significant all right," Sterrio responded. "Hopefully we got the facts from Klosov, even though he was obviously in a drugged state."

"He certainly seemed to express himself clearly enough to specify the Ebola virus," Gamba said as she recounted the frightening words that came from the imprisoned Russian.

"Antidote, hmmm?" Sterrio added curiously. "They obviously have something planned to protect the people on their side. Maybe he'll tell us more if we give him another dose."

Shortly after their call with Gamba, Fresco called Chief Aritan and gave him the results of the sodium pentothal test on

Klosov. "Un-friggin' believable," Aritan growled with a tone of dread in his voice. "If these people are planning something with an Ebola virus, we need to step-up our response to find out more – fast. The S.O.B.s must be crazier and more desperate than I ever imagined."

33

After bringing Thaddeus Pohl in for the attempted murder of Oli Klosov, Officers Bella Gamba and Enzo Ferno needed to check on some other leads in the investigation of The New Global Order. Marco Fioso was the guy who sent Klosov a package that was intercepted at the hotel, and they needed to learn more about him.

"We've got an address for Fioso on Via Ovidio, not far from the Vatican City," Ferno offered. "Let's see what he might tell us since he obviously took orders from the enemy."

Making their way through Rome traffic was always a challenge but they finally made it to Fioso's apartment and parked on the street. "He's an older guy so he may not be very active," Ferno suggested. Later that afternoon, Fioso left his apartment, got into an old Mercedes, and drove down the street.

"I'll see what I can find in his place if you want to keep an eye on him," Ferno requested as he got out of the car and began checking out the apartment building. There was a small deck in the back that he was able to climb to. After jimmying the door lock, he entered.

On the way to his destination, Fioso thought to himself, *Need*

*to get more action. Got to pay my bills. Another job will come soon
enough. Now I need a few drinks. Watch the Roma soccer boys kick ass on
TV. Nobody can beat the maroon and orange when they're healthy.*

Gamba followed Fioso to a small restaurant called Cucina
Romano. When she entered and found a secluded table, she saw
that Fioso was alone at the bar being served a tall beer. A soccer
game was on several TVs. All the patrons seemed to be enjoying
the football, occasionally screaming for their team. Later, Fioso
ordered something off the menu and soon a waiter delivered a
large bowl of pasta with bread rolls, which he savored with his
beer.

"Not much happening here," Gamba reported. "Guy's just
having dinner and watching soccer."

"Got his place taken care of," Ferno responded. "Be here
when you get back."

After the soccer game ended 1-nil, Fioso downed his fourth
beer, paid his tab, and got up to leave. Gamba cautiously
followed him out the door and tailed him back to his place, with
Fioso weaving a bit in his car. When he arrived at his apartment,
he locked his car and went inside. Ferno rejoined Gamba and
they sat for a while to see if anything would happen. Soon, the
sounds of Fioso's TV came through the planted listening device,
which would interfere with any conversations he might have.

While waiting on some interesting activity from Fioso,
Gamba called the station and spoke with another officer about
the wiretaps on the escort services. One of them was
responsible for sending the call girl, Barba Sevilla, who tried to
murder Klosov. The phone call records from the hotel also
indicated Klosov had called Evening Shade, which must have
been her company. Its phone was tapped but nothing out of the
ordinary was coming through other than the usual requests.

"What do we know about the escort service Evening Shade?"
Gamba asked. "Let's see who owns that place." She did a search
on her Interpol computer link and found that the owner was

named Viola Solo. Gamba ran a criminal check on her and found that she was indeed a person with a criminal past. She found an address and made note of it.

"Looks like we need to pay Ms. Viola Solo a visit, Ferno," Gamba stated. "She lives on Via Mecenate on Parco del Colle Oppio. Nice location. She obviously does quite well."

"Let's turn the monitoring of Fioso over to our people at the station and see what's happening with Solo," Ferno suggested. They drove to her residence and kept watch outside a beautifully restored Italian villa that overlooked the park. They plugged into the wiretapped phone and waited patiently to see if there was anything new. After several hours, nothing unexpected took place.

THE INTERPOL STATION in Rome continued to monitor Reid Enright's home for more conversations. Officers Kara Sterrio and Alberto Fresco had left and gotten some sleep, but the next day they returned to keep an eye on his house. During their absence, there were no suspicious calls, but they expected more. Later in the morning a phone rang, and Enright answered. "Yes, sir...don't know what happened to Pohl...Klosov was not in the hospital...Police must have moved him somewhere...I don't think we have anyone inside at Interpol...I'll have to investigate our options...Yes, sir."

"Very interesting," Sterrio mused. "Need to make sure everyone has been securely checked, especially the nursing staff that comes into our station. They may be the only people we haven't thoroughly evaluated." She then called headquarters to make sure they were doubling their efforts to screen anyone who entered the facility, even the medical staff treating Klosov.

Suddenly, another call was taking place in Enright's home.

"Yes, who can we bribe to get into the Interpol station?"

Enright inquired of his contact. "We need to take out Klosov...
he's being held there...we can't trust him...money is no object...
let me know when you have a solution."

The next afternoon, after doubling efforts to check on all the
staff at the Interpol station, one of its veteran police officers
made his way to the jail cell area. Glancing suspiciously to see if
anyone was watching, he used his keycard badge to open the
barred access door to the hallway leading to Klosov's medical
cell. The policeman didn't seem to care that he was being
monitored by the surveillance cameras. The officer monitoring
the TV screens immediately recognized that the intruding officer
was not authorized to be in that part of the facility.

He quickly called Officer Bella Gamba who was not far away.
She sped to the access door and yelled at the officer to halt, but
he ignored her. "One more time, STOP, or I'll fire," she yelled.
Just then, he turned with his sidearm raised, but she was too
quick and fired at his midsection. He tried to get a shot off but
Gamba blasted him again. He dropped to the floor. Prisoners in
the nearby cells screamed and cursed, backing away from the
chaotic gunfire.

As she neared the traitorous officer, she kicked his weapon
away and cuffed him. "Who the hell paid you to do this,
Morto?" she yelled. "You are a sworn officer of the law, but you
have jeopardized your life with this idiocy." Just then, Officer
Enzo Ferno came running in out of breath.

"Good work, Gamba. Can't believe they got to one of our
own people. Guess money can buy a lot. In this guy's case, he
just sold out for nothing." With medical staff on site, they were
able to treat the bullet wounds but needed to send him to the
hospital. "Call an ambulance," Ferno shouted into his com
device. "Need to make sure he lives so we can find out who got
to him."

AT HIS ISOLATED estate outside of Rome, The New Global Order kingpin, Adamis Baum, was going through the plans for *E-Day*, and the release of the Ebola virus into water systems throughout the world. While sipping on a cup of hot tea, he called the man who was heading up the operation, Douglas Greaves, for an update. "Where are we with the antidote, RGB101, Greaves?" Baum inquired impatiently while sifting through his itinerary and the grid of the critical events ahead.

"Yes, sir, all systems are on schedule," Greaves reported. "Our man at the biotech company, Regan Zultz, informs me that RGB101 is nearing FDA approval in the United States, and the manufacturing processes are ready for mass production. As reported earlier, no humans have had any adverse reactions. Even the top-secret trials of people who have been exposed to the Ebola virus have thrived with no ill effects after taking RGB101. It has proven to be a viable antidote. Once we have supplies on hand, we will be prepared to move forward with E-Day."

"Excellent, Greaves. This means we are only weeks away from the operation! How is the recruiting of new technical and military staff in various parts of the globe?"

"The leadership in all sectors report that they are on target to have people trained and ready for E-Day, sir," replied Greaves as he stared at the expansive, detailed plans posted on the large wall in front of him.

"Splendid, Greaves," Baum responded in his nearly maniacal manner. He then sat back in his chair and reveled in the painting masterpieces that hung in his lavish study. Sipping his tea, he contemplated plans to add to his collection in the weeks ahead when the priceless Caravaggio would be up for bid. His greed was insatiable.

34

After the unexpected attempt on Klosov's life by one of its own policemen, the Interpol station increased its security and exchanged everyone's badge. Only a select few would now have access to the prisoner cells.

The next day at the hospital, Officers Gamba and Ferno visited Donato Morto, the traitorous officer who attempted to take out Oli Klosov. It was shocking to everyone at Interpol because Morto was nearing retirement and had been a faithful member of the team. As a charge nurse was finishing dressing his wounds and replacing the bandages, Gamba asked, "Well, Morto, how did you get mixed up in such a sordid deal to go after Klosov?"

"I don't know how I could have been so stupid, Gamba," Morto replied as he stared down at his wounds, picking at the bandages. "I recently found out I have incurable cancer and not much time left. I was approached by someone who said he would make sure my family was well compensated if I murdered Klosov. At the time, I figured, this will set my family up after I'm gone."

"Who was this person? Did you know him? How did he pay you?" Ferno asked in rapid-fire succession.

"Never saw him before and don't know how he picked me. Maybe because I'm old. He offered me 100,000 euros and said my family would receive another 100,000 after I did the job. Actually, I didn't think I'd get out of the station alive after trying to kill Klosov."

"Would you be able to pick out his photo?" Gamba wondered.

"I'll try," Morto responded dejectedly. With that, the two officers spoke to the guards watching Morto and ordered them to be very cautious of anyone who tried to enter.

That afternoon, they returned to visit Morto with a computer loaded with images of potential criminals suspected to be associated with The New Global Order. Morto had been napping but woke to look through the photos. After nearly an hour, he spotted someone he thought was the person who paid him. "Here's the guy, I think, but it was dark when we met," Morto stated. Gamba pulled the computer around so she and Ferno could study it.

"Hmmm, looks like Danello Deline. He's been suspected of several crimes but has never been charged," Gamba read aloud. Deline was an older man with gray hair and a full beard. "Let's see, here's his last known address from a year ago. Let's check him out."

On their way to Deline's place on Via Vicenza through hectic Rome traffic, Ferno remarked, "It's amazing how many bad guys are connected to the enemy."

"No question about it!" Gamba replied. "It's a wonder that we've been able to keep up with so many of them."

When they arrived at Deline's small cottage, they parked and waited to see if anything was happening. As they watched the house for more than an hour, a car pulled in and parked in the driveway. A woman who looked to be in her late 50s got out with sacks of groceries and went inside. Then a man who resembled the crime photo of Deline came out to the car, grabbed a few more bags and took them in.

"Looks like we have a family affair here," Gamba remarked. "Might make it harder to get inside."

"Well, we know this guy was hired by Reid Enright, but how he was able to locate Morto is puzzling," Ferno commented. "Could it have simply been random selection, or do we have someone else on the inside who is providing information?" To fortify the station, Ferno contacted the security staff at Interpol and ordered a screening of all officers to verify they weren't missing something.

"We may be in luck," Gamba said as Deline and the woman left the house, got into their car, and drove off. "I'll follow if you want to get inside." After Ferno got out, he managed to break into the house, plant bugs and look for any evidence.

During their drive, Deline and his wife were arguing about the criminal life he'd led. "But it pays the bills, love," Deline protested. "Where'd we be without a little side money to buy you things you need, like the dress you've had your eye on."

"Don't give me that crap, Danello," his wife shot back, gesturing wildly with her hands. "Better hope you don't get caught!"

Gamba tracked the couple to a little dress shop with a cafe, where they had lunch and a few drinks after shopping. The wine sweetened Mrs. Deline's temperament. Two hours later, they returned, which gave Ferno plenty of time to complete his job.

"Nothing unusual in the house, Gamba," Ferno remarked when he rejoined her. "Who knows how often this guy gets a call." I didn't find any phones, so he likely has a mobile with him. Let's turn the monitoring over to the headquarters and head back."

THE INTERPOL STATION in Rome was now busily tracking conversations and wiretapped phones at multiple homes, trying desperately to get a break that would lead them to someone high up at The New Global Order. Reid Enright seemed to be the one most closely connected and an apparent intermediary. The other criminals had been called by him to carry out various crimes. Officers Kara Sterrio and Alberto Fresco were back at the office, occasionally checking on the monitoring of the various suspects being conducted by their analysts.

Fresco decided it was time to give Interpol's leader, Chief Samuel Aritan, a call. "Hello, Chief, Fresco here. We continue to track multiple people connected to crimes initiated by The New Global Order. We're hoping we get a breakthrough with Reid Enright, who looks like the highest-ranking member. Any next steps you recommend?"

"Time to try another dose of sodium pentothal on Klosov?" Aritan inquired as he lit up another cigar and blew smoke rings. "Last time was pretty effective. Maybe he'll spill the beans about somethin' else."

With the order from Aritan, Fresco asked Officer Gamba to do her thing. Once again, she quickly changed into a nurse's uniform and brought in a dose of the truth serum to inject into Klosov's IV. He was still sleeping much of the time but was occasionally alert. After several minutes sitting next to his bed with the recording device ready, he woke in a daze and glanced around the room. "We're protecting you, Mr. Klosov," Gamba said softly. "We want to make sure you have the antidote for the Ebola virus."

"Uhh...yeh...need be safe... director want many killed...but we be safe," Klosov muttered.

"Who is the director, Mr. Klosov?" Glamba inquired, stunned by Klosov's revelation.

"Yeh...he...wants...kill...many in...water...need stay safe..." Klosov responded, occasionally opening his glassy eyes.

"Who is in charge of the significant events?" Gamba probed again.

"Baum...will lead...he...will...lead," Klosov said and then he drifted back into unconsciousness. Gamba sat a while longer but he was out, so she returned to the office to share the recording with her team.

"Baum? Who's Baum?" Ferno stressed loudly after listening to the Klosov recording from Gamba. They were joined by Officers Kara Sterrio and Alberto Fresco.

"Holy Toledo, Gamba! This could be a breakthrough," Fresco said enthusiastically. They then called Chief Aritan in Innsbruck and played the recording.

"Amazing!" Aritan barked. "Let's get on this immediately. Don't know a Baum or even how to spell it, but it could be important. The threat of killing many in water – Ebola in the water? That's a significant event alright. Scary as hell."

With Aritan staying on the line, the team eagerly jumped onto the computer and began searching for someone named *Bomb, Bam, Baum,* even *Brahm.* It wasn't long before they located several Baums, but there were no recent addresses. None of the other spellings seemed to work. There was a Horatio Baum, but he was deceased. However, he appeared to have connections with The New Global Order.

"Horatio had a son, Adamis Baum, who had a checkered past in illegal financial activities, but no known connection to the organization," Gamba remarked. "Adamis Baum would likely be alive today. He's done a good job staying under the radar and hiding his past – and present."

"If anyone knows this Baum guy, it would be Reid Enright," Fresco offered.

"Right," Sterrio agreed. "How can we get to him other than making an arrest? These guys all seem to be willing to take their own lives rather than talk. The threat of death is consistent with all of the people we've captured."

"We need to get access to Enright's phone," Chief Aritan barked. "I know you've looked and didn't find any. Need to stake out his place and get in there at night, drug him, and download whatever burner phones you can find."

That night, Fresco and Sterrio drove to Enright's villa ready to carry out Aritan's orders. Equipped with night vision goggles and other tools, they waited until after 2:00 a.m. and found a window that was easily jimmied. Fresco crept in and waited to make sure there were no alarms. Sterrio then followed. Slowly, they moved through the house and found Enright apparently asleep. Sterrio pulled out a syringe loaded with a mild anesthetic and injected Enright to make sure he wouldn't wake up while they were investigating his place.

Looking around his bedroom, they located a burner phone in a drawer and downloaded the SIM card. There was another one located in a bookshelf in his living room. They downloaded that one as well. After thoroughly looking in drawers and cabinets, they found one more, which was stored inside a cereal box. While in the villa, they also added more tiny video cameras. Then made their way back outside.

"Hopefully this gets us what we need, Sterrio," Fresco said confidently as they headed back to the office.

35

The next morning, Reid Enright sluggishly woke up in his bed and couldn't remember ever feeling so groggy. He wasn't a heavy drinker and wasn't on any drugs. Sitting up in his bed, he rubbed his eyes and then tried to stand, but was unusually wobbly. *What the hell?* he wondered to himself as he made his way to the bathroom. Splashing water on his face and toweling off, he started feeling a little better. *What did I eat?*

Back at the Interpol station, Officers Fresco and Sterrio were analyzing the downloads they got from the three burner phones in Enright's villa. Other team members were monitoring the audio bugs and video cams in several rooms that Fresco planted the previous night. Suddenly, one of the wiretapped burner phones buzzed, and Enright moved to the bookshelf in another room where he pulled a phone out from its hidden location. "Yes, sir," Enright responded.

"What's happening with Klosov?" the voice on the other phone asked impatiently.

"I haven't heard but I'm not getting a good feeling," Enright answered wearily. "Our man inside Interpol hasn't given me an update on the Klosov hit. I'll let you know as soon as I find out." With that the call ended.

"We need to flesh out this inside person immediately," Fresco whispered loudly. "But where do we begin? Also, did we get a phone number from the person who called Enright?"

"Yep, the call didn't last long. We have a number, but he wasn't on long enough to get a ping on the caller's location," one of the analysts responded.

"Security was supposed to be running an additional background check on each of the staff," Sterrio said in disgust. "But they must not have anything, or we would have heard." She then went to speak directly with head of security, Donald Brooke, to find out more. "Brooke, we've definitely got someone here who is working with the enemy. Do you have anything suspicious on anyone?"

"I'm still checking, but one of our relatively new officers is Ricardo Musselli," Brooke answered. "Only been here for a year and may be a possibility. He came here with excellent references from the Italian military police. Everyone else is solid."

That was enough for Sterrio. She nodded to Fresco and they went to an open office area where Musselli was usually located. "Where's Musselli?" Sterrio asked the policemen near his desk.

"Not sure, he didn't come in today. Called in sick or something," one of them responded with a surprised look, as the others exchanged puzzled glances.

After they moved away from the other policemen, Sterrio quietly said to Fresco, "Let's find Musselli, maybe he's at his house. We need to get him and check his phone. He could have some recent calls from Enright. The guy looks dirty."

Sterrio and Fresco hurried to their unmarked squad car and drove quickly to the address they had for Musselli. "I think he has a family, so we need to be cautious," Fresco advised as he scanned Musselli's file. When they arrived, they parked a half block away and moved stealthily to his small house. "I'll take the back and you watch the front," Fresco ordered. Looking inside the windows, Fresco saw a younger woman and two small children watching TV.

He continued around the back of the house, checking to see if there was any sign of Musselli. "I don't see him through the windows," Fresco said to Sterrio on his com device. There's a young woman and two small kids in the living room. Knock on the door and ask the woman where he is. I'll stay in the back in case he's here and tries to run."

When Sterrio knocked on the door, the woman opened and asked how she could help. Sterrio told her she was from Interpol. She was looking for Officer Musselli. "He's not here now," the woman responded. "He said he didn't feel well and was going to the doctor."

"Do you have your doctor's name and phone number?" Sterrio asked. The woman left and returned with a number.

"Is there a bar or restaurant near here that you and your husband go to?" asked Sterrio as she looked behind the woman at two small children who came near the door.

"There is one called La Mura two blocks down the street. Is something wrong?

"Sorry, can't really explain right now, but thank you for your help. Do you have a phone?"

"Yes, my cellular."

"Here's my number," Sterrio offered. "Please give me a call if you see him or hear from him. Do you have his phone number?" The woman gave Sterrio both of their numbers.

Sterrio alerted Fresco and they returned to their vehicle to see if Musselli was at the restaurant. On the way, she phoned the doctor's office, but he didn't have an appointment and they hadn't seen him in some time. When they reached La Mura, they got out and looked around before entering. "I'll come in the back way. You try the front," Fresco ordered.

When Sterrio entered the restaurant, she scanned the

patrons but there were a few booths where she didn't have a good view. She stood at the front for a few minutes and then noticed Musselli coming from the back, probably the restroom. He didn't spot Sterrio and went to the bar where he was nursing a beer. "He's here," she told Fresco on her com, as he entered through the back door.

Together, they both walked up behind Musselli who instantly caught sight of them in the mirror behind the bar. He spun and started to draw his pistol, realizing why he was being visited by Sterrio and Fresco. "Stop right there, Musselli," Fresco demanded. "You've got a wife and small kids. Don't want to leave them permanently, do you?"

"Crap!" Musselli mumbled disgustedly. "How'd you know?"

"You were the most likely candidate for someone working inside for the enemy," Fresco said as he took Musselli's weapon and grabbed the phone from his pocket. After cuffing him, they walked him outside and into their vehicle.

"How did you put them onto Morto for the hit?" Sterrio inquired during their drive back to the station.

"I was friendly with him and knew he was dying from cancer," Musselli replied. When they returned to the station, they charged him with aiding and abetting the enemy for attempted murder.

They quickly got all the information from Musselli's phone and scanned through his recent calls. "Bingo," Sterrio said excitedly. "There are several calls from one of Enright's phones, so this confirms his part in the failed murder attempt of Klosov."

The phone number they got from Enright's last call was not registered to anyone, so they weren't able to get an address. Was it Baum? They needed more information. And, they needed the calls to be longer.

"Chief, we found out who the inside man was here at the station," Fresco said in his call to update Samuel Aritan in

Innsbruck. "We're getting calls from Enright but will need one of them to last long enough to get a ping on a location from the caller."

"Right, have to hope there's a longer one soon," Aritan agreed as he fingered through his case notes. "Just as we figured, Enright is the intermediary, so he'll be the one to get the calls from the top guy, probably Baum. Here's a thought: Do you think it would work for one of you who sounds like your inside guy to call Enright and say that Morto was successful in killing Klosov? Or, could we force your inside guy to fake the conversation in exchange for a lighter prison sentence? Might help us get a longer call with Baum."

"Worth a try, Chief!" Fresco answered, thinking Aritan always comes up with something. Shortly after the call, they went into Musselli's cell and brought him to an interrogation room. They explained that if he would follow the script and report that Klosov was killed, they would help reduce his sentence. He agreed and they prepared for the call to take place.

The call started ringing in Enright's home and they could see him grab the phone from his bedside table drawer. "Hello, what's the latest?" Enright answered.

"Sorry it took so long to get back to you, but things have been pretty hot," Musselli said in his most sincere voice. "Morto was able to get into Klosov's cell and use his weapon to shoot him twice in the head. But Morto was gunned down almost immediately."

"Good work," Enright said and hung up.

36

With Interpol monitoring Reid Enright's calls, he appeared to phone his contact at The New Global Order within an hour after receiving the update from Musselli.

"Hello," Enright began, "we have word from our inside man that Morto was successful in terminating Klosov."

"Excellent," the voice responded somewhat gleefully. "Good to have Klosov out of the way. He simply outlived his usefulness."

"Do you have any assignments you'd like me to initiate, sir?" Enright replied thankfully.

"I'll get back to you soon," the voice confirmed. "As you know, we have major events that will be taking place in the next few weeks that I will need your help with." And the call ended.

"Did we get a location on that call – possibly Baum?" Fresco asked insistently.

"Sorry, still not long enough," one of the Interpol analysts responded. "Needs to be closer to a minute."

"Do we have a wiretap on the phone of the guy Enright called?" Fresco inquired.

"Yes, we have it ready to go if he uses that phone again," the analyst responded.

"Okay, that could be very helpful," Fresco enthused as he sat with Sterrio in a room with a dozen large video monitors being viewed by the team.

EARLIER IN THE DAY, Douglas Greaves, the head of the E-Day operation for The New Global Order, called Dr. Chester Kauff, the medical supervisor on the vessel docked off the coast of Italy in the Tyrrhenian Sea. This was the ship that was storing the Ebola Zaire virus that would be used to eradicate billions of people if Baum's plan came to fruition.

"Hello, Doctor," Greaves said, "I understand that a scientific facility in Russia that stores Ebola, HIV, anthrax, and other deadly strains recently exploded and went up in flames. Are you familiar with this incident?"

"Yes, Greaves," responded Kauff. "The laboratory is known for having developed vaccines for some of the Ebola strains. That is certainly very disturbing."

"We are concerned that the vaccines they have developed could be distributed and used to inoculate people in Russia and elsewhere," Greaves wondered. "What do you know of the effectiveness of their vaccines for the Ebola Zaire strain that you have contained on the vessel?"

"At this point we do not believe the vaccines and antidotes they are producing will be able to counteract the ravages of the Ebola Zaire virus," Kauff replied. "This strain is considered the deadliest, and we have every confidence that only the RGB101 will be able to counteract its effect on humans. As you know, RGB101 treats the immune system, which is how it also enables cells to fight off the ravages of the aging process, allowing people to live healthy lives past the age of 100."

"We know the symptoms of the Ebola Zaire virus are devastating on humans," Greaves replied.

"Yes, the infection begins within a week or two after the virus enters the body," Kauff continued. "Initial symptoms include sudden fever, fatigue, joint and muscle pain, headaches, and sore throat. As the disease progresses, a person experiences vomiting, diarrhea, rash, extreme weight loss, internal and external bleeding from the gums, and blood in the stools. Without a proven vaccine or antidote, death is inevitable."

"We assume that the containment of the virus on the vessel is very secure, Doctor," Greaves inquired.

"Of course, and we are confident that our on-board containment system will remain so," Kauff concurred. "Furthermore, we have shown absolutely no unusual health issues among our medical technicians and the armed guards on board."

"Excellent," Greaves said confidently and concluded the call with Kauff. He then phoned Regan Zultz, the head of the biotech facility that was producing RGB101. "Hello, Zultz, Greaves here. Any news on the development and manufacturing of RGB101?"

"Yes, Greaves, we are very enthusiastic about the results we've seen. As you know, our drug reduces infections in older people, so they are no longer susceptible to colds and flu which can be devastating for someone in their 80s or beyond. Their antiviral defenses are turned up when they begin using RGB101, which allows a person to avoid the pitfalls of aging."

"Wonderful, we understood that this was an important benefit of the drug," Greaves said impatiently. "What's the latest on the manufacturing?"

"All of our operations will be ready within a week for production through distribution channels. We are going through testing to verify product integrity, ensuring patient safety, shelf life, and uniformity of the drug through different production lots. We are also controlling degradation by the elements such as oxygen, moisture, heat, and prevention of microbial contamination."

"Thank you, Zultz!" Greaves said in conclusion. "Please keep me updated."

After his call to Zultz, Greaves decided to call his boss, Adamis Baum, to make sure he was current on the production of the drug. "Hello, sir, Greaves here. I wanted to let you know that all systems appear to be ready to move forward within a week according to Regan Zultz."

"Good to know, Greaves. Let me know when the timing of the supply distribution is closer. Alert the global commanders to make sure they have their people in place. As I understand it, the only drawback we are experiencing is paying off people responsible for the water systems in various locations. But we are learning that people are willing to do almost anything for a price." With that the call ended.

Unfortunately for the Interpol team, the phone used by Baum on this call was not the same used by Reid Enright, so they weren't able to track it.

TOWARD THE END OF JULY, it had been a week since Salvatore Amie left Rome to stay with his associates in Naples, Italy. Amie was another intermediary in the organization identified as the person who paid off Michael Raffone, who in turn paid Ivan Lasch to murder Jack McCabe's parents. Then Lasch attempted murders of Jack and Sara at the restaurant in Innsbruck. Amie was nearly captured in Rome by Interpol Officers Alberto Fresco and Kara Sterrio, but he was able to elude them and slip out of town.

Amie had an intense romantic affair with one of The New Global Order's key members, Lisbett Kant, an attractive, wealthy widow who had a luxurious villa in Venice, Italy. Amie had lived with her for nearly a month before she had to leave for a meeting with The Committee at Baum's estate in Rome. He missed her deeply and wanted to rendezvous soon.

"Amore," *what Amie called Kant,* "I miss you terribly and need to be with you," Amie begged after he reached her on the phone.

"Tigre," *what Kant called Amie,* it's so wonderful to hear your voice!"

"I can drive today and be with you tomorrow night," Amie offered seductively.

"It could be dangerous, but I want to see you desperately, Tigre," Kant responded breathlessly, imagining their bodies intertwined in passion.

That next evening, Amie made it to Kant's villa on the Grand Canal in Venice. They embraced, kissed deeply, and quickly stumbled into her lavish bedroom where they rekindled their nearly inexhaustible excitement for each other. An hour later, Kant put on her silk robe, left the bedroom and returned with a bottle of one of her finest champagnes for them to savor.

After catching up on their individual lives, Kant expressed her desire to bring Amie into the inner circle of The New Global Order. "Tigre, it is so incredible to be with you tonight. I wish it could last. I need to tell you that we have some extraordinary events coming soon. I would like to ask the Director if he would consider bringing you into the round table meetings of The Committee. I think you would be a wonderful asset."

"Oh, Amore, it is so generous of you to offer to give me a referral!" Amie replied thankfully, kissing her warmly. "I know I have asked you about this in the past, but the timing wasn't right. Why have you changed your mind?"

"If I wasn't sworn to absolute secrecy, I would share the information I have. Please be patient and I will contact the

Director in the morning to discuss bringing you into the fold. For now, let's enjoy the time we have together."

The next day after a sumptuous breakfast, Kant put in a call to Baum on her personal phone. "Herr Director, this is Secretary Kant," she began. "I hope I have reached you at a good time."

"Yes, Kant, I'm surprised to hear from you," Baum responded, a bit annoyed to receive a call from her unexpectedly.

"Sir, I wanted to ask if you would consider my referral of Salvatore Amie as a candidate for The Committee?" she inquired respectfully. "As you know, he has been a dedicated intermediary in the field for many years. I know him well and recommend him wholeheartedly."

"Let me think about it, Kant," he responded in a rather hesitant tone. "Hmmm. I'll give it every consideration." He paused and then said, "He may be valuable on the inside with all we have to undertake." With that, the call ended.

37

Unfortunately for Lisbett Kant, she used her personal phone to call one of Baum's burner phones that Interpol was tracking. It was the same phone used by Reid Enright to call Baum, so when the call came in, they were ready. The good news for the Interpol team was they now had Kant's phone number, allowing them to track it and determine where she was located: Venice, Italy.

Interpol was also excited to hear that Kant had a relationship with Salvatore Amie, who recently eluded them in Rome. He was one of the organization's key intermediaries in the field and was high on their most-wanted list.

The bad news was that the call wasn't long enough to identify the location of Baum, so he was still outside of their radar. But Kant was a huge discovery and they would explore her location in Venice.

Since Officers Alberto Fresco and Kara Sterrio lost Amie in Rome, they were eager to track him down in Venice. But first, they wanted to learn more about Lisbett Kant to whom the phone was registered.

Sitting at one of the computer stations in the analysts' office,

Sterrio ran a search on Lisbett Kant and found some details. "Let's see, she is apparently quite wealthy...obviously from German background...played a role in her deceased husband's illegal real estate deals, which led her to a connection with The New Global Order. She's quite the looker from this photo."

"Do you have an address?" Fresco wondered.

"The phone shows her villa to be next to the Venice Grand Canal Terrace. We can get a room there and keep an eye on both Kant and Amie," Sterrio replied. She then logged off and the two Interpol officers began packing for their trip.

The next day they found themselves traveling over Ponte della Liberta, the long bridge into Venice. When they arrived on the island, they parked, and made their way to their hotel via canal taxi. "This place never gets old," Sterrio remarked at the breathtaking charm of Venice. When they checked in as a couple, they made it to their room and set up their computer to continue monitoring Kant's phone calls.

Fresco was a lean, muscular Italian with dark features, and Sterrio – who was also Italian – was statuesque, tall and slender with long dark hair that she pulled back in a bun. Together, they easily posed as another young, attractive couple on vacation.

"I'll take a stroll and see if there are any sightlines to Kant's villa," Fresco said as he grabbed his sidearm, concealing it under his jacket. When he reached the walkway in front of the canal, he identified her villa but there was no immediate view inside. He walked to the Rialto Bridge and crossed to get a view from the south side of the Grand Canal. Eventually he made his way to Palazzo Dolfin Manin and took the stairs to the roof. Pulling out his binoculars from a small travel pack, he could see into Kant's villa. After nearly an hour, Kant and Amie suddenly appeared on her balcony with drinks. It was apparent they were lovers by their affectionate interplay.

With his communication device he called Sterrio with an update. "I've got them spotted from across the canal," he reported. "I'm going to give Aritan a call and see if he has some thoughts on our next steps."

Fresco then dialed Chief Aritan, Interpol's anti-terrorist leader, and looped Sterrio in a 3-way call. "Hello Chief, I've got Sterrio on the line and we're staking out Lisbett Kant and her lover, Salvatore Amie, here in Venice. Want to see if you have any recommendations."

"Good work, Fresco and Sterrio. Continue to track Kant's phone and see if there are more calls with Baum. Would it be possible to break into Kant's villa and set up some bugs? The two lovebirds may have some interesting discussions about the organization's plans."

"We've got the tools with us, Chief," Fresco responded. "We can get in there tonight and do our magic."

"Start with that and see where it leads," Aritan confirmed, flicking ash from his cigar. "Kant's the closest we have to the organization since we captured Klosov. She could be very helpful."

To kill some time before their break-in, Fresco and Sterrio walked to the Ristorante Pizzeria and ordered a pizza quattro stagione, salad, and sparkling water.

"I did a little nerdy research on Venice before our trip, Fresco," Sterrio began.

"Oh, now you're going to get all technical on me, huh?" Fresco responded as he grabbed another slice of pizza.

"Well, it's actually pretty interesting," Sterrio said as she pulled up the data she downloaded on her mobile phone. "It says that Venice is sinking at a rate of approximately two and a half centimeters per year. The sea level around Venice is rising at almost the same rate," she continued. "As a result of both the sinking of the city and sea level rising, flooding is becoming more common.

"Plank walkways must now be used a few times a year to allow people to get around large portions of the city. They also use a series of gates designed to keep water out during rising tides. So now you know what's going on when you're forced to walk the plank," Sterrio concluded with a laugh.

"Very funny, Sterrio," Fresco responded.

Late that night about 1:00 a.m., Fresco and Sterrio covertly crept to the façade of Kant's villa. Fortunately, it was the type with deep grooves between the stone blocks that permitted climbing. When they reached the balcony, they crept over the railing and, with their night-vision goggles in place, peered inside. It didn't appear that anyone was awake, or at least no one was visible. Slowly, Fresco tried the door handle. It was unlocked. Opening it slowly, they waited to hear any sign of an alarm. There was none that they could detect.

They both moved inside cautiously and waited to see if anyone heard them. They were immediately impressed with the lavish appointments to the villa, from the stylish Italian furniture to the elegant oriental area rugs to the tasteful paintings and wall hangings.

Fresco and Sterrio moved from one room to the next as stealthily as they could, planting audio bugs and a handful of tiny video cams. In minutes they had their job completed. Silently, they retraced their steps to the balcony, exited through the door and scaled down the brick façade to the walkway. They packed their gear and walked briskly back to their hotel.

"We can begin analyzing in the morning, Sterrio," Fresco advised. "For now, I picked up a great bottle of champagne from Kant's liquor cabinet. Let's enjoy." After changing into their sleepwear, they popped the cork and grabbed a couple of glasses to savor their discovery.

The next morning, they both felt the effects of the bubbly and were a bit self-conscious that it led to their first lovemaking encounter. Since neither of them was attached to anyone, it was a fun, if unexpected, night. Without saying so, they both wanted to explore each other's sensuous bodies again soon. From a professional standpoint, they had previously avoided any physical expressions of affection, but the champagne was the ticket to dissolving their inhibitions.

After eating room-service breakfast and drinking plenty of black coffee, they both started feeling back to normal. "I'll see what we've got from the bugs and video cams we planted," Sterrio said as she logged in and waited for the signals to boot up. "Looks like the lovebirds are up and at it already," she remarked watching Kant and Amie walking naked from one room to the next. Eventually they put on robes and made their way to the balcony with Amie carrying a coffee service to a table.

Not long after, a phone buzzed, and Kant pulled a mobile from her robe pocket and answered. "Hello, Kant, it's Baum. I've been thinking of your request. I will approve the addition of Amie to the round table for our next meeting."

"Oh, thank you, sir," Kant replied almost breathlessly. With that, Baum ended the call. "Tigre, this is wonderful!" Kant expressed as she reached for Amie's hand, leaned over and kissed him.

Sterrio and Fresco glanced back and forth and were eager to see when the next meeting would take place. They knew that if Kant and Amie were contacted for a meeting, they would lead them right to Baum.

38

During the rest of the morning until early afternoon, Officers Fresco and Sterrio continued to listen in and watch for anything revealing from Lisbett Kant and her lover, Salvatore Amie, at Kant's villa in Venice. Suddenly, Amie said he wanted to go out for a smoke along the canal. Kant said she would use the time to freshen up and get ready for the evening.

"I'll see where he goes if you want to continue tracking Kant," Fresco advised. He got dressed and had his revolver hidden under his jacket as he left the hotel and waited to spot Amie. Several minutes later, Amie came out of the villa in search of a tobacconist shop. It wasn't long before he found what he was looking for. He purchased a pack of Gauloises cigarettes and started to head back. Unfortunately for Fresco, the newspaper he hoped would hide his face, was not very effective. He was spotted.

"What the hell?" Amie almost shouted after recognizing Fresco, whom he remembered from his near capture in Rome. Amie immediately turned and started running down the canal. Fresco gave chase.

A few minutes later, Amie spotted some rental speedboats

docked next to the walkway pier. He jumped in one, kicked on the motor, and it revved up. Before Fresco could reach him, he put it in gear and sped out onto the canal. Fresco tracked close behind. Following suit, he commandeered another boat, quickly got its motor humming, and powered away from the dock. He then called Sterrio on his com to let her know that Amie ID'd him, and he was now pursuing him in a speedboat. "Holy crap, Fresco! Be careful!" Sterrio shouted.

"Call the Polizia Locale and let them know the situation," he screamed back. Amie would not be easy to catch. Fresco gave his boat as much gas as it would take, but he couldn't seem to gain on him. Amie veered north on the Grand Canal, then turned west until the canal veered south. Throughout the chase, gondolas and other small vessels moved from one side to another, allowing them to pass. Some crashed onto the banks of the canal, with people screaming and gesturing at the speeding boats that passed them.

Finally beginning to catch up, Fresco noticed the canal police following him. He saw that Amie was slowing and pulling his boat up to the edge of the canal next to Giardini Papadopoli, a large terraced garden with shade trees where Amie probably thought he could elude Fresco. Without tying his boat, Amie jumped ashore and ran into the garden. Moments later, Fresco pursued him to shore and noticed the police were not far behind. Amie ran as fast as he could and when he made it through the garden, he found a small canal bridge that he crossed, hurrying down the walkway into an alley near ancient Italian structures.

As Fresco got within shouting distance, he yelled at Amie to stop. Amie ignored him and kept running. Fresco was gaining as Amie glanced back and appeared to be getting winded. Fresco yelled again as Amie continued down a street between buildings. Pulling out his weapon, Fresco fired and hit Amie in the back of his leg. Amie began rolling, grabbing his wound. In seconds, Fresco was on him and pulled out cuffs to bind his hands behind his back.

"I've got him, Sterrio," Fresco shouted into his com. Just then, the local police arrived, and Fresco showed them his Interpol badge. "We've been tracking this guy. He's connected to a terrorist organization and has been wanted for attempted murder and other crimes," he reported to them. "He is very dangerous but will need medical attention. You must take every precaution in guarding him, understand? Our people will pick him up tomorrow to take him back to Rome."

Fresco then called Sterrio back. "Shot the guy in the leg and he'll need medical attention before he is taken to the local police station."

"Good work, Fresco. Can we trust the local police? Maybe you should tag along until our people get there to pick him up."

"Good idea. Stay alert to see if anything happens with Kant. She'll likely freak out when Amie doesn't return."

"Sounds like a plan. I'll call our station in Rome and then call Chief Aritan with an update."

After calling the Rome station for people to come to pick up Amie, Sterrio phoned Aritan. "Hello, Chief, Sterrio here. Fresco was spotted by Amie and had to give chase on the canal and then on foot. Finally fired and hit him in the leg. He's going to stay with him until our people pick him up tomorrow. We'll continue to monitor Kant to see what she does. Any orders from here?"

"Appreciate the update, Sterrio," Aritan responded as he scratched his beard. "Yes, we need to stay on Kant. She's a potential key to finding Baum." Watching the video cams of Kant, Sterrio could see that she was becoming extremely upset, pacing around her villa, shouting German curse words. Moments later, she picked up her mobile and made a call.

"Hello, Director, so sorry to call but something must have happened to Amie. He left almost an hour ago and hasn't returned. I haven't heard from him and don't know what I should do," she said as tears streamed down her face.

"Unacceptable, Kant," Baum replied. "I'll contact someone in Venice and have him check with the local police. We will have to intervene." And then the call ended.

Good to know, Sterrio thought as she listened to their conversation. She then called Fresco. "Kant just had a brief phone call with Baum who said he was going to contact someone in Venice to help Amie. Be on the lookout to protect yourself and the prisoner. Hope the local police aren't on their payroll."

"Thanks for the heads up," Fresco responded. "I'll stay alert and hope I can control the situation." Amie was taken by canal ambulance to a local hospital where the bullet was removed, and his leg was bandaged. Fresco stayed with him throughout and was prepared for anything.

Later that day, the hospital released him, and he was transferred to the local police station. When they arrived at the police station, Fresco reiterated the dangerous situation with Amie to the police. He advised them that his Interpol team would transport Amie to Rome in the morning. He also let them know that the prisoner must not be permitted to leave. "No visitors, understand?" Fresco ordered emphatically.

Early in the evening, a man called the police station stating he was from the local government and that he would arrange for Amie's release. The man was told that Amie was not permitted any visitors and that he was being held by orders from Interpol. The Venice policeman who took the call informed Fresco, who appreciated the information.

Moments later, "Chief, it's Fresco. Looks like the enemy is going to try to free Amie. Not sure what they will try."

"What the hell? I've got some people there that I'll contact immediately to help. Need to make sure no one tries to strong-arm the situation," Aritan growled as he began looking up the contact for his team in Venice.

An hour later, Fresco received a call from Dustin Karr, an officer he didn't know. "Fresco, Aritan called and I've got three men to assist you to make sure there isn't any trouble. We'll position ourselves around the police station to fight off any attempts to capture Amie."

After thanking Karr, Fresco called Aritan and confirmed that Karr was indeed legitimate. Having extra guards on hand alleviated his concerns, because an enemy raid could be imminent. Fresco then called Sterrio to give her an update. "Aritan came through again. He's got some local Interpol officers guarding the police station. If there is an attack, we should be ready. Any news on Kant?"

"She continues to act very frightened. Good to hear there'll be backup. Don't know what the enemy will try. We know they're very resourceful."

The four Interpol officers who were surrounding the police station were well-hidden and well-armed. Fresco remained inside not far from Amie who was sleeping from the pain pills he received at the hospital.

Two hours later, four armed enemy militia silently crept toward the station. Karr, who was at an elevated view near the front, saw them and alerted his other three men. "Get ready, team," he said calmly into his com device.

As the enemy militants came near, one of them ordered two others to approach from the rear entrance. Immediately, Karr yelled for them to halt, but two of them ducked and began firing. The two militants heading to the rear were shot down before they could reach their destination. The other two in front continued to fire and hit one of Karr's men in the shoulder. But Karr had a better position and blasted them in their heads before they could get off another round. Blood streamed from the two enemies as they were jolted back, falling limp onto the street.

Minutes later, "Looks like we were able to stop the bad guys," Karr called to inform Fresco, who was concerned at the sound of the gunfire. The Venice police came running outside to check on the sound of gunfire. The enemy militia were checked for signs of life, but none survived the fast response from Karr and his team. Attack averted.

"Good work! And thanks!" Fresco responded, feeling an immediate sense of relief. This was becoming an all-too-familiar circumstance with the enemy.

39

After the attack at the Venice police station, Officer Alberto Fresco called the Rome Interpol station and requested that they bring extra guards in an armored truck. "We don't know what to expect from the enemy," he said cautiously. "I want to be prepared in case there's an assault on the transport back to Rome."

Throughout the night until dawn broke, with sun reflecting off the canal, Fresco sat in the same chair near Amie's cell. He was able to get some sleep even though it was sporadic and uncomfortable. By mid-day following Amie's arrest, the armored truck from Rome arrived at a parking facility outside Venice. From there they took a canal taxi to the police station. When the armed guards entered, they presented their IDs to the local policemen.

"We've got four guards ready to take Amie back to Rome, Fresco," Officer Enzo Ferno reported. Fresco was happy to see him and knew the prisoner would be well protected. Ferno's reliable partner, Officer Bella Gamba, was also on the team.

Interpol Officer Dustin Karr and his men, except for the one who was injured during the gunfire, had stayed through the night. As they wheeled Amie to a police boat, Fresco thanked Karr again and said he and his men were dismissed if they were ready.

"We'll be happy to escort the armored truck out of town to make sure there aren't any unexpected surprises, Fresco," Karr offered.

"Much appreciated," Fresco said thankfully. After they loaded up and drove out of town in their convoy, Fresco got a ride back to his hotel from one of the local police boats. When he returned to the suite, Officer Kara Sterrio gave him a big hug and kiss, wrapping her arms around him. "Thank God you made it okay, Fresco!" she said as she hugged him again.

"Sorry my cover was blown but thought I was camouflaged by the newspaper I was pretending to read," Fresco responded. "He spotted me from a half block away."

"Good job commandeering the speedboat!" Sterrio remarked. "Guess I'll have to start calling you *Captain Fresco*," she chuckled.

"Anything happening with Kant?" he wondered since he knew she was probably frantic without Amie.

"Not much, but you must be wiped out after staying up all night," Sterrio replied. "Go ahead and get some sleep and I'll wake you if something happens."

That's all it took to convince Fresco to take her up on the offer. He jumped in the shower, toweled off, and hit the luxurious mattress in the suite's bedroom. In minutes, he was sound asleep.

ON THE WAY back to Rome, the armored truck carrying Salvatore Amie passed through Padua, then Bologna, and drove around Florence with no disruptions. As they entered the last stretch of highway E45 toward Rome, however, there was a roadblock that they were not expecting. Someone had placed a barricade on the highway that prevented them from continuing, so they began a detour which led them to a smaller road, Via Palombarese. After traveling 80 kilometers, they approached another roadblock, with no detour options.

"Somebody's playing games with us," Ferno stated, quickly realizing they could be in danger. As they started backing up to try another route, the crack of gunfire poured down on them from the hills on either side of the road. Their armored truck could withstand the attack if they didn't use any stronger weapons like bazookas or rocket launchers. The Interpol team tried firing back from within the truck, but they were limited in their view of the attackers.

Ferno called the Rome station, requesting immediate backup. "Do you have a couple of military helicopters you can send right away?" he asked calmly. "We're being fired on by snipers from the hills over Via Palombarese. Need to take care of them, pronto!"

In less than an hour of taking fire from the enemy, two armed helicopters emerged above the nearby hills, whirring loudly. The pilots spotted the gunmen in the hills. In minutes, they obliterated them, one after another. "Thanks for the help," Ferno responded to the base. Two of the Interpol guards got out of the armored truck and removed the barricade blocking the road. "We're heading in now. Looks like the coast is clear. Send a clean-up crew to take care of the dead enemy militia in the hills."

After making it back to the base, Salvatore Amie was charged with murder and aiding and abetting the enemy. He was then fingerprinted and moved into a cell. "We'll have to get some medical attention for his leg wound," Ferno ordered, "but he will only be allowed visitors with top security clearance, no questions asked."

LATER IN THE evening in Venice, Officer Albero Fresco rolled out of bed and rejoined Officer Kara Sterrio who was still monitoring the scene in Lisbett Kant's villa. Kant had continued to appear extremely upset, pacing her villa. The Interpol officers thought she would be summoned to a meeting with Adamis Baum, the ruthless leader of The New Global Order. They didn't yet know where Baum resided and needed a clue. Time was becoming an issue, however, because the team was aware of plans to weaponize an Ebola virus. What they planned exactly and when they would initiate it was still a mystery. It didn't sound good.

"I took a call from Officer Ferno," Sterrio advised as she manipulated the various video cam feeds that displayed on her computer monitor. "The enemy tried to interfere with the transport outside Rome, but our team got armed helicopter help. They were able to get Amie back to the base without taking any hits."

"Amazing!" Fresco said as he poured himself some fresh, hot coffee. "Those guys won't stop at anything. Thankfully our people were close to Rome and got support, fast."

WHILE EAGERLY ANTICIPATING the launch of *E-Day* – the dissemination of the Ebola Zaire virus into the world's water systems – Baum called the head of the operation, Douglas Greaves. "Hello, this is Baum. We need to initiate the encapsulation of the virus shipments to our various organizations around the world. Is everyone on alert?"

"Yes, sir," Greaves responded. "From all the reports I have received, we are prepared to commence the operation. What is your timetable for the shipments?"

"I will give you the green light in a matter of days, Greaves," Baum snorted as he tapped on a large grid in front of him. "You have all the contacts and addresses at our various organizations, correct?"

"Of course, Director," affirmed Greaves. "I have the drop points and contacts for the following:

Britain's Royal Institute of International Affairs
The U.S. Council on Foreign Affairs
The Canadian Institute of International Affairs
The New Zealand Institute of International Affairs
The Australian Institute of International Affairs
The South African Institute of International Affairs
The Indian Institute of International Affairs
The Netherlands Institute of International Affairs
The Japanese Institute of Pacific Relations
The Chinese Institute of Pacific Relations
The Russian Institute of Pacific Relations

"I've had discussions with all of the commanders in the field and they're set to launch E-Day upon your orders," Greaves responded respectfully. "Of course, everyone is a bit on edge about having ample supplies of the antidote RGB101."

"Of course," Baum stated affirmatively. "We will not launch until the antidote has been distributed to all of those who are working with us. As I said, when we are ready, we will initiate E-Day – but NOT before."

With the call from Baum completed, Greaves used another phone to call Dr. Chester Kauff, the manager of virus containment aboard the vessel off the coast of Italy. "Greetings, Doctor. Are the shipping containers and the individual virus capsules ready to prepare?"

"Yes, Greaves," Kauff answered as he looked over the storage supplies and his men working below his perch on the vessel. "Adamis Baum has issued an order to prepare the containers. He believes the time is near for the antidote to be distributed to all of our locations," Greaves confirmed.

"Very well, Greaves," Kauff said approvingly. "I will initiate the procedure with our technical staff."

Greaves then called the manager of the biotech company, Regan Zultz, to verify that he was accurate with his projections for the production and distribution of the RGB101. "Hello, Zultz, Greaves here. Are you still expecting mass production to begin in a matter of days?"

"Yes, sir. The production system has been thoroughly inspected to begin within a week."

"Splendid," Greaves replied almost breathlessly. "The Director will be most pleased to hear that the entire process is on schedule."

40

The next day, Lisbett Kant received a call from Adamis Baum. "Kant, this is Baum. I'm afraid you and your location have been blown. As a result, you won't be able to join us for the next meeting of The Committee. I am terribly disappointed about this turn of events."

"But, Herr Baum," Kant muttered with tears in her eyes, "isn't there a way I can overcome this and be with you?"

"At this point, I don't see how. Amie was captured and taken back to Rome, so he is out of the picture. Wherever you go, the police will track you. I'm sorry, Kant. You know what to do." And Baum concluded the call.

Having listened and watched as Kant spoke to Baum, Officers Kara Sterrio and Alberto Fresco looked at each other and wondered what the next step would be. "I'm going to call Chief Aritan," Fresco offered. "We might as well arrest Kant and take her back to Rome."

"Hello, Chief, Fresco here," he said as they continued observing Kant on the monitor. "Looks like Baum has cut off Lisbett Kant since it's obvious we know where she lives. Don't know what she will be able to do other than commit suicide."

"Go ahead. Take her in," Aritan confirmed, making notes. "Who the hell knows, we might get her to talk. Make it fast."

With their orders, Fresco and Sterrio prepared to capture Kant in her villa. "I'll go up the wall to the balcony. You try the front entrance," Fresco proposed while they put on their military gear. "Hope we get there in time." Even though it was still daylight, there was a section of the façade below her balcony that was hidden from public view. Sterrio made her way to Kant's entrance and Fresco climbed up the hidden balcony wall until he reached the railing. Looking over the edge, there was no sign of Kant.

"I'm coming in from the balcony, Sterrio," Fresco said on his com. "I don't see her." Sterrio tried the front door, but it was locked. She jimmied it and pushed the door open. There was no immediate sign of Kant. Sterrio stepped in with her weapon raised. She cautiously crept further inside the villa, hoping to capture Kant before she did anything to herself. She was on suicide watch at this point.

At the same time, Fresco easily made it through the balcony door. "Still no sign of her," he whispered on his com.

Suddenly, Kant appeared from her bedroom with a weapon. "Halt! Put the gun down," Sterrio barked, but Kant began raising the pistol to below her chin. Her intention was obvious. Before she could pull the trigger, Fresco fired. His bullet grazed her gun hand. The weapon flew across the room and Kant doubled over in pain, holding her wrist with blood beginning to stream out.

Sterrio rushed over, pushing Kant to the floor. Making sure there were no other weapons, she grabbed a nearby tea towel and wrapped it around Kant's hand and wrist, trying to stop the bleeding. Sterrio then advised her that she was being charged with her association with the enemy. They knew she likely had been involved in multiple murder attempts, but they weren't aware of which ones she may have initiated.

"I'll contact the local police. You take Kant to a medical facility to look at her wound," Fresco requested. Sterrio then escorted Kant outside where they got into a canal taxi and headed to the medical facility. Kant needed stitches and Sterrio wanted to make sure her wound was dressed properly.

Before leaving Kant's villa, Fresco began an exhaustive search. He knew that since she was in The Committee's inner circle, there must be some documentation about their plans. He checked bookshelves, drawers, under area rugs, around the beds, below counters, behind mirrors and wall hangings.

In her bedroom, he began poking around the jewelry boxes on her large vanity. He opened one that was a music box that played the German holiday melody, *O Tannenbaum*. Inside, he rummaged through earrings, beads, rings, and then noticed an unusual broach. Picking it up, he rolled it around in his hand and twisted the top. It unscrewed to reveal what looked like a tiny USB drive. *Hmmm, what's this? Maybe my Christmas present.*

After he completed his search, he grabbed some of her belongings, her weapon, and two phones that he found, placed them all in a bag, and headed out. When he got back to his hotel suite, he sat down to his computer and plugged in the oddly shaped, tiny USB drive. He quickly discovered he would obviously need a password. He tried several quick options, but none worked.

Fresco then called Sterrio to see where she was with Kant, "Hey, what's the latest?"

"We're just leaving the medical facility. How did you do in her villa?" Sterrio replied curiously.

"I think I found something that could be big. It's a tiny flash drive, but we'll need our expert to crack the password," he explained. "How are you feeling?"

"I'm good, what's up?"

"I'm worried about another attack since Kant is a big player in The Committee. Would you be up for leaving tonight?"

"We can do that, just need to pack up our gear," Sterrio said as she was also concerned about potential problems getting Kant back to Rome after the attack on the Amie transport. Kant was woozy from the pain meds the medical staff gave her, so she didn't resist when Sterrio escorted her to their suite.

Within minutes, they collected their belongings and equipment, checked out of the hotel, took a canal taxi to their vehicle, and headed back to Rome. To keep Kant comfortable during the trip, they injected her with another sedative. She slept most of the way.

On the trip, Fresco called Officer Dustin Karr to see if he and his team could do a sweep of Kant's villa in case he missed anything important during his search.

As they neared Rome early in the morning, switching off driving duties throughout the night, they were relieved to have avoided any of the enemy's surprises. After an almost seven hour drive, they pulled into the Interpol station, brought Kant in, and booked her.

Fresco met with the analysts to describe the broach that was really a USB drive. "This might have some very revealing information, but we need to decipher her password," Fresco said as he described the capture of Kant. "Which one of you is the top hacker who can get us into the files? Graff?"

"I'll take a crack at it," offered Interpol's computer wizard, Sarah Graff, who had broken through firewall systems, detected and removed spyware, trojan horses, rogue security software, computer worms, rootkits, parasites and dark web codes. In less than an hour she had it.

"Awesome, Graff!" Fresco responded after sitting patiently watching her do her magic. "Looks like a lot of files. How long will it take to download this stuff?"

"Not long, now that we're inside. It should be easy," Graff replied confidently. One file included names of all the members of The New Global Order, at least those who were now connected to The Committee. But there were no addresses or phone numbers, so they still needed to track down Adamis Baum.

Another file listed all the groups connected to The Committee in different parts of the world, from the U.S. to China. "Very interesting," Fresco muttered to himself. "We've got our work cut out."

There was documentation about the Ebola Zaire virus and the group's plans to disseminate the deadly strain in the world's water systems. "Holy Toledo!" Fresco shouted as he began scanning the information. "Where in the hell are they keeping this stuff?"

There was also a report about a wonder drug called RGB101 that would serve as an antidote for the virus and provide an anti-aging benefit to those who took it. "Amazing! I'd like to get some of that," Fresco remarked. "Baum would kill if he knew this information was exposed. Come to think of it, he'd kill for much less."

Another file described the execution targets cited in the group's recent Enemies List, including names they were familiar with: Jack McCabe, Hugo DeMann, Cyrus Burnett, and others. The organization's Environmental Disruption Initiative was spelled out, including how they had supported and weaponized the dramatic climate-change proposal and other political schemes to destabilize the U.S. economy.

After scanning through the files, Fresco called Chief Samuel Aritan to describe the incredible treasure trove of information contained in the tiny USB flash drive. "That gives us a lot to work with," Aritan snorted, exhaling a plume of cigar smoke. "We've got to dig deeper to find out about their sick plans to kill billions of people. When and how will they do it? Who is running the show besides Baum? You said there are no addresses or other phone numbers, right?"

"That's correct, Chief. We picked up a couple of phones at Kant's villa and we'll get information from those soon."

Later in the afternoon, Fresco got a call from Officer Dustin Karr, who performed a more extensive search of Lisbett Kant's villa. "Hello, Fresco. Found a laptop that you'll want to investigate."

"Wow, great work!" Fresco responded. "Where'd you find it?"

"We got lucky. The ornate coffee table in her living room had a hidden drawer that opened by pushing on a specific piece of inlaid tile on the side. One of my men accidentally found it. We'll get it to you tomorrow."

41

Officer Kara Sterrio was working with the analysts on the two phones Officer Alberto Fresco brought back from Lisbett Kant's villa in Venice. "Do you have the list of names and phone numbers from the phones?" she asked curiously. "I think this is what you need," one of the analysts reported as he gave her a printout of all the data they found.

One of the phones was registered to Kant personally, which was how they located her in Venice. The other was a burner phone. Working with Fresco, they began comparing the list of The Committee members they uncovered from the USB drive with those on the phones.

One that they recognized was Oli Klosov, the former Russian military officer who was now in one of their holding cells. The other names were unfamiliar to them, but they crosschecked the list and had the staff run background searches on all of them. Most of them had been prominent in business, finance, politics, military and government. Many had some sort of criminal background before joining forces with The New Global Order.

Still, there were no addresses. The phone numbers for Adamis Baum were ones they already knew, *except* one. "Let's get a wiretap on this number," Sterrio requested. "We'll see if it gets us anywhere." Shortly, they got the wiretap ready and began monitoring Baum's calls.

With the staff busy doing searches on the enemy names they discovered, Sterrio brought Lisbett Kant into an interrogation room. Sterrio and Fresco had turned on the recording device and asked Kant to be cooperative, but she looked at them with disdain. "You will never learn anything from me," Kant muttered. "I am loyal to my cause and will die before betraying it."

"We know your group has the Ebola Zaire virus. And you plan to use it to murder billions of innocent people, Kant," Sterrio stated firmly. "Are you willing to sit there and tell us you have no sympathy for much of the globe's population? Are you really that evil? I don't think so."

"It is our philosophy of global control. We must reduce the world's population in order to reach our destiny. Besides, the world's resources cannot support the number of people on earth as it is," Kant explained weakly. "I don't expect you to understand."

"Think of all of those children who will be murdered by your greed and hunger for power," Sterrio continued. "Do you really want to see the misery and horror that will come to pass if your sick dream is fulfilled?"

"We will do what we have to do to achieve our goals," Kant rebutted. "We know it will be difficult, but it is the price of our evolution."

"I can't understand why you don't believe in the power of love in this world, Kant," Sterrio continued. "Certainly, you felt love in your relationship with Amie."

"It's too late for you to prey on my emotions," Kant responded with disgust. "Everything is in motion and you will not be able to stop it. You're too late. That's all I will say." Then Kant turned her head to one side and stared off into space, trying to ignore them. After unsuccessful attempts to break Kant with more probing questions, the two officers escorted the prisoner back to her cell.

"Well, we tried," Sterrio said to Fresco when they returned to their office. Later that afternoon, one of the analysts asked them to join him because Baum was making a call on the burner phone they tapped.

"Hello, Greaves, Baum here. We need to ship the virus capsules to their destinations so they will be prepared for E-Day when the antidote arrives. Do you understand?"

"Certainly, sir. I will give the order immediately." And the call ended.

"Well, this Greaves guy sounds like he's in the control center for all their big plans," Fresco remarked. "Got his number, right?"

"Yes, sir, got it," the analyst replied. "We'll get his phone tapped as soon as possible."

"So, E-Day is the name of their plot?" Sterrio wondered aloud. "Ebola Day?"

"Can we determine if the Greaves' phone is registered to him?" Fresco inquired.

"We're running a check on it now," the analyst replied. Minutes later, it was learned that it was a burner phone that was not registered to him, so they wiretapped it as quickly as possible.

The wiretap came just in the nick of time, as Greaves made a call. "Kauff, this is Greaves. Baum wants us to begin shipping the virus capsules to their destinations so they will be ready when the antidote arrives. Is that understood?"

"Certainly, Greaves, the encapsulation is completed, so we will initiate the shipping procedures." And the call ended.

"Now we've got another guy...Kauff? Who the hell's that?" Fresco asked his team. "You got his phone?"

"Yes, sir," the analyst responded. "We'll see what we can find out about him."

Suddenly, Greaves was making another call. "Greetings, Zultz. Just checking in to let you know that we have orders to ship the virus to its destinations. I'm hopeful you are still on schedule with the antidote."

"Of course, Greaves," responded Regan Zultz. "All systems are set. We will be in production in the next few days." And they disconnected.

"Who was that call to? Could you tell?" Fresco asked.

"The area code was to the U.S., maybe East Coast," the analyst reported quickly.

"It occurs to me, Sterrio," Fresco asserted, "if they don't get their antidote, they won't disseminate the Ebola virus into the water systems. Make sense?"

"You're right, Fresco! Brilliant!" Sterrio replied. "Now we have to find out how we can interfere with or stop the production of the antidote." With this newfound information, they called Chief Aritan to see if he had a good connection with the FBI in the States.

"Hello, Chief, Fresco here. Looks like the antidote for the Ebola virus is being manufactured in the U.S. Do you have a good contact we can work with who will investigate the biotech company?"

"Didn't you say the name of it?" Aritan asked looking at his notes. "RGB101?"

"Right, Chief. I wonder if the Food and Drug Administration is aware of it? If so, we can locate the manufacturer quickly."

"Good thinking. I'll contact someone at the FBI who will probably help us and let you know." Minutes after sifting through his electronic rolodex in between gulps of coffee, Aritan located just the person he wanted.

Agent Myles DeLong was active in combatting FBI terrorist

threats. "Hello, DeLong. Samuel Aritan here from Interpol in Innsbruck. Hope you're doing well."

"Hello, Aritan, it's been too long. Haven't heard from you since our tour of duty in the Middle East," DeLong responded. "This is quite an unexpected surprise. Still enjoying those excellent cigars?"

"You bet. I'm afraid we've uncovered a dangerous situation here in Europe. Surely you've heard of the terrorist organization called The New Global Order?"

"Why yes, Aritan, nasty bunch from everything I've been told," DeLong responded, wondering where this might lead.

"Well, they have gone off the deep end. Hope you're sitting down when I explain this. They're planning to unleash a deadly Ebola virus in the world's water systems."

"Oh my God, you can't be serious!" DeLong said as he recoiled at this unfathomable information, pushing back in his desk chair.

"I'm afraid so from everything we've learned," Aritan confirmed while reviewing his notes. "Here's why I'm calling: there's a biotech company in the U.S. that's manufacturing a drug called RGB101. We think the company's located somewhere on the East Coast. This drug is supposed to be an antidote for the Ebola virus, but it also has miraculous anti-aging benefits. We assume that only the people who are in the good graces of The New Global Order will be given the antidote."

"This is really crazy!" DeLong agreed, shaking his head.

"Do you have contacts with the Food and Drug Administration?" Aritan asked hopefully. "The company may have been in clinical trials and applied for FDA approval at some point. If you can investigate them from that angle, you may be able to locate the company quickly."

"So, what do you want us to try to do if we locate them?" DeLong inquired.

"We've got to stop them from shipping any of the damn antidote – have to lock them down," Aritan advised. "We assume that without the antidote, they won't want to spread the Ebola virus in the world's water systems."

"Makes sense to me," DeLong confirmed. "You caught me at a good time since I just finished another case. I'll start making some calls, but I'll need authorization from the top brass to do what you want. Email the documentation to me and I'll submit it as a high priority."

42

After Chief Aritan ended his call with FBI Agent Myles DeLong, he contacted Officer Fresco and explained how DeLong offered to help. He also had another thought. "I'm wondering about that friggin' Ebola virus," Aritan questioned. "Where the hell would the enemy get such a thing? Who stores that stuff?"

"I don't know," Fresco replied. "Maybe organizations who are doing tests to find cures. Places like the World Health Organization? Centers for Disease Control?"

"It might be one of those, Fresco. The Centers for Disease Control and Prevention is in Atlanta, Georgia. I'm quite sure that the World Health Organization is in Geneva, Switzerland. I'll check with WHO and ask DeLong to get in touch with the CDC to see if they have discovered any missing viruses."

Moments later he redialed his contact. "DeLong, it's Aritan again. Sorry to bother you so soon but I've got another important request. We'd like to investigate the Centers for Disease Control and Prevention in Atlanta. Want to see if they've discovered any of its Ebola virus samples missing."

"Of course, that would be critical, Aritan," DeLong agreed.

"I'll get another field person working on that part of the problem." In short order, DeLong pulled two of his investigators into his office to discuss the issues. He assigned Agent Andrew Friese to the biotech company research and Agent Barbara Dwyer to the CDC. He explained the seriousness of the matter and ordered them to get back to him as soon as possible.

Andrew Friese contacted a source at the Food and Drug Administration to inquire about RGB101. "Hello, this is Agent Friese from the FBI," he said urgently while also confirming his identity. "We're trying to locate a new drug called RGB101 that may have been in clinical trials recently. We think the biotech company producing it may be based on the East Coast."

"If you can wait for a minute, I'll scan my computer files," the FDA representative offered. Five minutes later he got back on the line and stated, "Yes, there is a company called Nupharma Corp. in Boston that has been in trials with a drug called RGB101."

"Great, do you show someone named Zultz there?" Friese inquired.

"Let's see...there is a chief operating officer named Regan Zultz," he replied.

"Thank you, we'll follow up from here," Friese said as he concluded his call.

Minutes later Friese called DeLong. "Sir, we located a Nupharma Corp. in Boston that is manufacturing the RGB101. What do you want to do?" Friese requested.

"I have orders from our top brass to shut them down," DeLong replied as he made notes on the pad in front of him. "Take a team there and serve them with a warrant to stop production and any shipments."

The next day, Friese took two of his people to Boston, entered the headquarters of Nupharma Corp., showed the armed guards their badges and IDs and asked to speak to Regan Zultz. Initially, the guards appeared to want to resist the request, but when Friese and his men drew their weapons, they relented. One of the guards then said Zultz was occupied but would inquire about his availability.

"We need *to see him now*, sir," Friese demanded. "This is a federal case we are investigating." Moments later, the guards directed the FBI agents to Zultz' office.

"What seems to be the problem?" Zultz asked innocently, looking back and forth at the FBI agents, beads of sweat forming on his forehead.

"We have orders for Nupharma to cease operations until further notice," Friese said authoritatively. "Your company is known to be associated with a terrorist organization and RGB101 is suspected of being part of a sinister plot."

"There must be some mistake," Zultz pleaded as the agents began leading him to the production processing section of the facility. When they arrived, the agents instructed the plant workers to cease all production operations immediately.

"We will have federal agents remain on site until we are satisfied that the threat has been alleviated," Friese explained. They then arrested Zultz and ushered him from the building in handcuffs.

Shortly after his trip to Nupharma, Friese called to inform DeLong of the results of the raid.

"Good work, Friese," DeLong responded. "That was quick and I'm sure our people overseas will be happy to hear we accomplished the mission."

During that same time period, Agent Barbara Dwyer called the Centers for Disease Control, provided her identification, and inquired about the security of its virus samples. A representative who monitored specimens in containment said that there had been no reports of security breaches, but she would submit an inquiry.

The next afternoon, "Hello, Agent Dwyer," the CDC representative began. "I'm very sorry to inform you that, indeed, we have shown there was a breach in security, and we are investigating the staff to see who may be responsible."

"What do you show is missing?" Dwyer asked, amazed that this could happen.

"It looks like a large amount of the Ebola Zaire virus was somehow removed from containment," the representative said as she reviewed the computer report in front of her.

"Do you have any idea where it went?" Dwyer asked impatiently.

"I'm afraid we don't know yet, but as soon as we have answers, I will contact you. This is an extremely serious matter, and we will get to the bottom of it, ma'am. As you can imagine, we take every precaution with our security to avoid something as criminal as this."

Shortly after the call, Dwyer contacted DeLong and informed him of the crisis at the CDC. "They are looking into it, sir," Dwyer reported. "Their security system was indeed breached. At this point they don't know where the virus samples are."

After the call with Dwyer, DeLong called Chief Aritan to report on the two assignments he had given them. It was good news about the biotech company, but there was no information yet on the CDC samples that were inexplicably stolen from containment. Aritan had checked with the World Health Organization and they did not have any security issues, so it was only the CDC that they were aware of. *Where in the Sam Hill are those Ebola viruses now?* Aritan wondered anxiously.

Later he called the FBI again. "DeLong, please have your people search through the documents and phone records at Nupharma Corp. Find out who owns the company and if there're any phone numbers or addresses," Aritan requested eagerly. DeLong assured him that they were already in the process of going through records and would let him know as soon as something turned up as evidence.

"Hello, Fresco, Aritan here. Good news on the biotech

company. They've been ordered to cease and desist from any production or shipping, so the antidote won't be available to the blasted enemy for their crazy plot. We also discovered that it was the CDC that lost containment of its Ebola Zaire virus samples. Hard to believe!"

"Yes, it is amazing – and extremely frightening – to think that something as dangerous as this virus could be stolen. Now we have to find those samples and locate the madman in charge of the E-Day plot."

"Right. We discovered that Douglas Greaves is the person supervising the E-Day operation, but we don't know where he lives. He called someone named Kauff who is apparently involved with shipping the Ebola samples. We have Kauff's phone number but have no idea where he is.

"Also, the FBI is looking through Nupharma's corporate documents for any names, phone numbers, and addresses. Surely if Baum is behind this, which we assume he is, he wouldn't be careless enough to use his real name on the damn corporate documents."

"I agree. Baum will likely falsify the information if he owns Nupharma," Fresco concurred.

Just as they expected, DeLong reported that the corporate documents from Nupharma showed that the company was owned by a person named Anaken Sassin from Boston, Massachusetts. However, after investigating Sassin, they determined the entire record was fraudulent. The potential phone calls between Zultz and Douglas Greaves and those between Zultz and Baum were numbers they already had. Therefore, no new leads were uncovered.

"One of the files we got from the USB drive we found at Kant's listed all the groups connected to The Committee in different parts of the world, from the U.S. to China. What's the status of those investigations?" Aritan inquired.

"We're working on the people in leadership at those

organizations," Fresco assured him. "They must be in the loop about the Ebola dissemination plot."

"We'll need to initiate raids on all of those groups, locking down their facilities immediately," Aritan ordered. "Our team will have its hands full with this all-out counteroffensive."

Shortly after Fresco finished his call with Aritan, he was alerted that Officer Dustin Karr had arrived at their base. "Hello, Fresco," Karr greeted and handed him Lisbett Kant's laptop.

"Awesome, Karr," Fresco said excitedly. "Looks like we have another job for our computer hacker, Sarah Graff."

43

A week after he was freed from being kidnapped, Jack McCabe and Sara Bellamy had completed their testimony against Ivan Lasch, who had attempted to kill them. "Looks like we've done our duty to put Lasch away for a long time," Jack said to the U.S. Embassy's Tessa Steckles at her office in Innsbruck.

"I imagine you two are eager to get back home again in Indiana," Steckles replied. "Thanks again for making the trip for Lasch's trial. And thank God you are feeling back to normal after your harrowing experience at the hands of the terrorists."

"We'll be flying out tomorrow and pray that we won't have to face more threats on our lives," Jack said, although he suspected there could be more issues to deal with in the future. He just didn't know what to expect anymore. "This might sound crazy, Ms. Steckles, but I'd be willing to do what I can to help find the people who have created this crisis."

"I appreciate your offer, Jack," Steckles answered. "We'll see how things go and, who knows, we may call you again. You may be interested to know the name of the person who we think is running The New Global Order. I got this information from Chief Samuel Aritan."

"Sure, who is it?" Jack asked curiously.

"His name is Adamis Baum, the son of Horatio Baum, who was also connected with the organization. We have a lot of information about their insane plans but still can't locate Baum."

"Hmmm," Sara chimed in, "genealogy is one of my passions. I've done some work with an ancestry website to research your family's background, Jack. If I'm not mistaken, your great grandmother's name was Ada Baum. I need to look that up again. Holy cow! You could be related to Adamis Baum!"

"Oh my God!" Jack responded as he sat up straight in his chair and gripped the armrests. "Let's check on the laptop when we get back to the hotel. I'll call to let you know, Ms. Steckles." The mere thought that he could be related to one of the most ruthless, psychopathic criminals on earth made him cringe. *Could it be? Impossible!* He thought to himself.

When Jack and Sara returned to their hotel suite, Sara dug into her carry-on bag and pulled out the laptop. Within minutes, she was logged into the ancestry website and pulled up Jack's family history.

"Incredible, Jack! Your great grandmother, Ada Baum, was, in fact, the sister of Adolph Baum, who was the father of Horatio Baum. Can you believe it? Horrifying!"

"There's more. Ada Baum married George Weinbrecht and they had a daughter, Dorothy Weinbrecht, who was your grandmother, right?" Sara continued.

"Of course!" Jack confirmed as he sat on the bed, shivers running through his body. The thought of this relationship was staggering.

"Amos, your grandfather, obviously, and Dorothy had your father, Thomas." Sara said going through the lineage. "Dorothy would have been the first cousin to Horatio Baum. Your father,

Thomas, would have been the first cousin, once removed to Adamis. It's unbelievable! And Adamis had him killed and tried to kill you! He must have had no idea of the family connection. Total lunatic."

"And that would make me a first cousin twice removed from Adamis Baum!" Jack surmised as he followed the relationship logic, utterly stunned at this sudden and unexpected twist. "Does it show any other living relatives from the Baum family tree? Ms. Steckles said they can't locate Baum's address. I wonder if anyone in the family would have a clue?"

"Well, there is one person who is part of the family tree descending from Amara Baum, another sister of Adolph and Ada," Sara responded. "Amara's grandson is named Conrad Pfeif from Germany. I don't see any more Baums on the list. Adamis may be the last of the Baum line. Maybe for good reason."

Minutes later, Jack phoned Tessa Steckles to let her know the stunning ancestry details, and that there was a relative possibly still living in Germany.

"Thank you, Jack," Steckles responded with a surprised tone. "That is absolutely unimaginable. Hate to say the obvious but, what a small world, huh? Who would have ever conceived of this? I will pass the name of Conrad Pfeif onto Chief Aritan who can run a check to see if he knows anything about Adamis Baum. My guess is that Adamis Baum is totally isolated from his family. He has obviously been so wrapped up in the evil world of global dominance, the family was not a blip on his radar."

"Say, we have a little time," Jack offered. "Why don't we try to contact Conrad Pfeif and introduce ourselves since we are relatives? I will inquire about Adamis Baum and then tell you what we've learned."

"Sure, if you have time," Steckles replied. "I imagine it would be interesting to say hello to a newly found relative."

After an hour digging through search files on the website, Sara came across seven Conrad Pfeifs and began making calls.

When she got to the fifth person on the list, she thought she might have a match and gave the phone number to Jack.

"Hello, my name is Jack McCabe and I'm a descendant of Ada Baum, who may be related to Conrad Pfeif. I'm visiting in Austria and wanted to reach out to him," Jack said to the woman who answered.

"Yes, this is the home of Conrad Pfeif, and his grandmother was Amara Baum who may have been Ada Baum's sister," the woman said. "My name is Kathryn Pfeif. I'm Conrad's wife. Conrad is out now but I will be happy to let him know you called."

"Wonderful, Mrs. Pfeif!" Jack answered happily. "Do you know when he will return?"

"He went out early to fish at the nearby river but should be returning within a few hours," Kathryn replied. "I'm sure he will be very happy to hear from you."

"I'll call back later today and hope to reach him then. Don't want you to incur any phone charges. By the way, do you happen to know of another relative named Adamis Baum?"

"Conrad will know more than me, but the name sounds familiar," Kathryn answered. "I will be sure to tell him you called."

Jack and Sara looked at each other with mixed feelings. "Great job, Sara!" Jack said, knowing he could always count on her to come through. After the call, they went out to grab a late lunch, then got back to their suite to try to reach Conrad Pfeif.

"Hello, Mrs. Pfeif," Jack said with his phone on speaker mode so Sara could hear. "This is Jack McCabe. I called earlier. Has Conrad returned?"

"Why yes, Mr. McCabe, he's right here, I'll put him on."

"Mr. McCabe!" Conrad greeted warmly. "Kathryn told me that you called and that we are related through the Baum family tree."

"Yes, sir, so good to reach you," Jack answered excitedly.

They discussed their family connection and how his grandmother had married Amos McCabe after the War. Jack also learned that the Pfeifs had no children of their own, so there may be no other descendants from the family tree besides the two of them. "We are wondering if you know of any Baums who may still be living?"

"Well, let's see," Conrad said as he scratched his full beard. "The only one who may be living is Adamis Baum, but we don't hear anything from him. People tell me that he is quite wealthy and has owned several homes. He had one in Berlin and may own one in Rome, Italy. But we only hear things from friends of friends, so to speak."

After an extended conversation about their backgrounds, they wished each other well and Conrad invited Jack to visit any time.

"Well, that's fascinating, Sara," Jack said with a wide smile. "I'll call Ms. Steckles and let her know the limited information we received.

"Hello, Ms. Steckles, Jack McCabe here. Thanks to Sara, we were able to reach my relative, Conrad Pfeif, and had a wonderful discussion about our family. He is a very engaging gentleman, but he hasn't heard from Adamis Baum in decades, and only knows about him from mutual acquaintances. He did say that he heard Baum may have owned homes in Berlin and possibly Rome."

"I'm happy to hear you made contact with your relative, Jack. Very good to know about the two possible locations for the Baum residences. I'll relay the information to Chief Aritan and I'm sure he'll put his people to work on them. Thanks again, and I'll stay in touch." Before the call ended, Jack gave Steckles the Pfeif's phone number in case anyone needed to reach him.

"Hello, Sam, Steckles here. You will not believe what Jack and Sara discovered today. It turns out that Jack is a cousin of

Adamis Baum! Sara had done ancestry research and made the unbelievable discovery."

"I'll be a son of a bitch, no!" Aritan croaked, coughing on cigar smoke. "That's the last thing I would have ever imagined. And to think Baum was behind the killing of Jack's parents and tried to kill him and Sara!" It took Aritan a few seconds to focus after that thunderbolt.

Steckles went on to describe Jack's call with his newly discovered relative in Germany who told him about Baum's potential residences in Berlin and Rome. "Thanks, we'll investigate right away," Aritan said as he set down his coffee mug and shook his head in disbelief.

44

The man heading up the massive E-Day scheme, Douglas Greaves, attempted to call the biotech company manufacturing the RGB101 antidote and anti-aging drug. However, his call to Regan Zultz was not answered and it sounded like the phone was no longer functioning. And then, to his utter shock and disbelief, he called the main phone number and learned from a recorded message that *the operation has ceased production until further notice.*

The next call was one he dreaded making…to Adamis Baum. "Hello, sir, Greaves here," he said timidly. "I don't know how to say this, but it appears that the biotech company has been raided and is no longer in operation."

"What! This is beyond my comprehension, Greaves!" Baum roared into the burner phone. "How in the world could something like this happen? After all the intense preparations, I do not understand this! Totally unacceptable!" Baum raged, and threw his phone at the nearby fireplace in his spacious study. It exploded loudly against the stone façade, splintering into hundreds of tiny pieces of plastic and metal.

With his blood pressure spiking, Greaves sat alone and tried to get a grip on his next steps. Without the antidote, there would be no purpose in sending out and disseminating the deadly Ebola Zaire virus. *Where do we go from here?* he thought. *Bollocks, stalemate!*

Greaves then called Dr. Chester Kauff to see if he had shipped the Ebola specimens to the various commanders around the world. "Hello, Kauff, this is Greaves. We have hit a major snag in our plan, I'm afraid to say. The biotech company making the antidote has apparently been compromised and shut down! We're at a standstill."

"What? It's too late! We have shipped the capsules to their destinations, Greaves," Kauff replied, experiencing the sudden shock of the plan going awry. "I will send out notifications to all the commanders letting them know that the procedure should be aborted completely until further notice."

In the days following the discovery of the USB drive in Lisbett Kant's villa, Interpol officers in various parts of the world made progress investigating the organizations they were assigned to track down. Working with local law enforcement agencies in each vicinity, they were able to identify and arrest many of the leaders and place their facilities on lock down.

At the U.S. Council on Foreign Affairs, FBI agents nabbed its executive and D.C. socialite, Biff Wellington, to the horror of staff members and political dignitaries who were on the premises. Armed guards were ordered to stand down at gunpoint. Onlookers were aghast at such a turn of events.

In Japan, they arrested Commander Nomo Noki in his headquarters at the Japanese Institute of Pacific Relations, despite a military skirmish that lasted a few hours. Several people were killed in the gunfire.

Then, in Hong Kong, they brought in Kum Hia Nao at the Chinese Institute of Pacific Relations, with token resistance from his armed militia.

The police also nabbed the leader of the Russian Institute of

Pacific Relations, Ilya Chirkoff, even though there was a considerable backlash from local strong-armed militants. Two enemy guards were badly injured.

At the Australian Institute of International Affairs, Sir Harold Cumbelly was cornered and brought to the local police station for questioning amid tension and initial resistance from his guards. Several were killed on both sides during the bloody skirmish.

One leader of The New Global Order after another was being seized and dragged in for questioning. In each case, police ransacked the organization's headquarters and were able to locate the capsulized specimens of the deadly Ebola Zaire virus.

As Chief Samuel Aritan received the news of the raids that he orchestrated and the discovery of the virus samples, he felt like the worst could be behind them. But he knew he couldn't put anything past Adamis Baum, who was as ruthless and vicious as any criminal he had ever known.

Aritan also ordered the various headquarters be searched for any evidence pointing to Baum's location. They needed to check documents, phones, USB drives, computers, CDs, and any other forms of communication they could find. He had to assume that an intermediary would have done the communication with these people, but it was worth investigating. And from where were the virus specimens shipped? They still didn't know.

As he was going through his notes on the global counterintelligence, his phone rang. "Hello, Chief," Officer Alberto Fresco said eagerly. "Looks like we have a lead on Douglas Greaves, the guy running the E-Day operation for Baum and The Committee."

"How the hell did you get that?" Aritan replied with great interest.

"We know his last known location was in Rome, but we're not sure if that's a permanent residence," Fresco advised. "His address is on Via Ostilla near the Colosseum. Should we bug his place or bring him in?"

"Let's do a stakeout and plant bugs and video cams. I'm afraid that if we bring him in he'll stonewall us like Kant. Plus, they're all on suicide monitoring. If you need to, disguise yourself in your service repairman's uniform to get inside."

"Got it, Chief," Fresco agreed as he and Officer Kara Sterrio began preparing for the stakeout.

"Ready for another possible all-nighter, Sterrio?" Fresco asked in jest.

"That's our job, right?" she replied with a smile on her face.

As they got their gear loaded into one of the unmarked vans that was equipped with monitors and listening devices, they drove to Via Ostilla about a half block from Greaves' apartment and parked. It was late afternoon, so they waited until it was dark to try to get into his place. If they needed to get in during the day, they would use Aritan's idea of the repairman disguise.

Watching from their van, they didn't see anything other than the usual activity of people walking on the street. The apartment was one that apparently had multiple tenants, so they would have to determine the best way to approach his unit.

They got a photo of Greaves through the Interpol search, but it was not very clear. Suddenly, a tall thin man with a bushy mustache left the apartment with a bicycle and peddled down the street.

"I'll follow if I can. You want to check inside?" Sterrio offered.

"I'm ready for a visit," Fresco responded as he grabbed his gear dressed as a Pronto repairman with the company's logo on his hat and shirt. As Sterrio began driving down the street following Greaves, Fresco read on the apartment directory that Greaves' place was on the second floor. He had to wait for another tenant to leave before catching the secured front door and entering.

With no one in sight, he took the stairs to Greaves' apartment and began jimmying the lock to get in. Before he entered, an elderly neighbor lady poked her head out of her door, gave Fresco a quizzical look, but went back inside.

As Fresco opened the door, there didn't appear to be any indication of an alarm, so he entered. He was immediately stunned by a wall that Greaves had turned into a massive scheduling grid for E-Day. He pulled out his camera and began taking photos from wide views to closeups. He then initiated the planting of audio and video cams in different rooms. When he completed those tasks, he started rummaging through drawers, behind wall hangings, under carpets, and anywhere he determined was a potential hiding place.

Above a hutch he located a laptop. *Should I just grab it? Yes, it would take too long to crack the password here.* He also found a phone, and using his device, he downloaded the contents. Then he left, closing the door behind him. *Repairs completed.*

While he peddled through Rome traffic around nearby historic landmarks, Greaves thought to himself that things had certainly gone terribly awry. *Bollocks! How did everything go to such bloody hell in a handbasket?*

When Fresco was walking out the front entrance with his hat pulled down, Greaves was just getting off his bicycle and walking past him. *Good timing*, Fresco thought as they brushed by each other. He then rejoined Sterrio in the van.

"Don't know if this was the best thing to do, but I took his laptop," Fresco said, wondering if it would give away their stakeout.

"He'll notice it's missing immediately, but the contents might be worth it," Sterrio assured him.

Fresco then called Chief Aritan with an update. "Not sure if this was the wisest thing but I got into Greaves' place and swiped his laptop. Thought there could be some good intel on it. I also downloaded the contents of his phone."

"He'll know he's been blown but, I agree, it may have been worth taking. Get everything back to the analysts and see what we've got."

On the drive back to the base, Sterrio remarked, "Greaves basically rode around like he was getting some fresh air, muttering to himself, but it didn't take long. He just took a spin around the outside of the Colosseum. Not exactly a gladiator, would you say?"

When they reached the Rome Interpol headquarters, Fresco and Sterrio entered the analysts' office that was loaded with monitors showing video feeds from various locations they were observing. They could hear and see that the audio and video bugs were getting a signal at Greaves' place as he was seen frantically rummaging around his apartment for his laptop. Then he flopped onto a living room chair, put his shaking head in his hands and appeared to weep convulsively.

"I have a download of Greaves' phone and here's his laptop. We need to crack it and see what we can get," Fresco said to the top hacker, Sarah Graff. "Let me know when you get the password. Should be some valuable information."

"Hopefully it won't take long, sir," Graff replied as she began her magic.

Fresco also gave his camera to the analysts and asked them to blow up the wall diagram that he photographed in Greaves' apartment. "Quite a display that guy had! Hopefully it will never come to fruition."

45

A few days following the raids on the various regional headquarters of The New Global Order, the Interpol policeman who worked on the Japanese location called Chief Samuel Aritan to report an interesting find. The Ebola virus capsule had apparently been shipped from a loading dock in Santa Marinella, near the seacoast northwest of Rome.

After discussing the arrest of Commander Nomo Noki and other details, Aritan thanked him for the new intel, which could be valuable. Laying his cigar in the ashtray and picking up a pen to make notes, Aritan called Officer Alberto Fresco in Rome. "Looks like at least one of the Ebola viruses was shipped from Santa Marinella. Send your people there to see if we can uncover the source of the shipments."

"Sure, Chief," Fresco agreed, realizing it could be critical in identifying the people involved in the stolen specimens from the Centers for Disease Control. Fresco then asked Officers Enzo Ferno and Bella Gamba to see if they could discover the person or organization that made the shipments.

Later in the morning, Ferno and Gamba jumped into one of the unmarked squad cars, drove to Santa Marinella, and reached the shipping depot near the waterfront. They entered the facility, identified themselves, and asked to speak to the manager.

"Yes, sir, I'll see if I can get him," one of the clerks responded. Several minutes later, a heavyset, balding man rumbled out of a back office and introduced himself as Emberto Balmer.

"Mr. Balmer," Ferno greeted, "we're looking for the source of some recent shipments to multiple locations around the world. We know at least one originated from here and need to see who may have arranged for them." Ferno then showed Balmer the list of the various organizations they originally discovered from Lisbett Kant's USB drive.

"I'll have to do a little research, if you can wait," Balmer said as he scanned the list. "Were these large containers?"

"No, they would have been relatively small items, almost like medical specimens," Ferno replied.

Balmer then went back in his office while Ferno and Gamba waited. After nearly 10 minutes, Balmer returned with some documentation printouts. "This looks like the shipment order," Balmer cited, pointing to the various destinations and comparing them to the list they gave him. "They were all sent from this location."

"Very good. Now we need to know who signed for the orders. Did the person have a return address?"

"From what I can tell, these came from a boat that must have been docked here. But there was no return address. The man signed his name as Matthew Tress."

Ferno and Gamba exchanged glances, wondering how they could locate Tress. "Okay, thanks," Ferno replied. "Can I get a copy of that shipping receipt?"

"Did you or one of your people take this order?" Gamba asked. "We'd like to speak to him or her."

"Looks like our clerk, Rhea Curren, helped Mr. Tress,"

Balmer responded and led them to a young woman busily finishing an order from a customer. "Rhea, these people are with the police and need information about a customer you met with recently."

After she rang up the sale with her customer, she turned to the officers and they described the shipments to the various parts of the world. "Do you remember the person who sent a number of small containers to these addresses?" Gamba asked, showing Curren the printout.

"Well, let me try to remember," Curren said as she clicked a pen she held in her hand and scanned the details. "I do recall that the containers were all the same size and weight, fairly small, and I remember the addresses since they were going to so many countries. Pretty expensive shipment." She paused while she thought and then said, "I think the customer looked like a military guy, possibly a sailor. He was in his 40s, maybe early 50s, well built. Medium sized. Mustached with dark hair. That's about it."

"Okay, thanks," Gamba replied as she gave Curren and Balmer a number to call if they thought of anything else. When Gamba and Ferno got back in their vehicle, they agreed that there must be a boat that had contained the Ebola specimens.

"If these things were kept on a vessel somewhere at sea, it could be pretty difficult to find," Ferno supposed as they began driving back to Rome headquarters. On the way, they called Officer Fresco. "We just finished talking to the people at the shipping facility. All the virus containers were shipped from the same location and it sounds like they had been stored on some sort of boat."

"Good to know, thanks. Any description of the customer who brought in the containers?"

"We got a bit of a description. Military or sailor, middle aged, well-built, mustache, dark hair. Hoping the shipping clerk we talked to will come up with more details."

When Fresco got off the phone and walked back into the analysts' office, the agency's computer hacker, Sarah Graff, had some good news. "Sir, I was able to break the password on Greaves' laptop as well as Kant's laptop, and we have good intel to discuss," Graff reported as she scrolled through a series of files that she was opening.

"From Greaves' laptop, it looks like the specimens were held on a ship that was docked off the coast of Rome in the Tyrrhenian Sea," Graff reported. "The guy in charge was Dr. Chester Kauff and I've got his number, but it may be the one we already had. Wait, there were two numbers, one may belong to Kauff personally." She then emailed the new phone number to one of the analysts and asked him to run a trace.

It appeared that much of what she found, the team already knew from Lisbett Kant's USB drive, including the names of commanders and their organizations around the world. All the people who were active with The New Global Order were also listed. The analysts were doing searches on each of them. They knew about the biotech company and closed it down. Unfortunately, there was no information about Adamis Baum's location.

As she was describing the files, the analyst found the information they were seeking on Dr. Chester Kauff. "Looks like he had been associated with the Centers for Disease Control and lived in Atlanta. The New Global Order must have paid him a king's ransom to orchestrate the theft of the Ebola virus specimens."

"Sir, much of what we found on Kant's USB drive is also on her laptop, but I'm still digging through it," Graff said as she focused on the myriad of files before her.

"Got it, thanks, Graff. Now we need to find this scumbag Dr. Chester Kauff and bring him in. Based on the phone conversations he had with Greaves, Kauff was probably on the ship. Let's start a trace on Kauff's personal phone to see if we can get his location. I assume the trace of Kauff's phone shows a street address. I'll report to Chief Aritan to send the FBI to investigate."

"Chief, looks like Dr. Chester Kauff must have been the person who orchestrated the heist of the Ebola specimens from the CDC. He may well have been on the staff because his residence is on Gatewood Road NE near the CDC." Fresco then gave Aritan Kauff's personal phone number to help in the investigation.

Aritan immediately called the FBI and reached Myles DeLong who was heading up the work in the U.S. "Hello, DeLong, Aritan again. Looks like the guy who may have been involved in the Ebola heist was Dr. Chester Kauff. He lived near the CDC. Must have been paid a hell of a lot to do this crap."

"Thanks. I'll relay the information to the agent in charge, Barbara Dwyer." DeLong then contacted Dwyer and gave her the intel on Dr. Kauff to see if she could find anything on him in Atlanta.

Agent Dwyer called the representative at the CDC and asked about Kauff. "Hello, FBI Agent Dwyer calling again about the missing Ebola virus. Did you have someone named Dr. Chester Kauff on staff? We believe he may be the one who stole the specimens."

"Turns out we do – or should I say did – have Dr. Kauff on staff, but he resigned unexpectedly not too long ago. In fact, he had access to the virus storage, but I don't think anyone suspected him of this kind of thing. We'll check it out."

After her call to the CDC, Agent Dwyer contacted the home of Dr. Kauff, but there was only a recorded message. She drove to his home on Gatewood Road NE. Unfortunately, after searching around the premises, there was no sign of anyone at the residence.

"Sir, this is Dwyer," she announced. "It appears Kauff may be the culprit behind the Ebola breach since he formerly worked in the containment area. He just recently resigned his post. Couldn't find anyone at his address."

"Thanks, Dwyer," DeLong replied. "I'll call my contact at Interpol."

46

After he received an update from Agent Myles DeLong of the FBI on Dr. Chester Kauff, Chief Samuel Aritan was eager to learn more about the whereabouts of the former CDC employee. "Hello, Fresco. Sounds like Kauff is the suspect for the blasted Ebola heist. Keep me posted on any new developments you uncover."

"Will do, Chief," Fresco advised and hung up.

Later that day, the Interpol analysts captured a call to Douglas Greaves, the supervisor of the Ebola dissemination plot for The New Global Order, from Dr. Kauff. "Greaves, I have some terrible news from here on the vessel," he offered desperately. "I don't know how it occurred but one of the specimen containers was apparently damaged during the encapsulation for shipping. We've already begun seeing symptoms of the virus on many of the men aboard."

"Oh my God, Kauff," Greaves responded in an immediate panic, nervously pulling on his mustache. "What can I possibly do to help?"

"With the production of RGB101 shut down, I am not aware of any antidote," Kauff surmised as he found himself beginning to exhibit symptoms of the virus. "As a result, I may be forced to contact the CDC to send a rescue team to quarantine the vessel and transport the entire crew to a medical facility to try to save them. There is no doubt that we have all been infected, and it's only a matter of time before people begin dying.

"If you recall, the infection begins within a week after the virus enters the body," Kauff sputtered. "There is fever, fatigue, joint and muscle pain, headaches, and sore throat. Many of the people on board already exhibit these signs."

"I'm afraid I don't have a solution or an antidote available to help you," Greaves responded. "And I know it gets worse."

"Yes, as the disease continues, there are symptoms including vomiting, diarrhea, rashes, internal and external bleeding from the gums, and extreme weight loss. Without medical treatment, death is inevitable. I'm afraid calling the CDC is our only escape route at this point."

After the call ended, the analyst and Interpol team members stared at each other in amazement. "Not sure there is anything we can do except alert the CDC that we know what has taken place and track their procedure," Fresco advised. He then called Chief Aritan to inform him of the sudden dire turn of events for the enemy.

In response to the news, Aritan said, "I'll inform my FBI contact and make sure they are aware that all of the people on the vessel will serve time for their crime—assuming they survive this disaster." He then called FBI Agent Myles DeLong to fill him in on the terrible dilemma facing the infected crew.

"Well, very sorry to hear about this. We will be sure to stay in close contact with the CDC. They need to be fully aware that the people on board will be held responsible."

Not long after his call ended with Greaves, Dr. Chester Kauff perspired and his hands shook as he reached his contact at the CDC to alert him of their grave situation. "Hello, Dr. Iaria, this is Dr. Chester Kauff. I'm calling for several reasons. First, I'm admitting my vile theft of the Ebola Zaire virus samples and understand I will be punished for the crime. Secondly, I am aboard a vessel off the coast of Italy and we have all been infected by the virus. In short, we desperately need help."

"Kauff, I have to say I am stunned to learn of your admission to such a horrible deed," answered Dr. Darrell Iaria, one of Kauff's previous colleagues at the CDC. "Why and how could you have been swayed to steal these dangerous specimens? You know they were only to be used to study and develop medical treatments. I have to assume someone paid you quite a sum of money."

"That is the sad truth, I'm afraid," Kauff wheezed and tried to catch his breath. "Now we are all paying for it. I can give you the coordinates of our location. Please send helicopters to airlift our people and quarantine the ship."

"I will need to make arrangements with our team, so send me your exact position at sea, and I will initiate an evac order," Iaria consented. "I understand that the FBI has been involved in an investigation of this breach, so you and your people will certainly be brought to justice."

Kauff provided their coordinates in the Tyrrhenian Sea, where they had anchored closer to the coast of Italy. After filling in Dr. Iaria on the number of people on board, Iaria went to work organizing the rescue. Among the 12 crew members – most of whom were exhibiting growing disease symptoms – the assistance from the CDC was their only hope for survival.

Two days later, Kauff received a call from the CDC's Dr. Iaria. "Okay, we have medivac helicopters with medical staff leaving the U.S. to transport your people. Plan to have your crew ready to shower and change into special clothing when the team arrives. They should land by 9:00 a.m."

As Dr. Kauff and his crew scanned the horizon in anticipation, the sound of two large CDC evac helicopters emerged whirring loudly in their direction. Finally, the choppers descended on the surface of the vessel. Its medical team quickly began moving onto the ship in full hazmat suits carrying special apparel for the crew. They set up a large tent structure which had several rooms.

The infected crew was instructed to enter the first room where they were doused with a disinfectant shower, then a second room where they were dried and given medical apparel and headwear to use for the trip back to the U.S. As each crewmember was escorted onto the helicopters, other CDC staff collected the infected clothing, bagging it for containment. They also seized the broken Ebola cannister and sealed it for transport.

The CDC staff continued searching from room to room within the vessel, collecting everything they could from the cabins, kitchens, recreational areas, and other compartments, storing it all for quarantine.

After the crew had completed the sanitizing process and boarded the helicopters, they lifted off and headed back to the CDC in Atlanta. Once they were airborne, the CDC contacted the Italian Coast Guard to alert them of the situation with the vessel. It would require additional sanitation procedures while it was quarantined. The CDC planned to return.

Late that night, the helicopters reached the CDC in Georgia and the infected crew was led to a special containment area that was isolated from the rest of the compound. Each person was given a thorough examination by additional medical staff dressed in protective hazmat medical apparel, and treatments for the Ebola disease were initiated.

Dr. Darrell Iaria entered the containment area and spoke with Dr. Kauff. "Looks like we arrived in time as your crew is only in the early stages of the disease. Our problem is we don't have a foolproof antidote and our treatments may not be a panacea for the virus."

"I realize you are probably limited but there could be a

solution," Kauff mumbled, as saliva dripped from the corners of his mouth. "We produced an antidote called RGB101 at the Nupharma Corp. in Boston that has shown to provide curative characteristics. If we can manage to acquire that medication, we may be saved. It was proven to be effective on human subjects in trials against the Ebola Zaire virus."

"My God, Kauff!" Iaria nearly shouted, stunned to learn of the human trial for the virus antidote.

"Yes, it does sound extreme, but the drug was first proven on lab animals. There were no negative effects when humans were tested."

"I will contact the FBI to see how they want to handle this," Iaria stated as he left the contamination area. He got the name and number of the FBI agent, Barbara Dwyer, who had been investigating the breach, and gave her a call immediately.

"Hello, Agent Dwyer, this is Dr. Darrell Iaria from the CDC. As you may have heard by now, we have rescued the people responsible for the theft of the Ebola virus specimens. They were all accidentally contaminated on board their vessel and we understand there is an antidote that has proven effective against the disease. I want to know if there are doses of the antidote that we can obtain to help these people overcome the infection. They know they are responsible for their crime and will pay, if they can be saved."

"Yes, Dr. Iaria, there is an antidote at a biotech company in Boston," Dwyer answered. "I will discuss your request with my superior at the FBI to see if that would be acceptable. I know it's a life or death situation. It may be the patients' only hope."

47

A fter speaking with Dr. Darrell Iaria and his request to secure doses of the RGB101 from the Nupharma Corp., Agent Barbara Dwyer called her superior, Agent Myles DeLong at the FBI. "Hello, sir, this is Dwyer. Just discussed with Dr. Iaria of the CDC on how to best treat the infected men involved in the heist of the Ebola Zaire viruses. He is requesting that we access the RGB101 drug to see if that will cure them."

"Very interesting, Dwyer. I'll check with my Interpol contact to ask if he has any objections to trying to help these criminals." Later in the day, DeLong called Innsbruck. "Hello, Aritan. The CDC is aware of the antidote for the Ebola virus that was developed at the Nupharma Corp. Do you have any objections to accessing the medication to save the patients?"

"Good question, DeLong," Aritan responded as he paused to take a puff on his Dominican and consider the situation. "Certainly, it will be better to save them, and then they will be brought to trial. No, I don't object."

Following the call, DeLong reached Agent Andrew Friese and gave him the order to visit Nupharma Corp. and inquire about the availability of RGB101 that could be used to cure those infected. "See if they have an ample supply of the drug and make arrangements to ship it to Agent Barbara Dwyer," DeLong ordered and then he emailed the shipping directions.

The next morning, Friese and another agent traveled to Boston and reached the biotech company. It had been shut down with FBI agents standing guard. "Hello, we're here today on the order of Agent DeLong to acquire a quantity of the RGB101. Let's head to the manufacturing wing and see what exists."

Entering the production center, they found multiple cases of the medication, clearly marked, that looked like they were prepared for shipping. "Let's get a dolly and take four out to the van," Friese requested of the guards on hand. Shortly after leaving the biotech company, he stopped at a shipping facility and sent the containers to Agent Dwyer.

The next day, Dwyer received the boxes and made arrangements for them to be transported to Dr. Darrell Iaria at the CDC. As a follow-up, he called to thank Dwyer for her prompt action. Later, after donning protective gear, he spoke with Dr. Chester Kauff. "Looks like we have the antidote with instructions for the dosage. I'll begin administering the drug to all the crew and hope it performs as you assume it will." Iaria then distributed the antidote to the medical staff who were treating the patients. The symptoms were progressing in each of the infected people, so Dr. Kauff gave a thumbs up and hoped this would be the solution they were dying to receive.

CHIEF ARITAN CALLED Officer Alberto Fresco to give him an update and discuss the status of those being monitored by the analysts at the Interpol headquarters in Rome. "Hello, Fresco, wanted to let you know that Dr. Kauff requested the RGB101 antidote to treat the men rescued from the vessel. It'll be pretty damn interesting to see if it works as promised."

"Yes, Chief, and if they are taking the drug, they will receive other health benefits," Fresco responded. "As I've said, I wouldn't mind trying some myself."

"I've been thinking about the various people we've been monitoring," Aritan explained as he thumbed through his case files. "This includes Marco Fioso who had the package with the weapon and poison sent to Klosov at the hotel. Then there's Danello Deline who paid off Officer Morto to take out Klosov at our headquarters. Of course, we have Viola Solo, the madame at the Evening Shade Escort Service. She sent Barba Sevilla to kill Klosov at the hotel. Sevilla is already behind bars.

"Get your team together and round up Fioso, Deline, and Solo for questioning," Aritan ordered with a cigar clenched in his teeth. "Let's hold off on bringing in Reid Enright and Douglas Greaves for now. Who knows, maybe Adamis Baum will reach out to them or vice versa with other key information. With their organization falling apart, we may have the damn culprits backed into a corner. But we still need to find Baum.

"I'm also ordering Officers Phillip Wright and Melvin Loewe to bring in Suzanne Flay here in Innsbruck," Aritan stated. As you remember, she paid off Jack McCabe's kidnappers."

"Got it, Chief," Fresco responded.

"At this point, the other damn S.O.B.s from The New Global Order round table are on our radar. We'll be moving on them in the days ahead," Aritan advised.

After the call, Fresco met with Officers Kara Sterrio, Bella Gamba, and Enzo Ferno. "Okay, Sterrio and I will go after Viola Solo if you two can take care of Fioso and Deline. They shouldn't put up too much of a fight."

"Sounds like a plan," Ferno replied as he and Gamba began prepping for their work. "Let's head over to Via Ovidio near the Vatican City for Marco Fioso." As they drove through the busy Roman traffic on another steamy day in early August, they reached Fioso's home and went to his front door.

They knocked and the elderly Fioso answered the door. The officers presented their badges and asked if they could speak to him. "What's this all about?" Fioso questioned without opening the door.

"We know you were involved in sending a package with a weapon and poison to Oli Klosov at his hotel recently," Ferno stated. "We need for you to come with us for questioning."

"There must be some mistake, I don't know what you're talking about," Fioso explained as he held a pistol behind his back.

"We think you do, and we have evidence to support our charges against you," Gamba responded. Just then, Fioso pulled the weapon around and began to aim at the officers. But Ferno was too quick, shooting the weapon from his hand. Fioso grimaced in pain and staggered away from the door, holding his bleeding fist. The two officers entered and cuffed him without much resistance.

"Guess that tells us all we need to know, Fioso. I'll look around the place if you keep an eye on him, Gamba." After scanning the rooms, Ferno picked up and bagged the weapon, a phone, and an older laptop. "Okay, this will do to start, let's go. We'll send the team to follow up."

After getting back to the station and booking Fioso, they were ready to head out again. This time they would pay a visit to Danello Deline. When they arrived at his place, there didn't appear to be anyone home. "Last time we were here, he and his wife were at a café next to a dress shop," Gamba recalled. They headed back there and soon reached the parking lot to find Deline's Peugeot parked in front. In the café next to the shop, they spotted Deline and his wife finishing a late lunch.

Ferno and Gamba approached the couple and presented their IDs. "Deline, we have been monitoring you and have a witness who says you paid him to kill Oli Klosov," Gamba announced as the couple glanced at each other with stunned silence. "We need to go back to your place and pick up a few things of yours and head to the station."

"This is an outrage," Deline barked as he put his glass of red wine down roughly, spilling its contents on the red and white checked tablecloth.

"We know you paid Officer Morto to take out Klosov. Let's go," Gamba ordered calmly. "You can both come with us and we'll get your vehicle later."

After they returned to the Deline cottage, Ferno entered and Gamba kept watch over the elderly couple in the squad car. Ferno scoped around the small house where he located two phones that appeared to be burners. He also found what looked like a business ledger that included lists of his customers. Then he rejoined Gamba and the couple in the police vehicle and returned to the station. Along the way, the woman viciously cursed her husband for his criminal life.

"Mrs. Deline, you will be taken back to your vehicle if you are cleared," Ferno advised her. In the meantime, they held her in a small conference room until they checked to see if she was involved in any of her husband's illegal activities.

"How many times have I told you to stop this insanity, you old fool!" she groused, gesturing wildly.

While Ferno and Gamba had taken care of Fioso and Deline, Officers Fresco and Sterrio headed to the Evening Shade Escort Service to visit Viola Solo. It was an impressive Italian Villa next to a beautiful park. When they entered the front entrance, there was a video surveillance system waiting for them. After buzzing to announce themselves, a voice eventually answered and asked if they had an appointment.

Raising their badges up to the video camera, Fresco announced that they had an Interpol warrant for the arrest of Viola Solo. The voice answered that she would inform Solo. Two minutes later, the front door buzzed, and they entered an elegant reception area with two guards stationed nearby. One of them announced that the two officers could take the elevator to the second floor to see Solo.

After taking the slow-moving lift, they arrived at another luxurious space where they were greeted by a beautiful, middle-aged Italian woman in a bright, yellow pant suit. "Well, I'm Ms. Solo, what seems to be the issue here?" she asked with disdain.

"We have Barba Sevilla behind bars for the attempted murder of Oli Klosov and understand you paid her to make the attempted hit," Fresco stated firmly.

"Well, you must be mistaken. I'm not familiar with a Barba Sevilla. You obviously have the wrong business and the wrong person." Five stunning, scantily clad female staff members backed away, exchanging questioning glances with one another at the sudden turn of events.

48

Officer Alberto Fresco insisted that Viola Solo come with them to the station; she begrudgingly obliged. Solo grabbed her purse and they rode down the elevator. As they reached the first floor, Solo moved toward the front door with the two Interpol policemen behind her. Just as they were about to exit, the two guards tried to club both Fresco and Officer Kara Sterrio on the backs of their heads, swinging violently. But Fresco and Sterrio were ready and responded with force.

Fresco grabbed one of the guards by the wrist and flipped him down on the marble surface, quickly cuffing him. Sterrio punched the guard who attacked her. He momentarily recoiled, then rebounded and posed in a karate stance, leaping at her with kicks. But Sterrio was too fast and gripped the man's foot, twisted it, and slammed him hard on the floor. She jumped on him, immediately cuffing his hands as he screamed in pain.

"Base, this is Fresco," he shouted after the guards were taken care of. "Send some backup to Via Mecenate on the park at the Evening Shade Escort Service. We've just arrested a couple of guards who tried to attack us, but I'm in pursuit of Viola Solo who has a head start on me. Officer Sterrio will remain here with the two prisoners."

As Fresco raced outside, he spotted Solo speeding down Via Mecenate in her Ferrari 812 GTS. He ran to his unmarked Interpol vehicle which he knew would be no match for the Ferrari. But he would attempt to keep up. Solo took a quick right through the park on Via della Terme di Triaino as pedestrians yelled profanities and scampered out of the way.

Solo then took another right on Viale del Monte Oppio, and a sudden left onto Via Giovanni Lanza. Other cars careened from one side of the street to the other, honking frantically as Solo zoomed past them. It was all that Fresco could do to keep her in view. The rush-hour traffic in Rome was keeping her from leaving him farther behind. Solo swerved onto Via degli Annibaldi toward the Colosseum. With so many other vehicles in her path, Solo was frustrated that she was not losing her pursuer quickly enough.

She pulled into the parking lot of the ancient Colosseum and darted inside. *This may be my only way of eluding him,* she thought. But Fresco was nearing her. He also veered into the public lot, jumped out, and gave chase. There were hundreds of tourists inside, and Solo hoped she could find an area among the visitors and columns where she could disappear. She was happy she had left a gun in her car glovebox. She tried to conceal the pistol as she ran to the opposite side of the ruins, behind a series of pillars.

Fresco was beginning to feel that she had eluded him. He continued scanning the area and peering over the people who were milling around inside. Finally, he spotted a glimpse of the yellow pant suit she was wearing and hurried stealthily to her location. Suddenly, he had her in his sights, ran in her direction, and yelled, "Give it up, Solo, you're not going anywhere."

With her pistol ready, she fired. The bullet clipped his left ear and he felt the ooze of blood begin to drip on his neck. He ducked behind a large stone block as he felt the sticky wound. "I don't want to shoot you, Solo," Fresco shouted, but she kept up her defense, scooting behind another pillar.

Fresco decided he would stay low and move around the series of large stone blocks and come at her from another side. He reached an area that he hoped would surprise her. She was looking the other way. "Drop it, Solo," he barked as she quickly turned to fire, but she was too late. Fresco returned fire and hit her in the shoulder, causing her to double over and lose her weapon. Visitors in the vicinity shrieked in horror and dropped down to the walkway of the ancient gladiatorial arena.

He quickly raced to her and kicked the pistol away as he grabbed her hands, cuffing them behind her. He ripped the bottom of her yellow jacket and used it to tie a tourniquet around her upper arm to stop the bleeding. Then he pulled out his com device and called Sterrio.

"I had to chase Solo into the Colosseum. We exchanged some gunfire, but I've apprehended her," Fresco reported. "I took a slight hit to my ear, but I'll survive."

"Oh my God, thankfully her aim was off," Sterrio replied anxiously. "I was wondering how you would do chasing her through the Rome traffic."

"Her Ferrari was amazing but, fortunately, the rush hour kept her from losing me. I'll bring her in," he explained, grateful he was able to track her down. "Didn't think she'd put up such a battle, but the Colosseum is as good a place as any for that, I guess."

Sterrio chuckled and responded, "Our backup came and took the two guards in. We'll need to take a closer look around here to see if anything turns up. In the meantime, I've grabbed Solo's phone and personal laptop to see if there's anything we can use."

When Sterrio and Fresco returned to their headquarters, they updated the staff and gave the analysts Solo's phone and laptop to research for any possible intel. In the meantime, Fresco had his ear bandaged.

Fresco gave Chief Aritan a call and let him know that they brought in Fioso, Deline, and Solo. "Any new orders for Greaves and Enright at this point, Chief?"

"Give it a few more days to see if anything happens," Aritan responded as he put down a steaming cup. "We picked up Suzanne Flay here in Innsbruck. She didn't give us too much trouble."

———

DRESSED IN PROTECTIVE GEAR, FBI Agent Barbara Dwyer visited the quarantined medical center at the CDC. She spoke to Dr. Chester Kauff who admitted his role in the theft of the Ebola Zaire virus specimens. "Well Dr. Kauff, any improvement in the symptoms? It's been a few days now."

"Yes, I am feeling a little better and I understand the rest of the crew is exhibiting positive results. Temperatures have come down."

"Since we acquired the antidote for you and your infected group, you have agreed to cooperate with us on information. So, tell me," Dwyer continued as she turned on her mini recording device, "how much did your contact pay you to make the heist?"

"It was $5,000,000, quite a sum, but I was admittedly a fool for taking the bait."

"And who was your contact in this deal?"

"It was Douglas Greaves who is in the inner circle of The New Global Order."

"Well, I've heard that name from our contacts at Interpol," Dwyer said, feeling like she was getting somewhere with her prisoner. "And just how did you go about getting the specimens out of the containment area? You must have had help since the amount of the specimens was fairly significant."

"Two of the people who came with me on the ship assisted in the breach," Kauff admitted and identified them by name. "I had empty specimen containers created that were exact replicas of the ones that held the viruses. During the transfer of guards, we electronically manipulated the video monitoring displays, so the guards weren't looking at an actual live feed.

"As a result, we were able to move the live specimens out of the building through empty hazardous waste bins. I'm sorry to say it was easier than it should have been. During the next transfer of guards, I had the video displays transferred back to normal."

"Okay, that's helpful," Dwyer stated as she checked to make sure her recording device had been activated. "How about the vessel you acquired to store the specimens?"

"We shipped the bulk container of the specimens to a port outside of Rome. Greaves bribed the security office, so we didn't have to worry about an inspection. He also acquired the vessel for us to transport our cargo, with no resistance.

"Our team flew to Rome and met the vessel at the port. The ship was well equipped and stocked with food and supplies, so we were able to maintain our position at sea for several weeks while we waited for the RGB101 to be completed. Then all hell broke loose.

"Interpol must have known about our plans. They attacked all the international facilities of The New Global Order, retrieved the specimens, and shut down the biotech company. Of course, making matters worse, the accident with one of the capsules infected everyone on board the vessel."

"That's quite a story, Kauff," Dwyer responded, happy to have solved the case. "I suspect now you'll agree, crime just doesn't pay. Thank God it didn't because billions of people could have been sadistically murdered."

49

Despite the impending collapse of The New Global Order, Adamis Baum's ego would not be denied. He craved more. The fine art collection was among his most prized possessions and he had his eye keenly focused on a famous piece of art that was going up for bid very soon.

Finally, Baum was tipped off by a contact from an auction house in Chantilly, near Paris. The prized painting, *Judith Beheading Holofernes*, was previously retained by the French government, but was now deemed ready for private sale. Created by Caravaggio, it depicts the biblical story of Judith, who saved her people by seducing and beheading Holofernes, an Assyrian General.

Having closely followed the status of this masterpiece, Baum immediately sent his aide, Bendrick Dover, to the auction to make a substantial bid. The location in Chantilly was packed with eager buyers and he stayed in contact with Dover via mobile phone during the bidding. His winning offer was in excess of $100 million; he screamed out in joy, realizing the Caravaggio was now his. Dover was shocked at the sudden expression of emotion from his employer, who was usually intensely reserved and stoic.

"Wonderful, Dover!" Baum intoned gleefully. Moments later he gave instructions. "The painting measures 145 cm x 195 cm, so it will need to be carefully prepared for shipping to an art gallery here in Rome. The name and address are Sacripante Art Gallery c/o A. Baum, Via Panisperna 59, Rione Monti, 00184 Rome. I purchased several smaller items from them in the past and will advise the proprietor that it will be coming. When you return, make arrangements for it to be transported to my estate. Understand?"

"Certainly, sir," Dover responded respectfully. He then quickly followed up the bid by providing for a wire transfer of funds to the auction house and made arrangements for the crating of the canvas. He also gave them the shipping instructions to the gallery in Rome. After Dover was satisfied that everything was in order, he closed his brief case and took a train back to Paris.

As BAUM's recent bad luck would have it, the news of his fine art purchase inadvertently leaked to the artworld press. It was supposed to be an anonymous acquisition, but news spread, and rumors were rampant within a very select audience. Over the next week, Baum's name became associated with the Caravaggio purchase. Word got back to Berlin and eventually to one of his unknown relatives, Conrad Pfeif.

Later at the Pfeif home, Kathryn remarked to her husband. "Well, Conrad, I heard the most interesting thing today while speaking with a friend at the market," she said with excitement. "I believe you have a relative named Adamis Baum, correct?"

"Yes, of course, but you know we haven't heard anything

from him in many years. Jack McCabe was inquiring about the Baum family when we spoke recently."

"Rumor has it that an *A. Baum* bought a very expensive painting from an auction house near Paris. I think it was a Caravaggio. According to the news tidbit I heard, the artwork was shipped to a Rome address. You don't suppose that could be your long-lost cousin?"

"Hmmm," Conrad mused at her startling revelation as he put down his coffee cup. "Maybe I'll give Jack McCabe a phone call and let him know. He might be surprised to hear Baum's name surface again after all these years – assuming it's the same Baum."

The next day, Conrad called Jack and greeted him warmly. "Yes, Jack, hope all is going well with you now that you are back home."

"Hello, Conrad," Jack said in delight. "To what do I owe this pleasant surprise?"

Conrad then relayed the information that Kathryn told him about the Caravaggio painting and its purchase at an auction house near Paris. And that the artwork was being shipped to an art gallery in Rome in care of *A. Baum*.

"That is incredible news, Conrad! I certainly appreciate it and will let my contact in Innsbruck know very soon. It's possible it could lead them to Baum in Rome, assuming it's the same person."

After ending the call with Conrad, Jack phoned Chief Samuel Aritan to give him the news that could be a possible lead. "Hello, Chief, this is Jack McCabe calling from Indiana. My relative from Germany gave me a very interesting piece of information that you may want to look into." He then detailed the story of the fine art acquisition he heard from his cousin and wished Aritan well in exploring it further.

"Thanks very much, Mr. McCabe!" Aritan responded as he

made notes on the pad in front of him. "I'll get my people from Bruges on this right away. See what we can uncover."

"Hello, Payne, Aritan here. I just got a potential tip from Jack McCabe that an *A. Baum* purchased a famous painting by Caravaggio near Paris that was shipped to Rome."

"That could certainly be a good lead in finding the mysterious Baum, if it's the same person, Chief," Officer Cameron Payne responded. "Paris is not far from here, so we can easily investigate." That afternoon, Payne researched the recent purchase of the Caravaggio painting and identified the art gallery in Chantilly, just north of Paris. They also got a warrant to investigate the purchase.

The next day, Officers Payne and Jeanette Poole flew to Paris and rented a vehicle to drive to Chantilly. When they arrived at the auction house, they asked for the shipping supervisor and presented their warrant to investigate the address for the Caravaggio painting. The representative was initially reluctant to share the information but quickly relented when the warrant was presented. "We appreciate your cooperation in this matter, madame," Poole said in her best French accent.

They learned that the shipment of the large canvas was sent to the *Sacripante Art Gallery on Via Panisperna 59, c/o A. Baum.*

"It shipped nearly a week ago so it should be there soon," Poole said as they returned to their rental car.

"Chief, this is Payne. It looks like the painting was shipped to an art gallery in Rome in care of *A. Baum.* If your people in Rome hurry, they might catch it before it goes to the Baum residence." He then gave Aritan the name and address and ended the call.

"Fresco, this is Aritan. We may have a way to track down Baum," he said excitedly, chewing on a recently lit Nicaraguan. "Jack McCabe gave me a tip about a famous Caravaggio painting that an *A. Baum* purchased at an auction near Paris." He then gave Fresco the name and address of the gallery.

"Sterrio, let's get going," Fresco said urgently as he pulled her away from some research she was conducting on her desktop. "We may have a lead on Baum." On the way to the Sacripante Gallery, Fresco explained the news that Aritan got from Jack McCabe about the recently acquired painting. They hoped they weren't too late to see if it would lead them to Adamis Baum's address.

The Sacripante Gallery was ready to close when they arrived. Fresco presented his badge and ID and told the proprietor he needed to find out about a painting that may have been shipped from Paris.

"Yes, in fact, we just received the Caravaggio and it is still crated in the back," Renata Sanse advised them. "We are expecting the owner to arrange for it to be transported to his residence any day now."

"We appreciate your cooperation in this matter and ask that you not mention our visit to your gallery," Fresco requested. "Would it be possible for us to see the crated item before we leave?"

"Well, I am closing, but I will allow it if it can be done quickly, please," Sanse agreed. They moved through a maze of sculptures and paintings on easels to a storage area. Inside they saw the crated shipment and studied the label to *A. Baum*. Sterrio then snapped a few photos with Fresco standing next to the crate for perspective.

"Would that be Adamis Baum?" Sterrio inquired gently. Sanse nodded reluctantly that it was indeed Adamis Baum. "Interesting," remarked Sterrio as she admired the wooden structure encasing the masterpiece. "I'd love to see the painting sometime. What's it called?"

"It's titled *Judith Beheading Holofernes* and illustrates the brutal decapitation of an enemy by a young Judith from a biblical story," Sanse explained. "It was a theme painted by several famous artists of the era." She went on to describe more details of the painting's dramatic story. "Compelled by the threat to her people and filled with faith in God, Judith was prepared to put herself in harm's way. She coiffed her hair, dressed in her finest clothes, and bravely entered Holofernes' camp under the guise of bringing him information that would ensure his victory. Struck by her beauty, he invited her to dine, planning to seduce her later.

"As the biblical text recounts," Sanse continued, "Holofernes was so enchanted with her that he drank more wine than he was used to and became inebriated. Judith saw her opportunity. With a prayer in her heart and a sword in her hand, she saved her people from destruction. Depicted in detail, streams of blood wash over the white linen of his bed when she chops off his head."

"Wow, that's one brave and amazing woman!" Sterrio said in response to hearing the daring story of Judith. After departing the art gallery and thanking the proprietor, Sterrio chuckled. "A large painting of a beheading would certainly warm up Baum's home, wouldn't it?"

They knew they would have to carefully monitor the movement of the painting when it was delivered – hopefully to Baum's residence. Fresco called the station and ordered a rotation of guards at each entrance of the art gallery. They couldn't let this opportunity with the painting brush by them.

50

I t took them longer than they had anticipated, but Detective Lewis Tenant and Deputy Jerome Atrich from the Culver Police finally received the information that the lab was retrieving from the phone of Senator Russell Fossett. Fossett had been called by a person from Rome, Italy, and they now had his number.

Based on the timing of the call ordering the hit on Jack McCabe in Culver, they began to wonder if it was someone connected to The New Global Order. Tenant decided to give his contact at Interpol a call. "Hello, Chief Aritan, this is Detective Tenant from the Culver Police in Indiana."

"Of course, Detective, what do you know?" Aritan replied, scratching his beard, curious to hear why he would call. Tenant went on to describe the failed attempt of a hit on Jack at his cottage on Lake Maxinkuckee and how the Indianapolis police had wiretapped the phone of criminal Patrick Downe. As a result of the effort, they traced the call to Fossett. Even though the senator committed suicide, they retrieved his mobile and found the phone number that originated from Rome, which Tenant provided to Aritan.

"Very interesting, Tenant!" Aritan said with keen interest. "I will get this number to our station in Rome to investigate. Much appreciated. Hope it leads us to one of the top people we've been tracking."

After the call to Aritan, Detective Tenant looked over at Deputy Atrich who was polishing off a cinnamon twist donut and said, "Hope this makes their day, Jerry! What's that old saying about cutting off the head of the snake?"

"Doesn't that have something to do with eliminating a larger problem by aiming at the source – often the leader?" Atrich replied. "When you cut off the head of the snake, the rest of it will naturally die off." Atrich and Tenant both chuckled and went back to their work.

"Fresco, it's Aritan. I've got a phone number I need your team to trace. I just got it from the Culver Police in Indiana who found it on a senator in D.C. who had arranged an attempted hit on Jack McCabe."

"Great, Chief," Fresco replied, "I'll get our team on it right away." Less than an hour later, the analyst said the personal phone number did indeed belong to Adamis Baum and displayed his address near Rome.

"Holy spumoni! It's amazing that Baum's personal number would come to us all the way from Indiana. Wherever Culver is, they just came through for us in one of the biggest terrorist investigations we've ever had."

After getting this breakthrough information, he said, "Chief, looks like the number is indeed Adamis Baum's!" Fresco shouted excitedly as he and Aritan shared long-distance high fives. "We'll start checking out his location. We also have the painting that should be delivered to the actual address, assuming he still lives there."

It didn't take the analyst long to come up with the location and description of the estate. "Looks like Baum's place is in the Castelli Romani area, near Albano Lake, about 14 kilometers from Rome. There are 13 bedrooms, four floors, a large living room, private library and study, spacious hall for meetings or dining – perfect for the round table group, plus a walled exterior. You name it, this place has it," the analyst said as he finished his review.

"It likely has security and surveillance systems, so we'll need to plan carefully to avoid alerting him," Fresco claimed. Little did they know the extent of Baum's security: a vicious combination of high tech and old school.

"Sterrio, let's drive out near Baum's place with a video drone and look at the layout of the property. We'll see if there are any major obstacles." The next day when they arrived within a kilometer of the property, the drone was airborne and sped to the Baum estate.

Inside the van equipped with monitors, Fresco and Officer Kara Sterrio watched the video feed. "There's a high stone wall surrounding the property, but that shouldn't pose a problem," Fresco noticed immediately. "Okay, there are a couple of mean-looking guard dogs roaming around – Doberman Pinschers – which we'll need to sedate with a dart gun."

As the drone continued its aerial reconnaissance, it picked out something else quite intriguing: four separate spring-spear booby traps. "Oh my God, Fresco, I don't believe this," Sterrio remarked in spotting the traps. They were difficult to see but the sunlight glinted from the tripwires located off the beaten paths. "Hopefully the dogs have an electronic boundary fence, so they don't get close to those deadly things."

When the drone neared the building, they kept it at a safe distance to avoid being detected by the video surveillance cameras they spotted.

However, with a telephoto lens adjustment, they could see inside several windows. "Can't tell for sure but it looks like someone inside, possibly in the study. Could it be Baum?" Sterrio wondered out loud.

Additionally, they were able to identify the various points of entry. This told them they had a variety of options when they were ready to get inside. Hopefully to capture Baum.

The next day, Fresco got a call from one of the men on the stakeout at the art gallery. "Hello, Fresco, looks like the large painting is being transported from the art gallery. Do you want us to tail it?"

"Okay, confirm it's headed to the Baum estate near Albano Lake," Fresco responded. The Interpol guard and his partner followed the delivery van out of Rome on route to the Baum compound. They stopped a distance from the gated entry to keep watch. The delivery man must have announced that he had arrived. Minutes later, the Interpol team watched the large metal entry gate swing open and the van drove in. A half hour later, the van exited the property.

"Sir," the guard explained, "looks like the van apparently finished its delivery and has headed back."

"Good to know, thanks," Fresco responded. "Return to base and we'll plan our next move."

While inside the villa, the art gallery delivery man had helped Baum uncrate the painting and set it up in his study, surrounded by many of his other fine art masterpieces. Baum sat and admired his new possession, which brought tears to his eyes. *Judith Beheading Holofernes* was indeed impressive. He had a spot picked out for it but, for now, he was able to appreciate its classic grandeur where it stood. Baum, with the help of his assistant, planned to hang it later.

In a meeting with Officers Enzo Ferno, Bella Gamba, and Kara Sterrio, Fresco decided that all four of them return to Baum's estate. No telling what might be in store for them. They would take the video drone which Gamba could monitor in the van, and alert team members as the situation warranted.

That night after midnight, they headed southeast out of Rome and parked a half kilometer away. The drone was airborne and Fresco, Sterrio, and Ferno were equipped with night-vision goggles as they neared the wall.

"We'll probably run into the dogs. Have the sedatives ready to shoot them on sight. Don't want them making any noise," Fresco advised. As they climbed the stone wall and peered around, there was no immediate sign of the dogs, so they jumped over.

"Ferno, head to the garage area. See if you can locate a circuit breaker to shut off the electricity," Fresco ordered. "Sterrio, see if you can find any windows on the first floor that you can get into. I'm going to climb up to the second floor to try to get in."

Suddenly, the two Doberman Pinschers came sprinting around the corner of the house next to the garage. "Ready with the sedative," Ferno announced on his com to the others. The dogs began speeding toward him but stopped short, growling ferociously, preparing to pounce. He pulled out his dart gun and fired. In seconds, the dogs froze and gently fell to the stone sidewalk. "Okay, they're going to sleep for the next hour, at least," Ferno reported as he moved toward the four car garage.

"No sign of movement in the house," Gamba reported from the van as she watched the video from the drone.

All the garage doors were locked. Ferno decided he would attempt to jimmy the lock of the entry door. After a minute, he was able to open it and waited to see if there was any sign of an alarm. None sounded, so he opened the door and moved inside, scanning the environment.

51

With his night-vision goggles in place, Officer Enzo Ferno perused the large garage. He quickly identified the impressive vehicles parked inside, including a Porsche, BMW, Mercedes, and Land Rover. "Well, the guy's got good taste in cars," Ferno quipped on his com device. "I'm in the garage looking for the circuit breaker." He moved around the vehicles and started checking inside a series of cabinets. He found it and announced to his team, "Got the breaker box. Ready for me to cut the power?"

"Okay here," Officer Alberto Fresco responded quickly from the second story, as he began cautiously looking in windows.

"I'm good," Officer Kara Sterrio confirmed while she continued checking windows on the first floor.

"Here goes," Ferno alerted them. He pulled the circuit switch to disconnect the power to the house. Immediately, they could all see there must have been a backup generator kick in as a series of auxiliary lights came on in various parts of the villa. "Well, he'll wake up now if he wasn't already," Ferno said softly.

"I see movement in the house on the second floor, northwest

corner bedroom," Officer Bella Gamba said, looking at the drone video feed.

Suddenly, through the window he was peering into, Fresco saw a man dart down a hallway. "There could be a security alarm go off when we break in, so be prepared for noise," he warned. "I think I saw Baum or someone running down the hall on the second floor." As Fresco jimmied the lock on a second story window, it opened and the siren began to wail, jolting the three officers. Lights were also strobing on and off throughout the house.

Sterrio was ready. She forced one of the first story windows open but waited momentarily. Suddenly, two metal arrows aimed at the window were unleashed from a tripwire security device. They crashed through the glass just as Sterrio ducked down. She waited a few seconds more, then opened the window to sneak in. At this point, with lights flashing and the siren blaring, she knew she wasn't surprising anyone. "Be prepared, there are booby traps on the windows on the first floor, and maybe more," she warned as her pulse pounded.

Fresco opened the second story window further and waited to make sure something wasn't fired at him. Seconds later, he climbed inside the house and scanned the area. No sign of anyone. "I'm in," he said as he began stealthily moving into the room.

After Ferno disengaged the garage door lock, he opened it quietly and stood back momentarily. Just then, a shotgun blasted the door, riddling it with buckshot. Ferno was partially hit in the leg but not crippled. He peered in to see Baum's assistant, Bendrick Dover, at the end of the hallway reloading his shotgun. "Halt, police!" Ferno yelled, but Dover started to raise his shotgun again. Ferno pulled his sidearm and hit him in the shoulder, stopping him in his tracks. The shotgun skittered off to the side. Blood splattered from his arm.

"I've taken a hit, but I'm okay," Ferno announced as he

moved inside with the lights flashing and a siren blaring. Just then, he spotted the alarm control panel in the hallway and fired at it. Plastic and metal flew everywhere. Immediately, the siren stopped but the lights continued to flash. He was near the spacious kitchen, grabbed a towel he located on the counter and wrapped it around his bleeding leg.

Behind him, Dover was lying on an oriental carpet, blood pooling from his shoulder. "I'll take care of you later," he growled as he picked up the shotgun and put it on the kitchen counter.

"Just saw a man heading to the basement level," Gamba reported from the van as she monitored the drone feed. "You okay, Ferno?"

"I'll survive, just took out one of Baum's people," Ferno mumbled as his leg began to ache. He then moved through the kitchen and entered the large dining hall that included the famous round table where The Committee meetings were held.

Sterrio was inside on the first floor and began looking for the stairway to the lower level, lights still flashing. Fresco was searching the second story and went from one bedroom to the next to the see if anyone was in the house besides Baum and his assistant. He opened the door to the fifth bedroom, which could be a master suite.

Before he could move, a metal spear whistled toward him, partially piercing his arm before he could get out of the way. He screamed and jumped back into the hallway.

"I'm hit, another booby trap on the second floor!" he groaned and checked on the wound with blood beginning to seep out. He searched for a bathroom and found a towel that he used to compress the bleeding.

"That S.O.B.'s gonna pay," Sterrio barked as she moved toward the lower level stairway. "Take care of yourself, Fresco. I'll take care of the guy that headed downstairs."

The lower level of the villa was Baum's collection of

armaments, filled with an array of exotic weapons, new and old. Swords hung on the walls along with crossbows, knives, shotguns, pistols, maces, axes, shields, and more. Sterrio began slowly creeping down the stairs, wary of an attack at any moment. The lights were dimmer at this level but still flashing. Sterrio squatted down on a step and looked around. No sign of anyone.

As a diversion, she fired at a full suit of armor at the bottom of the stairs, with echoes from the metal resonating throughout the room. Just then, a bullet raced in her direction but missed. Suddenly, she did a partial pirouette, jumped over the railing and rolled on the ground behind a large white pillar. Bullets from Baum's weapon blazed toward her. She managed to elude them as they lodged in the pillar with deadly intent. She fired back repeatedly but Baum was shielded behind another pillar across the room.

"If that's you, Baum, give it up!" Sterrio shouted as more ammo was unloaded from his weapon.

"You're a fool!" Baum yelled as he began to reload his weapon. "I can't be defeated, don't you see?"

Sterrio thought she might have a chance to gain an advantage. She rolled back closer to the stairway, then crawled to another column near a wall loaded with knives and swords. Baum saw her and began to fire his shotgun again, but he only blasted holes in the column in front of her.

When he emptied his round, she realized her own weapon's clip may be out. She quickly grasped a shamshir, a large, curved saber – an ancient Persian sword – from the wall behind her and sprang toward Baum who was still reloading. She grabbed him by the head and yanked on a clump of his long dark hair. Pulling his head down, she swung violently with the sword. The blade caught him just below the chin, severing his head.

Blood began spewing in streams of crimson that pulsated with the strobing lights flashing around them. Baum's basement had become his dungeon of doom. The beautiful Kara Sterrio had vanquished her enemy.

She released the hair intertwined in her fist and let the disembodied head drop hard onto the marble floor below, blood quickly pooling at her feet. She stepped away with the sword still firmly in her grasp and peered down with disdain on her fallen prey.

Just then, Fresco and Ferno hurried down the stairway as Sterrio stood over the fallen Baum, blood dripping from the tip of her sword into the pool.

"Oh my God, Sterrio!" Fresco shouted with amazement. "You did it, you put an end to this monster's reign of terror." He then called Gamba who was aching to know what the hell happened. Fresco explained how Sterrio dramatically took down Baum. "Call an ambulance and backup, Gamba," Fresco reported. "Mission accomplished. With all the evil Baum planned, I'd have to say he lost his head a long time ago."

Moments later the three Interpol officers moved back upstairs. Ferno returned to the garage to turn the circuit breaker on to restore the power. Baum's assistant, Bendrick Dover, curled in a ball on the same oriental rug, was alive and in obvious pain from the bullet wound.

Sterrio and Fresco made it into the impressive study and immediately saw the large Caravaggio canvas of *Judith Beheading Holofernes* leaning against the wall. "Well, Sterrio, see any resemblance between you and Judith?" he joked, then turned to look at Sterrio, more impressed and in love than he ever thought he would be.

"We've got to get you and Ferno to the hospital to take care of those wounds," Sterrio said as she hugged Fresco and kissed him tenderly.

THE NEXT DAY, after Fresco and Ferno were released from the hospital, they sat in on a conference call with Sterrio, Gamba, and Chief Samuel Aritan. They had reported the defeat of Baum to Aritan prior to leaving his estate the day before but wanted to check back for any further orders. "Chief, looks like the bad guys are on the run or out of business for now," Fresco proposed as he adjusted the sling holding his bandaged arm.

"Great work, team!" Aritan growled as he put down his coffee mug. "I knew you could do it, just wasn't expecting such a decisive battle. We can go ahead and bring in those other people we've been monitoring, Reid Enright and Douglas Greaves. And the rest of the people we've been tracking from The New Global Order are on the run. Don't think Enright or Greaves will be getting important calls any time soon.

"I'll be contacting Jack McCabe and the police officers in Culver, Indiana, to thank them for their help and give them the good news," Aritan continued. "It's possible that Baum doesn't have any other relatives. We'll learn soon enough if he has a last will and testament. Could be that Baum's closest relatives, Jack McCabe and Conrad Pfeif, will inherit the Baum fortune."

The next morning, Chief Aritan reached Jack on his mobile phone at the cottage on Lake Maxinkuckee. They chatted briefly and Aritan told him how the Rome Interpol team took care of Baum. "Mr. McCabe, I'm happy to hear you're doing so well," Aritan bellowed. "Who knows, you could be in store to inherit part of Baum's billions, plus a pharmaceutical company and an incredible art collection."

"Wow! That's *one* of the best things I've heard in last few days, Chief," Jack responded, smiling broadly as he peered out over the lake. "But the best news is that Sara and I just learned we are going to have a baby."

END

ACKNOWLEDGMENTS

While many people provided guidance and support in the development of FAIR WAYS and FOUL PLAYS, I want to express my deep appreciation to editor and proofreader, Marguerite Hufford. Her dedication and keen literary skills helped me evolve as a first-time novelist. Another important contribution was made by Trisha Fuentes, who helped design and format my cover and book. Additionally, I would like to thank my wife, children, eight siblings, relatives, and numerous friends who gave me encouragement and positive feedback as I progressed from one version to the next. Finally, I am grateful to all the self-publishing gurus who instilled confidence in me to move forward as an independent author.

ABOUT THE AUTHOR

J. T. Kelly learning how to drive a speedboat with his father and sister at the lake.

J. T. Kelly gained a love for the European continent while living in Rome, Italy, for a year and traveling extensively. Prior to developing FAIR WAYS and FOUL PLAYS, he honed his writing skills as an award-winning communications pro.

Like the protagonist, Jack McCabe, the author spent part of his summers at Lake Maxinkuckee, where the experiences became a wonderful part of his life. His grandfather, who purchased the cottage in the 1940s, provided him and his large family many years of enjoyment with priceless memories. Yes, the "big hill" really exists.

As one might imagine, the author graduated from the University of Notre Dame and even enjoyed a short stint on the rugby team. One of his good friends at the lake, another Notre Dame grad whose family also owned a cottage, was an accomplished barefoot skier and remains in good health.

MORE FROM THE AUTHOR

To learn more about my upcoming books and special offers,
please visit
www.kellyfairways.us

**If you liked this book, please leave a good review at the
location where you bought it. Thank you.**